JANE

Book of Hours

Culture Crime Series – Book 2

Foreword

BOOK OF HOURS – BOOK 2 – Culture Crime Series.

A web of deceit...

Book two in the Culture Crime Series features unconventional heroine Mikky dos Santos, a protagonist who is brilliant, idiosyncratic and who does not always do the right thing.

Mikky dos Santos, artist and photographer, is lured back to Malaga with the hope of rebuilding her past. When an old friend asks her to determine the authenticity of a rare manuscript she is drawn into a web of lies and deceit. Travelling to Bruges and Canterbury she must use all her experience and resources to face the trauma of her past and to find justice.

After a shocking discovery, a Janus figure in the art world forces her to make an exchange and she comes face to face with her friend's murderer. Will the price be too high for the retribution she seeks?

With a background in travel and a love of and fascination for other cultures Janet Pywell creates a strong sense of time and place, taking the reader from Canterbury (England) to Bruges (Belgium) and to Malaga (Spain).

Acknowledgement

Many thanks to all the people who have helped me with my research for this novel: Kitesurfer Stefano Biagini. Sarah from Aquilo Kiteboarding and Steve Pentelton from Hawkuav. Mariluz from the Hotel Dos Mares in Tarifa. Lawrence Everett, Lynn Mitchell, Mirium Marcos and Ros & Robin Counsell. Heidi Conroy for her invaluable professional guidance and support. Tian Perry and students from Canterbury Christchurch University for their contributions toward social media. Amanda for her love, friendship and constant support.

Chapter 1 - Prologue

Under the cover of darkness he followed the solemn Good Friday procession. One of the most revered in the whole of the calendar year and a deeply held religious tradition; a social ritual of pomp and pageantry with solid historical conventions, entwined brotherhoods and elaborately decorated tronos. The Virgin de Soledad weighing almost five tonnes carried on the shoulders of over two hundred and fifty men, rocked and swayed; left to right, in small shuffling half paces that took balance and practice. It was accompanied by a hollow, lone, drum beat.

He'd followed the brotherhood down La Alameda and into Calle Larios watching the Virgin's halo glowing in the candle light, her palms turned upwards in a gesture of despair, a dagger embedded in her heart and a look of pain etched across her face as she mourned the loss of her only son.

There is no God. Why couldn't these bystanders see it? They'd been tricked by the church, manipulated by their lies and controlled by fear. He was sick of them in their long robes and pointed hats and the women who dressed all in black and he refused to be haunted by the mournful saetas, and the drums and trumpets that accompanied this eternal pageantry.

The sooner it was over the better.

He'd trailed her for hours and once again he went up on

his toes to look over the heads of the crowd searching for her blond hair. Streetlights had been extinguished and he squinted in concentration. He wasn't going to let her out of his sight and he pushed roughly past a small group. The April breeze, carrying a sharp tang of incense, followed him as he dived between hoards of people lining the streets squashed into narrow alleyways and crowded into doorways. He focused on her bobbing head as she weaved in and out toward the cathedral.

He'd preferred the atmosphere earlier in the week when other tronos had passed and the mood had been lighter and people had cheered and clapped from the balconies, shouting, 'Olé,' 'Guapa,' and 'Bravo,' and rose petals had floated down onto the heads of those waiting below but now as the Virgin de las Servitas passed only a dull bell tolled and a single drum beat echoed in the otherwise silent procession.

Jesus was dead.

It had been her intention to follow the Las Servitas to the Cathedral but it was past midnight and her earlier enthusiasm for being part of a crowd had faded. There had been several parades each day for a week, some had taken place at night, lasting more than five hours. She'd seen most of them but now as she tucked her blond hair behind her ears, she was weary and her feet ached. At first she'd embraced the ceremonious parades and welcomed the morbid ceremony. She'd filled her aching heart with haunting, plaintive tunes that accompanied life-size icons, fuelling the lament, hoping to ease the growing pain tightening in her chest. She wanted the loss and suffering of others to stop her from mourning but each day it had intensified; the anguish and torment had become raw and sore like an open wound gorged upon by thirsty leeches and

2

her sense of betrayal and devastation was turning from self pity to frustration and anger.

Alain was never coming back.

He'd dumped her by text from France.

How dare he treat her like this?

She staggered though the crowds her vision blurred and her judgement hazy, filled with too many vodkas. Loneliness sloshed inside her soul and she hoped to see a friendly face.

She didn't want Alain now. She never wanted to hear his name again and she was sick of all this morbidity, tired of this historical ritual. She needed some fun. She needed company. She needed a drink. She ducked into the nearest bar and tried to attract the attention of the busy barman. Her thirst and anger turned her into a restless demon as she pushed her way past the crowds and tapped red nails on the counter waiting to be served craving the taste of alcohol on her lips.

He followed her inside relieved to get away from the insistent priests and the Lord's Prayer. The words were meaningless, alien to him and he didn't believe them. He was a communist. He had only one love and it could buy him whatever he wanted. He took up position just inside the door and watched her.

The girl's blond hair fell like a curtain across her face and when she flicked it over her shoulder she knocked her glasses from her nose. Straightening them with clumsy fingers, she flashed a hopeful smile at a man old enough to be her grandfather but when he ignored her, her face crumbled with disappointment and she turned away spilling vodka down her shirt. She wiped her chin, licked her hand and tottered on high heels to the doorway where she surveyed the hushed crowds with hazy vision.

She hiccupped. She hadn't eaten all day and suddenly she

was hungry but the sombre mood only served to harden her thoughts and angry bitterness rose in the back of her throat. Her life wasn't over yet. She needed fun and laughter. She wanted to live. She wanted to feel something other than this dark depression - anything was better then this mawkish self imposed solitude and the negative scene of death and darkness that paraded past accompanied by a rhythmic, solid, empty drum beat.

'Are you okay?'

He appeared at her side like a ghostly presence and she stepped back to focus on him. He was slightly taller than her with broad shoulders and a body that said he worked out. His head was shaved but it was his grey, green eyes and the dark mole under his left eye that she noticed and when he smiled she felt she had known him all her life. Her heart tweaked in its isolated, solitary cavity and she smiled.

'This is depressing, isn't it?' he whispered.

His warm, intoxicating breath on her earlobe caused goose pimples to rise on her arm. Somehow her hand was holding his and when he stroked her fingers, his touch was firm and sensual.

She followed his gaze to where the brotherhood were resting. They laid the throne in the street and waited in silence. Around them the crowds fell silent but cameras still flashed and mobile phones were held aloft as images of the Virgin were recorded forever.

'Tourists love it,' he smiled, nodding at a group of Japanese.

She responded with a tilt of her head, trying to place his accent, unwilling to take her eyes from his hypnotic gaze and handsome smile. Aware of the heat rising between her legs, she imagined his naked back and muscled thighs pressed

4

against hers and when he manoeuvred her away from the door and out of the way of a couple leaving the bar, she moved willingly, trusting him to guide her.

'Will we get out of here – away from all this?' His suggestion was tempting but with a sudden flash of sobriety, she replied.

'I must watch this bit.'

He nodded but took charge, pulling her fingers into his hand and drawing her close to him. He leaned outside against the brick wall and stood behind her with his arms loosely around her waist and when he placed his head over her shoulder, his cheek was soft against hers and she let her body relax. She nestled against him, inhaling spicy cologne and she sighed, enjoying his strength and the heat of his body, feeling safe and protected.

Anyone who may have noticed them leaning against the wall might have thought they had been together for years; boyfriend and girlfriend, husband and wife. They would never have guessed the complexity of their meeting nor the purpose of their tryst.

The new couple watched in silence as the extinguished candles were relit, the bell tolled and the brotherhood in matching black suits and ties once again raised the Virgin aloft. Behind them the hooded fraternity – the Nazarenos – followed, making their way slowly through the city centre winding toward the Cathedral, accompanied by a lonely drum beat and a tang of heavy incense.

'This dates back to the Middle Ages,' she said. 'The colours, hoods and robes signify different brotherhoods in the city. They practise for hours, all through the year and the men have to be the right size and strong enough to bear the burden of the trono. It's an honour for them to carry...'

Her words were lost on him. His soft chin brushed her cheek and his hand travelled under her jacket. He unbuttoned her blouse and his fingers began gently rubbing her breast and when she didn't protest he moved aside her bra and rolled her right nipple between his thumb and forefinger. She gasped and arched her back, pushing against the hardness in his jeans and when a deep, guttural moan filled her ear, the primeval sound made her want him more.

Some of the crowd moved forward with the procession, passing them in the darkness; families, couples, groups and single people and when no one registered their slow, sexual movements against the wall this excited her more. She parted her legs hardly daring to move in case he stopped and when his right hand travelled down her thigh it sent a rush of desire between her legs.

It was like nothing she had felt before. She forgot about Alain. She was desirable.She was attractive. More importantly, she was wanted.

He placed the palm of his hand on her cheek and turned her face to him. Their lips barely touched, the tip of his tongue tested the tenderness of her mouth and when he kissed her deeply she was on fire, burning, consumed by his smiling, complicit eyes. She giggled but then in the half light, he suddenly released his grip and the magic disintegrated and she shivered.

She looked puzzled until he whispered into her hair.

'I want you.'

Her heart jolted then surged with pleasure and she barely hesitated before she followed him into the narrow alley behind the bar. He placed his lips firmly on hers, his tongue gently probing the contours of her mouth, sucking, drawing her into him. She shuddered when his hands traced the contours of her neck and his confident fingers lifted her simple skirt and caressed the roundness of her bottom. Stroking the inside of her thighs, he pushed her knickers aside and she opened her legs wider; wet and waiting for him.

The stranger unzipped his jeans and pulled her roughly to him. He entered her, filling her with reassurance, reaffirming her confidence and attractiveness and she knew then that nothing else in the world mattered. Her hands clutched his shoulders and she gasped, clawed his back and closed her eyes then s1§2Ish§ahe let out a strangled screamed and bit into his skin.

Alain was dead.

She was alive.

She didn't notice the stench of the overflowing bins, nor the maimed cat that crouched in fear, nor the glow from the cigarette of the restaurant worker who stood silently watching in the dark.

There was nothing more.

Chapter 2

"If you only read the books that everyone else is reading, you can only think what everyone else is thinking." - Haruki Murakami, Norwegian Wood

A cross the Straits of Gibraltar the Rif mountains rise into a hazy sky and liquid April sunshine. I turn my back against the strong Poniente, a warm dry westerly wind, and concentrate on the controller and iPad in my hand, raising the Phantom 4 drone to over one hundred and fifty meters. Although I squint into the sky, I can't follow it with my naked eye but I know it flies effortlessly against the relentless buffeting wind and the camera's gimbal stabilisation system continues to send me smooth video of the coastline. I track the drone's progress and focus on the sharp image as it follows Eduardo, my golden Adonis, kitesurfing out at sea. I track his gracefulness on the water and as the wind boots him maybe fifteen metres into the air with acrobatic moves I laugh, wondering if I'd be happier making sport videos rather than photographing precious artefacts for museums and art galleries.

After a few minutes I turn the drone toward the windswept beach and the old Roman town of Baelo Claudia behind me. During the reign of Emperor Claudius between 41-45 AD, it was an important town supplying garum, a fish paste, to the whole of the Roman Empire. Much later the industry was almost destroyed by an earthquake and following that the area became almost uninhabited. Today only the ruins of the temple, basilica and the fish-salting factory are a testament to the once thriving and busy town.

The deserted, wide sandy beach is reached by a narrow road from the N340 that stretches from Malaga around the southern tip of Spain's peninsula and west along the Costa de la Luz toward Cadiz. The road down to the beach of La Bolonia is seven kilometres long and is reached by passing over two rocky hills, the Sierra de la Plata and the Lomo de San Bartolomé. It's a hidden gem and a paradise for kiters like us.

Although it can get busy in the summer now it's out of season and deserted. It's all mine - ours - and has been or the past month, where we've practise our sport, sometimes here in isolation or further toward Tarifa where we've socialised with other free-minded souls.

A dusty grey Volkswagen travels cautiously over the last hill and I'm irked by the presence of other people arriving at my private site. I lower the drone and track its progress waiting for them to continue and park at the ruins but they don't. They turn into the sandy car park. My hope falls and my annoyance increases when they park beside my 4X4 BMW, beside the boarded up Cabaña that will open sometime next month when the sun is warmer and the hot Sirocco blows from the Sahara. Then it will be alive with music and cocktails and inhabited by kiters and sun worshippers alike who gather to listen to music, occasionally smoke pot and watch the sunset. Most of the other kiters hang out closer to the town beach or at the hippy camp at Valdevaqueros but this is my beach.

This is where, depending on the wind, Eduardo and I pick up a downwinder and we have the Atlantic to ourselves. This is where my adrenaline is unleashed and my heart pumps faster, where I learn to forget and I become calm and relaxed as I ride the ocean, revelling in the intoxicating wind and the surge of adrenaline travelling at great speed through my body.

I sigh and a wave of irritation gushes over me. There are no boards strapped to the Volkswagen's roof. It's not a hippy van - it's a townie. It belongs to a sightseer - someone who won't appreciate the waves, the wind nor it's direction or speed.

What do they want?

Why don't they just go home?

I'm about to turn the drone away and focus on Eduardo but the passenger door opens. Distracted, I pause the hovering drone, watching the controller in my hand and a woman steps out. There's a familiarity to her that makes me catch my breath. She zips up her navy jacket and flicks coal black hair from her eyes. Large sunglasses cover her face but she still shades her face and looks up at the drone suspended above her head. When she removes her glasses I'm left staring into dark eyes I haven't seen for over four years.

She doesn't move.

I lower the drone, gazing alternately at the motionless figure standing in the wind three hundred metres away and at the screen in my hand.

What does she want?

Her boots are clumsy and her gait is laboured as she steps into the sand and begins to walk toward me.

The drone's twenty minutes of battery life is fading fast and its fail safe mode, 'return to home,' kicks in but I cancel immediately. I'm unwilling to stop filming. Her skin is pale and a dark frown and heavy eyebrows give a clumsy handsomeness to her oval face. She has put on weight and she steps with care, wading through fine sand with graceful energy, holding her hair from her eyes and clutching the neck of her jacket against the wind.

The drone sinks. It's battery hits ten percent and it performs a controlled landing between us kicking up a plume of sand and I'm walking purposely toward it when she shouts.

'Are you still nuts, Mikky dos Santos?' She tugs her jacket closer to her throat. 'It's FREEZING out here.'

I bend to retrieve my new toy, flicking, blowing and wiping sand from its propellers.

'It's been too long, Mikky. I thought you were never coming back. I can't believe it.' She tip-toes across the sand and when she reaches me, she laughs and she flings her arms around my neck, holding me tightly. I'm overwhelmed by the scent of her Armani and the warmth of her love but I pull away.

'Never is a long time, Carmen.'

'Are you still mad at me?' She tilts her head to look me in the eye.

I shake my head and although I say nothing, it's still a lie.

'What have you done with your lovely mass of curls?' She reaches up to ruffle my already windswept hair and her hand lingers on my shoulder.

'It's my new look.' I move away, the truth would be too difficult to explain.

'Dolores said you were kite surfing again.'

'How did you know I was here?' I ask.

'They told me at the hippy camp.'

'Valdevaqueros?'

I'd kept a low profile in the month that we've parked the

van there. I thought they would have been more discreet and a small part of me feels betrayed. I've been found.

'Are you annoyed?'

I don't reply, instead I concentrate on the blades of the drone.

'Are you in disguise?' she persists.

'No.'

'In hiding?'

'No.'

She looks beyond me and I turn to follow her gaze and we watch Eduardo rotate his body and land smoothly toeside.

'Wow, is that him? Dolores told me you'd met someone special.'

Dolores was our art teacher from the University of Madrid ten years ago who has since retired and opened an art gallery in Mallorca. Although we have never been there at the same time we have both stayed in her art studio.

'Is it love?' she teases. 'Those currents out there can be dangerous. Did you teach him?'

'Yes and no, but not necessarily in that order.'

'You look happier, Mikky but I guess that wouldn't be hard after what you've been through.'

Her light comment assails me like the wind, slapping me in the face with unwanted memories and I wipe my eyes with the back of my hand.

'You look in good shape.' Her gaze travels down my wet suit. 'I'm surprised. Dolores told me about your accident last year.'

The wind whips my cheeks and Carmen's hot stare causes me to blush but I refuse to meet her gaze. I know she is studying me carefully, waiting for a reply but I say nothing. I don't take my eyes off Eduardo who is riding fast toward us, boosting himself off the water, his kite making a three hundred and sixty degree rotation on its axis. He makes a smooth transition and ventures back out to sea.

'We used to come here a lot – do you remember?'

How could I forget?

I walk toward my kite canopy that I've weighed down with sand beside the rest of our gear but she follows and links her arm through mine.

'I didn't realise you were back – you never contacted me, Mikky.'

'I haven't been here long,' I lie.

'Where have you been?'

'Here and there.'

'You didn't answer any of my calls.'

I blow the remaining sand from the drone, brush it with an old Rolling Stones T-shirt and place it safely in the bag but I'm distracted by a flock of kite surfers out at sea; a colourful array of canopies, spinning and floating in the sky. A kiter jumps and the wind keeps the board pushed against his feet.

'Is your father still living in Estepona?'

I shrug.

'You haven't seen him either?' she asks.

'No.'

'I'm sorry.'

'Don't be.'

'Are you working?'

'I've taken a few months off,' I reply.

'What about Josephine – do you see her?'

'Sometimes.'

'I like her.'

'So do I.'

'She thinks you have serious talent. I wish I could have shown her your artwork when she came over - you know, after your - accident. Are you still painting?'

'She wants me to prepare for an exhibition but I'm not ready...'

'Because of what happened?'

I shrug.

Her worried frown deepens and there's something in her manner that makes me think she isn't as carefree as she once was. Perhaps we've both got older; more troubled, more serious.

I ignore her, crouch down and begin to pack my gear; chicken loop, harness, bar and lines.

'I need your help, Mikky.'

'I doubt you would want my help, Carmen.' My smile is as false as the bitterness of my tone.

My back is against the wind. and for something to do I grab a handful of fine sand and let it slide through my open fingers. It dwindles like an hour glass and she crouches beside me.

'Well, it's not actually me that needs you - it's Father Ignacio.'

She hurls his name and it's all over me, clawing, wrapping and winding its way around my throat and neck in a tangled mass of memories, regrets and frustrated anger.

I haven't thought of him in years and I'm ashamed at my conflicting emotions. I reach for my rucksack and pull out a bottle of water and gulp quickly.

'He needs your help and he asked me to find you.'

We stand up, shoulder to shoulder, watching Eduardo un-hooking from his kite harness, the wind throwing him into a boost and the kite at forty five degrees. He looks beautiful,

14

stretching his body and arching his back horizontally like Superman and when he lands effortlessly, I smile.

'Mikky? Did you hear me?'

'Yes.'

'Well?'

'I can't help anyone,' I say.

'He says, it's urgent. He must speak to you. He asked me to come and find you. He wants to speak to both of us - together. It's important.'

So, Carmen hadn't come all this way to renew our friendship. This isn't about the bond we had shared when we were at university and the friendship we'd once had. She's here because Father Ignacio sent her.

'What does he want?'

I had been twenty-three. Almost ten years has passed and I haven't forgotten the effect he had on me. I wonder what he looks like now and if he's changed. I hadn't seen him since restoring the Holy Chapel of the Virgin near Ubeda, one of the best examples of Spanish Renaissance architecture. It was a masterpiece. I'd been fortunate to be involved in the project but to my shame I'd fallen in love with the novice priest. I'd been overwhelmed by his calm kindness and in my eagerness to impress him I'd even painted a canvas of Christ ascending into Heaven. He had loved it but he was unable to accept a gift from me and I had refused to sell it to him. The church though, unable to afford an original Old Master, were delighted to accept it and I had atoned for my sins, guilt and lust and the young priest's reputation had been saved. There had been no damage. Only my heart had been broken.

'Mikky? Will you come to Malaga and meet him? He says he must see you. Please Mikky, we were good friends once and l -

15

I miss you.'

Her words hang between us and I wonder where the four years has gone and how drastically my life has changed.

Out at sea Eduardo is a beautiful athletic angel and my hero. In the past six months his patience, understanding and kindness have restored my faith in mankind but probably more importantly, he makes me laugh and I'm beginning to learn to love again.

I lift my arm and wave at him, thinking how lucky I am to have met such a wonderful man and wondering how long our relationship might last until I mess up and ruin any hope I may have of a normal life.

'I must talk to you.' Carmen places her hand on my arm. 'Come to Malaga with me. I want to show you something. It's serious and we need your help.'

'I can't help you,' I reply.

'You can and there's no one else I trust. Please Mikky. I could lose my job and just about everything else.'

I glance at her. She's shivering and I wonder how she could be that cold.

'Are you still the Curator at the Picasso Museum?'

'The Provenance Curator - yes.'

'What's happened?'

There's so much to tell you, Mikky. Please, not here, come with me-'

'I can't-'

'If it's about what happened - forget it! We all have to face our past at some time, Mikky. This is your time now. Come back to Malaga. Let's get rid of the demons that haunt you. Let's get rid of them forever. I'll be with you. I'll help you. We can help each other and be the friends that we used to be...'

The warmth of her fingers reassure me and the familiarity of her touch restores a flicker of hope in my cold heart that I once believed had died forever.

Can I make amends for my past?

This is the opportunity I've wished for but never dreamed would happen.

Can I go back?

I'm standing at the cross-roads of my life. Can I right the past? Can I repair my mistakes?

I squint into the sun and realise I now have an excuse not to return to Mallorca with Eduardo. This can be my reason for staying behind on the mainland. He deserves better than me, someone normal with no mental anguish or hidden scars. This will save him from me. He can be free again.

'I'll come with you Carmen but only on one condition.'

'Of course, anything.'

'You must promise me.'

'Yes.'

'Just as long as I don't have to see Father Ignacio,' I say. 'I don't think I could face him.'

Carmen's apartment block is situated in a leafy street off the Paseo Reding near the port of Malaga, Muelle Uno. As I navigate carefully through the one way streets I'm frustrated; they're familiar yet changed. The promise of a new city metro has turned parts of the city in to chaos with roadworks and diversions. Progress and modernisation has its interim disadvantages.

I remember them building the new port and the development of Muelle Uno with its open air shopping mall, bars and restaurants and pathways lined with orange trees and the expensive yachting marina with views toward the Alcazaba, and Gibralfaro the Moorish hillside castle. Beyond the extensive quays, two huge cruise ships are berthed and disembarking passengers are making their way through the city streets eating ice cream while others climb into horse drawn carriages, all of them enjoying the warm spring sunshine.

The city has undergone amazing transformation with the Museum of Fine Arts, the Malaga Pompidou Centre and the Picasso Museum and I'd been part of its growth working on the restoration of different churches and galleries and, as I park my car, my step is light. I feel a sense of achievement and belonging I'd thought was long gone.

The Moorish-style apartment building has been recently converted from a bank and is more luxurious than I imagined. Inside, is an interior palm-frond leafy patio with a running water fountain and a naked Eros. The white marble reception is cool with a contrasting black Italian marble staircase. It's beauty is overwhelming and I pause to admire the wide sweeping staircase before walking up to the fourth floor, recognising the investment and refurbishment its undergone to maintain its cultural heritage.

At the top, I pause to lean over the banister and look down into the deep well. It would be easy to fall and I imagine a spreadeagled body lying on the cold marble below. Instinctively I pull back but not before a shiver echoes down my spine.

I ring the doorbell and when the hallway lights clicks off the timer I'm plunged into darkness. I smack the red light on the wall with my palm and although the lights flick on again my breathing is ragged and my hand shaking.

There's no answer so I turn to go and I'm descending the

first steps with my hand on the rail as the front door opens and Carmen peers out cautiously outside.

'Mikky? You're late.'

'That's a lovely greeting.'

I retrace my step and walk back up.

'I didn't think you'd come at all,' she replies. 'I thought you'd change your mind.'

I almost had. A few hours ago I dropped Eduardo at Malaga airport to fly back to Palma. He had held me close and kissed me saying.

'Are you sure you're doing the right thing?'

Was I?

I had replied, 'It will be good to catch up with Carmen again. We were very good friends...'

'Promise you'll tell me about it one day.'

'I will,' I lied.

'Hurry home soon.'

'As soon as I can.' It was another lie. They seemed to materialise without any effort and, as I let him go, I felt his reassurance and optimism leave me too. By the time I was in my car and heading for the city centre I'd convinced myself that he was better off without me. He might meet someone else. Someone who wasn't so screwed up; someone who could love him totally and wholeheartedly like he deserved.

Carmen kisses me on both cheeks. I inhale Chanel Number 5 and it brings back a rush of memories. She takes a step forward to glance down the stairwell and my photographer's eye takes in the details of her appearance. Today out of the wind and the sunshine of Tarifa, she looks pale and tired. A deep frown makes her dark eyes look closer together, as if she has difficulty focusing or concentrating. She has an expensively styled bob and although we're the same age, a plump waistline has added years to her. Wearing an old-fashioned maroon jacket, black skirt, and cream blouse, Carmen looks forty.

'You wouldn't want to fall down there,' I say, looking over her shoulder.

She looks at me as if suddenly remembering I'm here.

'Don't say that, Mikky. Come on in.' Her grip on my arm is tight and she ushers me inside and closes the door behind us and I am left staring in wonder at the long hallway in front of me.

'Have you moved the museum into your home?' I joke.

Carmen pulls on her hair and I remember it's a nervous tic that she hasn't lost and, as if avoiding my scrutiny, she links her arm through mine and pulls me down the corridor toward two double mahogany doors. Only the swing of her hips against mine as she walks, reminds me of the lithe, sexy girl she had been when we were students over ten years ago.

With my practised eye I take in the lavishness of the apartment; heavy oak furniture, gilt-framed pictures, wood carved urns, cut glass crystal, a marble bust and even a medieval mosaic tapestry.

'Have you been stealing from the Picasso?' I laugh.

'I may be the Curator but I am not a thief.'

I automatically raise my hand to my forehead where those exact letters had been carved into my skin barely a year ago but thanks to cosmetic surgery my forehead is clear and unnaturally wrinkle free.

'This apartment is...amazing.'

'It's not mine,' she replies.

I stop in my tracks. 'But you live here?'

'It's Yolanda's.'

'But you live together?'

'Yes, but - well, I don't own it - Yolanda does, well, her father owns it.'

'It's your home. You can't tell me this isn't your taste.' I stop to pause at an old Indian mask on display. 'You've always loved this old furniture and these antiquities from South America-'

'We can't all be minimalist like you.' The tone of her sharpness takes me by surprise.

'Where's Yolanda?' I ask.

'Out, and I don't want her to know about this. You must promise, you won't say anything to her - or to anyone.'

Carmen is half a head shorter than me but with high heels I look directly into her eyes.

'You know you can trust me,' I reply.

'I'm sorry, Mikky. I'll explain it all to you later. You mustn't tell a soul. Yolanda doesn't know and I don't want her to find out so please don't say a word.'

'Where is she?'

'Her mother hasn't been well so she went to Madrid for a few nights but she's due back any time. Come on, we haven't long.'

She releases my arm and opens both doors at the same time and the first thing I notice are the high ceilings, magnificent paintings and the large sash windows along the back wall overlooking the tall trees in the boulevard below.

It's a far cry from the tiny studio she lived in with Yolanda four years ago in a less impressive part of the city and I've worked in enough museums and art galleries to have an appreciation of light, air temperature and space.

I'm impressed but as I walk slowly into the room my eyes are drawn to a lone figure sitting on a gold-leaf coloured couch.

'I'm sorry Mikky,' she says. 'I know you didn't want to but-'

I don't recognise him at first. His cheeks are fuller, his hair is greyer and his stomach rounder. He wears dark glasses and sits straight-backed which makes him look uneasy and uncomfortable. He's no longer the skinny, young, dark haired priest filled with vibrancy, urgency and life.

Is it him?

How has he aged so much and so quickly?

He tilts his head toward me and lowers the glass of water raised half way his lips. He places it carefully on the table and I'm reminded of his slow and thoughtful movements and how solemnly he moved between the aisles and the pews and how he knelt to pray and genuflect before Christ. They had once been gestures I'd found beautiful and endearing but now he's an old man and for some reason I feel cheated and betrayed.

'Mikky?'

His voice still holds that youthful, excited urgency. One, that you would expect from a lover and it quickens my heart and I bite my lip. I cannot move.

'Mikky? Is that really you?'

I'm lost in the past but what pulls me sharply back to reality is not just the dog collar he wears at his throat but also the white stick laying at his feet.

Chapter 3

"There is a great deal of difference between an eager man who wants to read a book and a tired man who wants a book to read." - G.K. Chesterton

armen is clutching my arm in a vice-like grip and she propels me across the room toward Father Ignacio.

'Mikky?'

I don't know what to say.

Carmen squeezes my arm.

What do I call him?

Is he really blind?

'It's been a long time, Mikky - seven years?' he persists.

'It's been ten - ten years.'

His frown is replaced by a warm smile and he rises to his feet holding onto the edge of the couch.

'I'm sorry, an unfortunate accident has left me with no sight. May I...' he pauses and holds out his hand and I remember his long slim fingers and the gentleness of his touch.

Reluctantly I hold out my arm and he draws me closer and raises his fingers to my cheeks.

'Do you mind if I touch you? It's something I've learned to - do you mind?' he asks.

'No.'

But I do mind.

I mind very much. I don't want him to touch me.

His fingers travel over my face, touching my chin, my cheeks and my forehead. It's an intimate gesture and a shiver tingles through my body at the contact of his clipped nails. It is at once sensual and familiar, then with complete tenderness, he reaches for my shoulder and pulls me close to kiss me on both cheeks. His breath is sweet and his lips soft. All traces of boyhood youth and innocence have disappeared and against my my will, he raises my hand to his lips and kisses my fingers.

That's when my heart dances.

'Not very appropriate for a priest,' I tease and when he laughs only a glimmer of excitement shows in his wry smile.

'My senses tell me you still look lovely,' he says 'What happened to your forehead?'

'You may not be able to see but you don't miss a trick, Father,' I reply emphasising his status and I move away, dismayed that he can see beyond the expensive cosmetic surgery and he didn't mention my missing curls.

'What happened to you?' I ask.

Carmen who has remained silent during our exchange points to a chair near the coffee table and opposite Father Ignacio. I'm irked by her calmness and I feel manipulated. She ignored my wishes; I told her I didn't want to see him. She has betrayed the trust we might have built and I have a feeling that this has been orchestrated deliberately and that he has been waiting for me to arrive. It's like I've been invited to their party and I wonder what they want with me after all these years.

We sit opposite each other and he begins speaking.

'I was in South America - working on a mission and we were travelling from a small village in the mountains in a violent storm. The car hit a tree and we ended up at the bottom of a ravine - I was lucky - the driver died.'

'It must have been awful,' I whisper.

'It was five years ago. The doctors thought I might see again or regain some of my sight but after several operations it hasn't been possible.'

'I'm sorry,' I whisper.

'Don't be. We both know there are others less fortunate and besides, I still have my intuition and the Lord guides me in my daily work. One doesn't need eyes to see.'

'If only He was as generous to others in the world, as He is in guiding you.'

Father Ignacio tilts his head and his smile fades.

'Are you disillusioned?'

'He's never helped me.'

'You have lost your faith?'

'I don't know if I ever had it to lose-'

'We don't have long, Father,' Carmen interrupts and she looks apologetically a me.

'Yes, of course - sorry. It's a very difficult situation.' Father Ignacio leans forward balancing his elbows on his knees and he clutches his hands as if in prayer.

'It's very delicate Mikky and there is no-one that I trust-'

'That's why he came to me,' Carmen interjects. 'He knew that I would find you.'

I look from one to the other but my eyes rest on the man of cloth who is now a stranger to me.

'What's this about?'

'May I show, Mikky?' Carmen asks him.

Father Ignacio opens his palms as a gesture of compliance and I find it hard to tear my glance away from him. For almost six months we had worked together under the roof of the same church. We had sat for hours in the dark recess of the church listening and talking, debating the merits of Christ as if He really existed. We had argued, disagreed, discussed and honed our beliefs. There were times when I had argued and had been very angry and I had shouted:

Where was Christ in my life?

Where was He when I was growing up? Where was He when my adoptive parents had been cruel and unkind – when they went from bar to bar, and Papa had smoked hashish and I suffered the rages of Mama's jealous fits? But as a novice priest Father Ignacio had argued back. He said that Christ had been by my side. He had been there for me. He had guided me to my destiny, to this small church near Malaga.

I doubted that then as I do now and, to reassure myself, I rub the ugly six inch scar on the back of my left hand remembering when I was twelve and how Mama had tried to slash my face with a bread knife.

He hadn't been there then and I raised my hand to protect my sight.

Had Father Ignacio known more about my life, he might have suggested that Christ had been with me last year when I was saved from a burning building. But no, it had been Karl Blakey and not God who had carried me out of the fire and saved my life. Although we were enemies, Karl had lifted my beaten body to safety and then charged back inside through the flames for the stolen Vermeer. Greed had taken over from his common sense.

Where was Christ then?

Carmen clears her throat and reaches for a dirty, old hessian cloth lying on the mahogany coffee table and hands me a package.

'Look at this, Mikky.'

It's too small and heavy to be a miniature painting and I peer under the cloth, lifting the the corners gently and when the last piece of hessian falls aside, I'm holding the most exquisite gold-leaf book.

My skin tingles with anticipation and my heart is ignited with an intensity that only beauty can stir. It's slightly larger than the average modern paperback. It's also thicker and probably twice as heavy and it's illustrated in fine gold.

'Wow,' I cannot hide my surprise. 'This is beautiful...amazing.'

I turn it in my hands admiring the gilt engraving and the gothic introduction. It's bound in moroccan leather and a pattern of flowers covers the front. The main text of the manuscript is Latin apart from a prayer at the back of the book that's written in Spanish.

'La oration de Sant Gregorio Papa,' I read then I look at Carmen. 'I can't believe it. It's a tome, a medieval masterpiece.'

Her eyes shine.

'What do you think?'

'I'm no professional book expert. You'd need an antiquarian bookseller or auctioneer.'

'But you spent a lot of time in Bruges. Didn't you work with a man who knew about these things?'

'Theo - yes - he loved these illuminated books. He was a small auctioneer and he worked with book dealers - amongst others,' I add. 'Many of these Book of Hours were made in the Netherlands; Ghent, Bruges were particular places for scholars who-'

'Is this an original?' Father Ignacio interrupts.

27

'It's hard to say. It would have to be verified.' I turn it over in my hands. 'The script on the vellum is Gothic and the binding looks like calf–'

'I've heard about the Rothschild Prayerbook, a Renaissance manuscript,' he says.

'That was made during the Flemish Renaissance, I think it originated in Belgium in the 1500's. This looks quite similar to the work of...' I struggle to remember the name of the Flemish miniaturist – and then it comes to me. 'Gerard Hereabout,' I say aloud. 'He served at the court of King Henry VIII.'

Father Ignacio exhales loudly.

'He was well know for this intricate type of work,' I add.

A slow smile spreads across Carmen's face.

'It looks similar to one the Rothschild's commissioned that sold in London a few years ago – over eight million pounds.'

'It appears intact,' I say. 'Malicious dealers have been known to rip pages out and sell them separately for more money. It's beauty is overwhelming.'

I'm subdued by the ancient hand work that would have been involved to create such a detailed illustration and I spend a few minutes turing it in my hands, admiring the decorative borders and the scripted text.

'It's all handwritten, see these ornate initial letters in each section?' I hold out the book and when I remember he can't see, I offer it to Carmen. 'All the illustrations around the borders are miniatures and very often there's a calendar of holy days in these type of books, look, see this – the scribes wrote in red ink the most important days. That's where the phrase, red-letter days, comes from–'

'You haven't lost your touch.' Carmen's frown is replaced by a sincere smile.

Father Ignacio's face muscles don't move. He seems lost in the darkness of his own world.

'You know more than I do,' I reply. 'You're the Curator.'

'These Book of Hours were popular in the fifteenth century,' Carmen explains to Father Ignacio. 'These books were very popular with the wealthy and devout Catholics who prayed at least eight times a day and recited prayers or liturgies.'

I turn a page, observing the small details marvelling at the beauty of the artwork and I add. 'These books were also seen as a status symbol, something of a fashionable accessory.'

I study the ornate lettering, the decorative boarders and the small drawings of animals, rabbits and squirrels and then other scenes depicting the stations of the cross.

'There was one made for the Spanish Queen - Joanna the Mad - Juana la Loca and there is a rumour that a second book was commissioned by her but there's never been any real proof of its existence but this could...'

Father Ignacio straightens his back and takes a deep breath.

'Where did you get this?' I ask and although I look at Carmen my question is directed at Father Ignacio.

He sighs and grips his hands together in prayer as if the weight of the revelation is too much for him to bare and when he eventually raises his head, his voice is low and measured.

'After Father Benedict died, I've been sorting through the library archives in the Monastery. I never thought we had anything of any value but then I found this. It had been hidden at the back of a vault...'

I'm suddenly reminded of Father Ignacio's soft voice echoing in the empty church and the warmth and security that I felt in his company all those years ago.

'Hidden by who?'

29

'I don't know.'

'Were there any other papers or documents?' I ask gently to deflect my memory.

He shakes his head.

I smile and stand up.

'You'll have to do better than this – both of you. Unless you both tell me the truth you're wasting my time.'

'Wait, Mikky. Please sit down.' Carmen holds my arm and says to Father Ignacio. 'I think you have to tell Mikky the whole story that you told me.'

Father Ignacio clears his throat and I sit back down then he whispers.

'Father Benedict was my friend. We had know each other for many, many years. He was old, almost ninety-eight when he died but he was still sensible. He knew his mind but the cancer spread rapidly toward the end, and he asked me to hear his last confession. He had considered taking his secret to the grave but then he said, he felt guilty – with so many, needing so much – and that I was to use it to some good. To help those in need. He told me, that he had been entrusted with a special book during the Civil War. As you know, Spain took no part in the Second World War they were fighting their own war against Franco. I will not go into the politics at the time but as you know families in Spain were divided and a number of foreign volunteers also arrived in Spain to fight the Fascists. Some were intellectuals, some were writers and others poets. The war divided the country and Father Benedict told me of a wealthy family from Granada who supported the Communists. They sold off many of their worldly possessions to fund, The Cause but they entrusted him with this special book. The family wanted this Book of Hours to remain with the church.They didn't want it funding the war between Spanish families.'

'What was the name of the family?'

'He didn't tell me.'

'So where was it kept?' I ask.

'It was hidden in a monastery outside of Granada.'

'And you found it?'

'Father Benedict hid it. He told me where to find it.'

I cannot see his eyes. I cannot tell if he is lying.

'When was this?'

'Last week - at Easter.'

'And you brought it here?' I say.

'Yes.'

Carmen's voice is filled with enthusiasm. 'I've done some research and you're right. Mikky. Juana la Loca had a second Book of Hours commissioned. It has only been referred to in one historical document and I believe this could be it-' Her voice takes on an edge of excitement but I cut into her eagerness.

'The first one is where?'

'Harvard University,' she replies.

Why she has involved me? What am I doing here? She's the curator of the Picasso Museum. She's the expert.

I turn the manuscript in my hand. 'What are you going to do with it?'

'We need to get it authenticated and valued. It could make a huge difference to the church,' replies Father Ignacio.

'Ah yes, it will help all the poverty in the world. It will provide food for the starving in Africa and help the uneducated-'

'Mikky, don't!' Carmen's voice is stern.

'It will be used to do good.' Father Ignacio says calmly. 'I

31

will ensure that it adds value to the lives of many. I promised Father Benedict.'

'Like to those living in the Vatican?' I suggest.

'Mikky, please. This is not about religion it's about art – culture – Spanish history. This is about a rare manuscript...' Carmen shakes her head and brings a finger to her lips as if warning me to say nothing more in front of the blind priest. 'We must make the right decision and help Father Ignacio.'

'Do you think it's authentic?' I ask.

She shrugs. 'Maybe. I don't know. That's the problem.'

'But that's your job – it's what you do.'

'It's not that easy...'

'You must know plenty of people,' I insist.

'Not people I trust with something as valuable as this. It could be dangerous.'

'Dangerous? You could make enquiries...Christies or Sotheby's?'

'It's not that simple.' Carmen tugs on a strand of hair.

There's something she's not telling me.

'So, who have you spoken to? Who knows about it?' I persist.

Her eyebrows furrow in concentration and she stares at the book in my hand, unwilling to meet my eye.

'It's my fault,' says Father Ignacio. 'I told her we must be careful who we tell. Father Benedict warned me. He said that there have always been rumours that this book exists and its value is presumed to be very high. Let's say that there are different factions, within the church, who would want to - for want of a better word – take it and use for other purposes...'

'What would you do with it, Father?'

Carmen holds up the palm of her hand and says. 'We must get it valued before we start dreaming about what anyone would like to do with it. It might be worth nothing or it could be worth millions - we just don't know.'

'Then go to one of the big auction houses in Madrid or London - Bonhams or Sotheby's,' I reply.

'It's complicated,' Carmen sighs.

Father Ignacio rubs his temple and holds his head in his hands.

Carmen raises a finger to her lips as if warning me.

'Don't worry, Father. Mikky is here now,' she says sooth-ingly. 'We'll sort it out.'

'Who knows about the book?' I count on my fingers. 'There's you, Carmen. Father Ignacio and now me. Are we the only ones who know about this?'

'Yes,' she replies and turns away.

'There was no-one else who heard the confession?'

'No.' Father Ignacio seems to rally and he leans upright.

'So, no-one else knows about the existence of the book or has seen the book? Father, forgive me for asking but how did you find the book, if you're blind?'

My bluntness causes Carmen to look up sharply.

Father Ignacio appears to choose his words carefully before replying. 'I was with one of the young Brothers. He helped me...'

'So there is someone else who has seen it,' I say, 'and where is this Brother now?'

'He has gone to a Mission. He wanted to go to Africa. He told me, the night before, that it was a responsibility that he could not stand. He thought he would be unable to keep the oath of secrecy that I had sworn him to. He was my eyes to find it and it's a terrible burden.' Father Ignacio looks wretched and he hangs his head.

'Is the church that divided?'

'It could be...'

'It's not just the church who would want this book,' Carmen says. 'Any artefact of any value, if not registered or claimed could belong legally to anyone - if there's no provenance attached to it - who's to say it doesn't belong to someones great aunt who had it hiding in a cellar?'

'But you can provide the provenance,' I argue. 'Knowing what you know about it.'

'You know how easy it is to forge these things and if it fell into the wrong hands - then what?'

'Did this Brother or did you, tell anyone else about this manuscript?' I insist.

'I don't think he did.' He shrugs. 'But how would I know?'

'Have you been to the police?' I ask.

Carmen looks up sharply. 'No.'

'Do you think someone from the church is after this book?' I speak quickly. 'Have you shown it to anyone? If anyone either inside or outside of the church know that you have this rare manuscript that has lay hidden for seventy years and is valuable - then they will come to you, Father. They might want it at any price.'

Although I think he looks at me, he cannot see the anguish in my eyes.

'How do you know that Father Benedict didn't tell anyone else? Why did he tell you?' I insist.

'He trusted me to do the right thing or perhaps he believed I was young enough to keep it a secret until my deathbed.'

'So why keep it a secret, now that the war is over?' I argue.

'That's why I wanted to speak to you, Mikky.'

I gaze at Father Ignacio wondering how a blind man in the

34

church, will keep such a secret even if he wanted to.

'There's no guarantee that other people in the church aren't aware of it or even people outside the church who will do anything to get their hands on it. We must act quickly. You might be in danger,' Carmen adds.

'Is there somewhere you can go?' I ask.

'I can go on a retreat. I will be safe there.'

'Good,' I reply unable to hide the relief in my voice.

'He wanted you here,' Carmen says as if Father Ignacio is not only blind but deaf too. 'He insisted that we work together and between us we can find out about the manuscript and work out the best thing to do with it.'

I nod my head still unclear of my role thinking about the young priest who carries this secret in Africa.

Carmen nods at the wall behind her.

'I can keep it here. Just until we work something out.'

'It would be safer in the museum,' I say.

'That's true,' she says. 'Leave it with me, Father.'

'I feel this is an imposition to you both. Now that I have come to you and told you everything I feel that I'm asking too much. I hope I haven't done the wrong thing-'

His voice is weary but there is an inflection of relief and his shoulders sag. He looks exhausted and drained.

'It's my job,' she says softly. 'It's what I do. I research the provenance for artwork like this and Mikky has lots of experience and contacts too. You mustn't worry. Trust us. Come on, Father. You need to rest. Let me get you a taxi.'

'You're right. I must return to the monastery. I must ask the Lord for guidance. He will help us.' Father Ignacio hooks his hand under Carmen's arm and she lifts the white cane from the floor.

35

I watch him move cautiously, navigating his way between the unfamiliar furniture with her help. He wouldn't be much of a guard for a rare and expensive manuscript. He looks like a broken man and I think a retreat might do him good - or a month on holiday in the Caribbean.

He kisses my cheeks and this time his slight whiskers scratch my skin and his breath smells of sweet almonds.

'Thank you, Mikky. I'm happier knowing you're here. It's been a long time but I've followed your career with pride.'

'It has been a long time, Father,' I agree returning the pressure of his fingers on mine.

I had once called him Antonio, but now he belongs to the church. The years between our last meeting have changed us both. In the ten years that have passed we are two different people and seeing him again, is like reading the end of a book after only reading the first chapter, and a hollow emptiness creeps through me. I feel deprived of the missing pages in-between and the conversations that we might have shared and the friendship that could have been ours, and as if reading my thoughts, his voice holds a wistful tone when he says.

'Your painting still hangs above the alter in the Chapel of St. Peter.'

'I'm pleased to hear it.'

'Goodbye, Mikky.'

'Take care, Father.'

Carmen leads Father Ignacio from the room and when the front door closes I go to the large sash window and gaze down at the palm-tree lined street and the busy traffic leading to and from the Port. I wait and watch Carmen in the street flagging down a white taxi. She settles him into the backseat, slams the door then raises her hand to wave, as if he can see her, until the car disappears around the corner.

To a stranger Carmen would appear thoughtful, perhaps even wistful but I know her. The self assured tone of her voice didn't fool me as she spoke. I have seen her acting a part, pretending she was someone else while inside her head and inside her heart her soul was withering and dying. And, like someone on the outside looking in, once again, I see the telling signs of her nervousness. The way she tugs her hair and how she taps her index finger against her lips.

It's a cry for help.

But why does she need me?

When Carmen walks back into the room I'm standing gazing at a painting with swirls of colours; splashes of reds, scarlets, mauves, oranges and black and a flamenco skirt rising into flames as the dancer spins.

'Flamenco en Llamas, by Sasha McBride,' I read the small sign on the wall. It's displayed as if in an art gallery.

'Sasha got divorced and went back to Argentina last year.'

'Wasn't she a friend of Yolanda's?' I say.

'They're cousins. Their mother's are sisters from Buenos Aires.'

'She's a good artist.' I move on to look at a replica of a Caravaggio - Boy with a Basket of Fruit - only a copy but a clever reproduction and I wonder if Carmen purchased it from our ex art teacher's art gallery in Arta where my accident happened last year. Dolores' gallery was famous for copies.

'Do you still paint - ever?' she asks, smoothing her skirt under her bottom before taking the seat Father Ignacio occupied.

'Rarely.'

'Dolores said you began again.'

37

'I've stopped.'

'I don't know why you do this. You waste your talent, Mikky.'

'It's not wasted, it's just diverted into other creative areas.'

'You're an artist - why do you keep denying it? Don't you ever just want to paint and do nothing else?'

'No. Do you?'

'My talent wasn't real like yours. That's why I became a Curator. Even Yolanda is more artistic than me...' Her voice trails off and I know her eyes are on me as I stroll around the room and I can't help but wonder what she makes of me.

I remain quiet, admiring handicrafts from Peru and India while absorbing and puzzling over the details of our encounter with Father Ignacio.

'Do you believe him?' I ask turning from an elaborately decorated Mexican urn.

'Of course, why wouldn't I?'

'I don't know.'

'He wouldn't lie.' She sits with her legs crossed winding a strand of hair around her index finger.

I finish my tour with a growing sense of unease. Within twenty-four hours I have been faced with two good friends from my past. People who I had left behind - people I'd hoped never to see again - and I'm trying to separate the conversations from the facts and also from my gut reaction but a growing sense of dread continues to flourish unaided inside me.

'So why do you need me, Carmen? What's going on?'

I sit beside her.

'That guy you worked with in Bruges - Theo, you said his name was - he knows about these books?'

I frown trying to remember. 'Carmen, that was years ago...'

'Then what about the other expert from Cambridge - when you were doing Fine Arts? Can you remember his name - you were good friends? I can Google him.'

She picks up her iPad.

'Carmen, wait.'

'He moved, didn't he? Where was he based - Oxford or London?'

There's an urgency to her voice and I reach out but she shakes my hand away before flicking her hair behind her ears.

'Carmen, there must be lots of rare book dealers or auction houses that you can go to,' I insist calmly. 'What about all your contacts at the museum? You must know all the specialists-'

'I don't want to go through the usual channels.'

I lean back and stare at her. 'But this is your job, you're a Curator. This is what you do.'

'Not this time.'

She bites her lip and a ripple of concern shudders through me like a sheet of corrugated steel.

'Why not?'

'What's his name, Mikky?'

'Fuller,' I reply. 'Simon Fuller but he moved from Cambridge.' I walk over to the window and look down onto the wide Boulevard.

'You trusted him, didn't you?' she insists.

'He was good at what he did but that was a long time ago-'

She taps the keys on her iPad.

'Look. Here he is - Canterbury - he's in England. Phone him for me?'

'Not until you tell me the truth.' I fold my arms and stare at her.

She tugs on a strand of hair, chews her lip and then picks up the old book. Holding it tenderly, she gazes at the illuminated pages and we both know that if it's the original, she should be wearing gloves but it's as if she has lost all rational and reasoning. She turns a page and I wonder what she is thinking.

'Carmen?' I prompt. 'What the hell is happening?'

'You've really no idea, have you?' Her eyes fill with tears and she turns away.

'What?'

'Can't you see how awful my life is?'

I laugh. 'You are joking?'

When she doesn't reply I hold out my arms.

'What? With all this…. You're not happy? Isn't this what you want, Carmen?'

'Of course it is, but–'

The 'but' hangs in the air and in that split second my heart sinks and I've a feeling that everything is about to implode and I'm about to be sucked into the backdraft of her emotional vortex.

'Are you having an affair?' I ask.

'Don't be ridiculous.' She stands up.

I exhale slowly. 'So, tell me?'

'He's frightened,' she says. She is at my side and although her face is turned to the busy street below, she seems lost in thought. 'Father Ignacio is very frightened. Why do you think he brought it to us and didn't just hide it?'

'To be valued?'

'He brought it to us because he's blind. He doesn't know who to trust. Imagine that - there's no-one else he can go to with this secret - and why?'

I shrug.

'Because he doesn't really believe any more. He's lost his

faith. Couldn't you tell?'

'Not really.'

'You wouldn't understand.' She moves quickly and snatches up the book.

'Explain it to me.'

'It was a mistake asking you to come here. I knew I was asking too much...'

She moves aside the oil painting, Flamenco en Llamas, and reveals a wall safe. She dials a number, opens the door and after folding the illustrated manuscript carefully in the hessian she places it inside the safe.

'Aren't you going to take it to the museum?'

She closes the door and returns the painting to its original position hiding the secret in the recess behind it. She does all of this silently then she turns around and looks at me.

'I'll take it later.'

'What wouldn't I understand? Am I insensitive or stupid?'

'You have money,' she says simply and with those few words I cannot argue but she doesn't know how much I have. No one knows about the deal I made last year with the Isabella Stuart Museum for returning Vermeer's stolen painting, The Concert – apart from Josephine Lavelle – and I can guarantee her silence.

'Tell me this isn't about money, is it?'

'I'm sick of looking after other people's things. Every day I'm surrounded by Picasso's painting and other works of art. I take care of them. I arrange and show continuously changing exhibitions of famous artists but they're not mine – the paintings – nothing belongs to me.'

I laugh. 'They can't be yours, any more than a banker can have the money he looks after – or a young kid who works in

41

a clothes shop can try everything on. It's like working in a restaurant and always eating the food. That's life, Carmen. That's how it is.'

'But I want my own things. I want something for me. I'm sick of it.' She folds her arms, squares her shoulders then she moves around the room, straightening cushions and lining up the dining chairs at exact distances from the heavy table and when the chair legs scrape against the oak floor I say nothing in her silence, waiting for her to speak and when she does, her voice is filled with emotion.

'You just don't understand what it's like, Mikky. What I've been going through. It's awful. It's just too...'

'Do you mean at the museum? I thought you liked your job?'

'I do. But I'm only ever the custodian, the guardian, the person who decides on the exhibitions. I negotiate and arrange the safety, insurance and transport and I check their provenance and authenticity – and I'm sick of it.'

'Then get a new job? There must be–'

'I don't want a new job!' she shouts. 'You don't understand. I want this book.'

Her words resonate in the room, bouncing off the walls and like an echo they reverberate my head.

'The book? The Book of Hours?' I nod my head at the safe. 'That book?'

'Yes.'

'But it's not yours.'

'Who says?'

I grin. 'Stop messing around, Carmen.'

But her face is deadly serious and my mind whirls rapidly as I'm thinking of what she's planning to do.

'You want to steal it?'

'It's in my possession.'

What about Father Ignacio and the-'

'Church?'

'He came to you in good faith. You can't steal it from him.'

'I can negotiate on his behalf and get something out of it for me.'

'Without involving the museum?'

'Exactly.'

'You'll get fired.'

'I'm leaving anyway.'

'Why are you leaving?'

She turns away. 'You wouldn't understand...'

'Try me.'

'I want out.'

'So, why am I here? Why do you need me'

'He wouldn't have handed it over to me otherwise.'

'How do you know that?'

'He phoned me last week. He told me that you were the only person he trusted.'

I take a few minutes to digest what she said, then I ask.

'What do you really want, Carmen? Why are you doing this? Are you so unhappy? This isn't you - this isn't the Carmen, I remember.'

'Do you think you're the only one who's changed, Mikky? Are you so self indulgent that the world only owes you an apology and the rest of us have to lump what we're given in life and put up with it? Do you think you're the only one affected by bad things and us ordinary mortals can just carry on with the daily drudge, never changing, never hoping, never wishing, never dreaming...'

'No, of course not-'

43

'I want freedom,' she raises her voice. ' I want the same freedom that you have, to do what you want - and the same freedom that Yolanda has to do what she wants.'

'Yolanda?'

'Yes.'

'But Yolanda works hard-'

'Yes - and she has Daddy's money to support her.'

I frown, uncomfortable at her jealous tone. 'But she has her own business.'

'He paid for this apartment,' she spits. 'He pays for everything. He controls her - both of us - with his constant demands.'

'What demands?'

'We go to exhibitions - we have to go to the opening of galleries and parties and special dinners. We have to meet people. It's all prestige and he uses me and my name and my position as the Provenance Curator of the Picasso.'

'But what does this have to do with stealing the book - money? Is that what you ultimately want?'

She doesn't reply so I continue.

'Carmen, this is your home. You're well paid. You take holidays abroad and weekends away, and I imagine you eat out and you rarely cook. You lead a very happy and successful life. I can't see why you would want to do this...'

'You don't understand my life, you never will,' she shouts. 'What do you know or care about anyone? You're so bloody selfish, you walked out four years ago without a backward glance and you never even stayed in touch. You never sent a word or even a text message to say you were alright.'

'I understand you, more than you will ever know,' I reply calmly, 'and I couldn't contact you or anyone. I was in a terrible state-'

'How do you think I felt?'

'It was better that I left. I had to go. Be honest, Carmen - tell the truth, wasn't it?'

She hesitates for a second before taking a deep breath and then she nods.

'This is the life you have created for yourself - this life with Yolanda. This is your home.'

'But I want-'

'What?'

'I want it to be mine,' she shouts and waves her arm at me. 'You have no idea about me or my life, Mikky. But I want it. I want to own something. I want something that's mine, that I can keep - that will get me out of here - out of this mess. I want to be in control and lead my life-'

'You're not making sense. If you're not happy with Yolanda then leave-'

'This isn't about Yolanda, it's about me.' She stabs a finger at her chest. 'It's about what I want. For once it's about me. I've had enough.'

'You can't go through with this.' My heart is beating rapidly and I feel disorientated as if the world has tilted from its tiller and we are both adrift on a choppy and treacherous sea.

'I'll do as I please, Mikky. I'm sick of it all. I'm sick of sticking to the rules and obeying everyone. Doing as I'm told. Where has it got me?' Her face is contorted with anger and determination

'Father Ignacio wanted me to have the book and you've put it in your safe. You're not keeping it, Carmen. I won't let you. Whatever problems you have - stealing this manuscript won't solve them.'

We're both glaring at each other and that's when the front door clicks open.

'I'll call the police if I have to,' I whisper.

'Hola?' A voice shouts out. 'Carmen, cariño?'

'Not a word,' she hisses. She blinks and suddenly her face becomes mask-like. She straightens her skirt and steps away from behind the dining table as if it's a shield that will protect her and takes a deep breath. 'Don't you dare mention a thing to Yolanda.'

'We need to finish this conversation,' I reply but she stalks out of the room.

I wait a few beats, waiting for my heartbeat to slow down then I follow her. I pause in the doorway. At the far end of the corridor Carmen throws her arms around Yolanda neck. She kisses her hard on the lips and for some reason I'm reminded of Judas's kiss in the Garden of Gethsemane.

'Welcome home, cariño, I have a lovely surprise.' Carmen's voice is light and fun, and all signs of our angry exchange has dissipated. She steps aside and waves a flamboyant hand in my direction like a magician would produce a white bunny rabbit from his top hat.

I smile and raise my hand.

Yolanda's smile dwindles. Her mouth drops open and her eyes blaze with anger. 'What the f-'

Her reaction is far worse than I had anticipated.

Chapter 4

"Always read something that will make you look good if you die in the middle of it." - P.J. O'Rourke

The following morning as I cross the wide shady boulevard of Paseo del Parque, a warm breeze flickers around my baggy Iron Maiden T-shirt raising tiny hairs on my arms amongst the vivid and colourful painting of Edvard Munch's The Scream, wrapped around my right arm. The long, despairing face is near madness and the vibrant colour represents my confusion. It's my talisman and it serves as a reminder to the dark days in which I lived and the state I was in four years ago when I lived in Malaga. It's a work of art, crafted on my arm that has been admired by many people but shocked even more.

I pause under the shade of a date palm to play air guitar to Gary Moore's, Parisienne Walkways and I smile when a man crosses the road and a young girl pushing a baby's buggy take a detour to avoid me.

There are quicker way to get to my destination but I want to see the changes and familiarise myself with the transformation this city has undergone. I stroll past the entrance to Muelle Uno and pause at the entrance to Calle Larios to look up at the statue of the Marques de Larios. It reminds me of Nelson's column but this man introduced sugar cane to the region that was turned into gin under the same brand name – Larios.

Although I was born in England, Spain is my home. I studied in Madrid and afterwards I moved to Malaga. For a while I was happy here. I'd met Antonio; Father Ignacio who spoke to me about life, love and religion and some of our conversations still resonate in my head. He was my friend and seeing him yesterday has made me feel incredibly sad. While I have lived, worked and studied, his life's path took him on a different route. Yesterday I saw a man who now appears lost, disillusioned and a little helpless.

Where did he go? Where did the young enthusiastic priest go?

I had loved him but where is that love now?

Where does love go when it disappears?

It's mid morning and there's something about the lazy and relaxed way the shops open their doors, deliveries are made that fill my heart with contentment. I breathe in deep lungfuls of air and the aroma of rich coffee beans. I want to fill my senses with smells from this city whose streets still bare witness to the Easter processions; pavements are being cleared of metal barriers and grandstand seating is loaded onto trucks. Street cleaners with swirling brushes clear plastic takeaway cartons, water bottles and squashed cans all debris from last night's revelry.

A waiter stands smoking in a small alleyway. Crouched beside him on an overflowing bin is a ginger and white cat with a torn ear and gouged eye. I pause to watch him rubbing her chest and feeding her bits of chicken. His tenderness surprises me and I wish I had my camera with me.

'Hola guapa,' he says to my inquisitive stare.

'Buenos dias.' I smile, turn away, and make my way through the narrow, cobbled, backstreets of the city, around the corner from the Picasso Museum. It had been a favourite haunt of mine four years ago now I dodge tourists in the Pasaje Chinitas, taking photographs on their way to and from the Cathedral or the Museums. I duck down a small alleyway to a bar that has been there for years, handed down through generations of the same family, Café Central. I push open the door and the familiar smell of warm coffee, garlic and herbs assail my nostrils and warm feeling surges through me but before I can adjust to the dark light of the interior Jose comes around from behind the bar and pulls me into his arms.

'Mikky! Que guapa! You look as beautiful as ever - even with short hair.' He rubs my head with his fat fingers.

'And you've put on weight.' I pat his ample stomach.

His hair is greyer and his face more deeply ingrained but his greeting is the same as always - a big hug.

I sit up at the bar and we make small talk as if I've never been away and when he asks where I've been I gloss over the past few years and tell him I now photograph for art galleries and museums mostly in London.

'You should come back here to work. Had they opened the Thyssen Museum when you lived here?'

'I left the year after it opened.'

He nods. 'And the Malaga Pompidou Centre?'

'That's new. I'll try and go this week.'

'Is your friend still at the Picasso?'

'Carmen, she's the Provenance Curator.'

'We don't see much of her any more. The museum must

49

keep her busy,' he adds loudly, above the noise of the coffee machine as he makes my cortado. 'It's good to have all these Museums. The tourists need something to do when the sun isn't out – Malaga has changed.'

He places the coffee in front of me and my nostril are filled with its rich aroma. Caffeine rushes to my head at the first sip and I smile. I'm home.

My breakfast roll is filled with queso manchego, garlic, squeezed tomatoes and a drizzle of olive oil. I eat hungrily, reading the SUR, talking to Jose between customers and afterwards, I wipe my lips, ball up the tissue and toss it onto the counter.

When Jose finishes serving a couple in the corner he slides a second coffee over the bar.

'What do you make of this?' I hold up the headline of the newspaper.

He shrugs in a Gaelic fashion with the corner of his mouth turned down.

'Quien sabe? Mafia? The Russians killed a man with an injection in the middle of London. Anything is possible.'

'Mafia?' I pull the newspaper toward me and check the details. 'The dead man was an electrician. He'd had been working on the installation for the new metro links in the city.'

'A gun with a silencer in the Easter processions...,' Jose replies. 'It's like a film. This place is changing, Mikky – the whole country has changed.'

'Why didn't anyone see who did it?' I ask.

'There's more Mafia here than the press will report on,' Jose says, wiping the counter in wide sweeping circles as he talks. 'Russian Bandits – it's even changed since you were here,

Mikky. They kill one and then another one takes over. There's a protection racket that would get you killed if you were to talk about it to the press. It's these foreigners - they bring trouble - first it was the English with their drunken teenagers and then it was the Americans bringing their fast food restaurant and now it's the Russian Mafia. They're taking over the coast and bringing their bad ways with them.'

The stranger sitting at the bar beside me begins nodding in agreement and blaming the influx of foreigners; Syrian and Moroccan refugees for the decline in the Spanish economy, and England's Brexit. Europe is collapsing.

I fold the newspaper, leave it on the bar and pay the bill, promising Jose I'll return.

I'm crossing the road when my mobile rings and I check the caller's ID.

'Josephine?' I say, standing under the shade of an old fir tree to let a group of teenagers pass. 'This is is a lovely surprise. How are you?'

Josephine Lavelle, once a world famous opera diva, is my birth mother but I still can't bring myself to call her Mama, Mum or Mother. Last year she came to find me. She commissioned my flat-mate, Javier to paint her portrait but it had been a ruse to meet me. Now I'm still not sure if I'm annoyed or flattered by the new role she is playing in my life but after the brutal beating I received last year Josephine not only insisted on paying for my private hospital treatment but she also cared for me with far more tenderness and kindness than I ever received from my adopted parents.

She wanted to make amends for her past and while I was too ill to protest we developed a tentative friendship and spent more time together, recuperating in a villa near Palma then on

Lake Como with her friend, another famous soprano, Glorietta Bareldo. It was an interesting and pleasant experience but then I came back to Mallorca to Eduardo, my intensive care nurse and now boyfriend. He encouraged me to work on my fitness levels and core muscles, I had started jogging then we had gone kitesurfing together in Tarifa.

'Where are you, Mikky?' Josephine asks. 'I've some great news! My friend in New York wants to exhibit your paintings.'

'I can't.'

'You must. It's a fantastic opportunity.'

'I'm not ready.'

'It will do you good and it will showcase your talents,' she insists, and in spite of myself I smile. I've never had the support of a parent and only Dolores,my ex art teacher, has shown any real interest in my art work.

'Where are you?' she asks.

'I'm in Malaga.'

The line goes quiet and I wonder is she can hear me.

I dodge the traffic and run across the road narrowly missing a noisy Vesper that careers around the corner. I shout at the driver, he doesn't turn around but raises a middle finger.

'Are you with your father?' Josephine's voice is distant. 'Is he still living down in Estepona?'

I pause under a palm tree and watch the street scene in front of me.

'I have no plans to see him - ever again - you should know that, Josephine. I'm staying with Carmen in Malaga.'

I can hear the relief in her voice when she says. 'I need you to come to London. Miles Davenport is prepared to fly over this weekend from New York and meet you.'

'I can't. I'll try and get time next month.'

'But this is important, Mikky. He wants you to do an exhibition next winter. I think you could have over twenty paintings. I've spoken to Dolores and she's prepared to lend us some of your earlier work. You will have more than enough time-'

'I'm not ready, Josephine.'

'I think you are, Mikky. You need to have more confidence in your ability. This is just the sort of opening and opportunity we talked about last year. This exhibition will get you noticed. Miles is the very best at-'

'I can't hear you,' I shout removing the phone from my mouth and holding it out to the noises of the street so she can hear the busses, the squealing brakes of taxis and the clip clopping hooves of horse and carriages. I hold the phone at arm's length. 'The line is bad. I'll call you as soon as-' I hiss like static crackle down the phone and hang up.

She may be my birth mother but she doesn't have the right to turn up in my life thirty-two years later and tell me what to do.

I play air base guitar to Foals, Inhaler and sing as I twang the chords. 'Don't follow me, You push and shove. I've had enough. You best believe...'

By the time I've familiarised myself with the new pedestrian streets at the foot of the Alcazaba and reacquainted myself with the shopping areas, it's eleven thirty when I make my way past the Thyssen Museum to the shop.

It's how I remembered it. Although when I open the studio door I realise its been redesigned. The floor is like a chequered chess board and a beaten up black leather sofa has been pushed

53

against the far wall. On the right, behind the reception, is a giant ink drawing of a naked woman reclining on a beach. I study the lean figure and I'm aware of soft padding steps behind me.

A voice cuts through the silent reception.

'Carmen drew it. Can't you tell?' Yolanda is tall, lithe and broad shouldered. She also has wide grey eyes and a hostile stare.

'It's beautiful,' I say.

'She drew it from a photo, one that she took that last summer in Tarifa, when we were watching the sunset and smoking pot. Remember?'

'Yes.'

How could I forget? We'd spent countless weekend travelling down the coast. Windsurfing had been my hobby but now kitesurfing was my passion.

'You used to take a lot of risks on the sea. You were always looking for danger.'

'Did I?'

'You were constantly seeking attention, like a child.'

'Really?'

'I never liked you.'

I smile. I won't let her rile me as she had tried to do last night. Once she had recovered from the shock of me standing in her apartment the three of us went out to a tapas bar. At first, Carmen and I reminisced about our University days and Yolanda had been sulky and quiet then she became irritable and irate. She had tried to talk about the incident four years ago but Carmen had deftly changed the subject. Ten minutes later Yolanda had pleaded tiredness from the drive back from Madrid and gone to bed.

54

Carmen had shown me to their spare room and when I ventured into the lounge to resume our interrupted conversation about the Book of Hours, she was making a few phone calls and she silenced me with a finger to her lips. After I left the room she closed the door behind me. Dismissed I'd gone to bed. This morning, after I returned from my morning run, they'd both gone to work early and I returned to an empty flat.

Yolanda didn't know I was going to turn up to her studio this morning. It's clearly an unwanted surprise, and she's provoked like a sleeping viper.

'Does Carmen still paint?' I ask.

'She's lost her confidence but out of all of my possessions this would be the one I treasure most. I would walk into a burning building to save this drawing,' she laughs. 'Although, I probably shouldn't say that. Don't you have an aversion to burning buildings?'

'Yes.' I return her smile.

'What do you want, Mikky?'

'I want to talk to you.'

She raises her eyebrows. 'Me?'

'About Carmen,' I add.

The door to the street opens and a familiar voice calls out. 'Hola, Mikky - is it really you?'

I turn and smile in greeting and we kiss on both cheeks.

'Enrique. You look good.' I hug him tightly.

He's skinny, waif-like and willowy with a shaved head and trimmed dark beard he looks like a male model. Originally from Morocco he has warm brown eyes and soft olive skin. He's a few years younger than me and he walks on his toes which make him appear young, enthusiastic and exited. His arms and neck are covered in an array of Aztec motifs and designs but across his chest, under his open shirt, is a small tattoo of an eagle in flight.

'You look gorgeous,' he says. 'Didn't you have some sort of accident? Didn't someone set fire to that lovely place where Yolanda and Carmen stay in Mallorca?'

'It was the art studio, behind the gallery,' I say.

'Was it deliberate?' he asks.

I shrug.

'Who did it?' asks Enrique.

'Did they ever catch the guy?' asks Yolanda.

'No. He disappeared.'

I don't tell them Roy Green, my ex neighbour's son, set the building on fire is in hiding somewhere in Europe.

'You were lucky...' Enrique rubs my short hair. 'I like it.'

'You're still working here – putting up with Yolanda?' I tease.

'She's the Queen and my dream boss.' He gives her a camp salute and I laugh.

'He's the only one who will work with me.' Yolanda looks down at the diary on the reception and points at the register. 'Enrique, who's this? Did you make this appointment?'

He looks over her shoulder and frowns at the scrawled writing.

'Guilty... as charged. He asked for you personally and we had a cancellation. He just wants a consultation.'

'Do you know who he is?'

I can't remember. Have you come to be inked again?' Enrique asks me. 'You'll need a appointment. Yolanda's well-known now...' He plugs in the kettle, turns on the CD and the salon is suddenly flooded with a recording of a familiar voice singing Tosca. He hums along in a false falsetto.

'Isn't Josephine Lavelle your friend?' Yolanda asks. 'She

came to Malaga last year to collect a package for you. Carmen and I had lunch with her near the airport.'

'Yes, Josephine has been very kind to me,' I answer truthfully.

'I didn't think she would be your type,' Yolanda glances up at me.

'She's a lovely person and a good friend.'

'What does she see in you?' Yolanda's smile is predatory.

I shrug.

She pours coffee into mugs and when she passes one to Enrique, he says.

'Yolanda's the celebrity tattooist for movie stars, footballers and other important celebrities...People adore her artwork. They appreciate the art and the craft involved – she's in great demand now – she's famous.'

'Reputation is everything,' I say, taking a mug of coffee.

'Okay, you'd better come through, Mikky.' Yolanda nods at me to follow her. 'We can talk in here until my appointment arrives.'

At the back of the building, a large room is flooded with natural light from overhead skylights. Two television screens are on mute but showing music channels with girls gyrating in scant clothing. Tattoo books, magazines and drawings hang on walls and cover tables. There are two reclining leather chairs, a couple of smaller ones on wheels and a table covered with electrical equipment, sterilisers and a box of plastic gloves.

She places her mug on an architect's table and picks up tracing paper and a pencil. She begins sketching a cover up of an old tattoo and when she speaks I hear passion in her voice.

'An Englishman – Steve – has got his girlfriend's name

57

tattooed across the back of his neck, see this photo? But they've separated and now he wants me to transfer her name into a serpent. I'm sketching ideas. It's never a good idea to get a tattoo of your partners name - I never recommend it - a tattoo lasts considerably longer than most relationships.'

I lean over her drawing board watch her artistic hand expertly pencil the serpent's tail. Art takes many forms and although she never studied with Carmen and I, her skills are amazingly deft and defined. I'd recognised her talent years ago and that's why I trusted her to ink my body with the masterpieces that meant so much to me.

'Do you regret yours?' she asks, as if reading my mind.

'They're a work of art. You did a good job.' She glances at The Scream on my arm; a colourful, emotional and traumatic image, scrutinising the anguished face, wide open mouth and silent howl.

'It's easy to imagine the tormented soul screaming in agonised torture. It's quite disturbing,' she says. 'Are you still so pessimistic?'

My body is a tribute to her artistic talents; The Scream on my arm, The Garden of Eden, then the darker images of The Betrayal of Christ, but the ultimate masterpiece is Salome's gloating smile and the seven coloured veils that wrap around my waist and the severed head of John the Baptist tattooed across my breasts.

'Some days are better than others,' I answer truthfully.

She lays down the pencil. 'Why are you here, Mikky? I hope you're not planning to stay.'

'I'm just passing through.'

'There's nothing for you here. Even Jorge has moved on.'

'I haven't come to see him.'

58

I block the chaotic images suddenly erupting in my head.

'So, it's Carmen you're here to see? I thought as much. She wants to organise a dinner tonight for you with the old gang but I don't think it's a good idea. Everyone has moved on...'

She turns the tracing paper.

'She's just being kind,' I counter and when Yolanda looks up, I ask. 'She seems tired – is she okay?'

'What's she said, to you?'

'Nothing.'

'Then don't start meddling, Mikky. None of this has any-thing to do with you.'

'None of what?'

Enrique pauses in the doorway. 'Your appointment is here,' he sings then he stands aside to let a man pass.

Yolanda shakes the stranger's hand and offers him a chair.

'This is my trainee.' She nods in my direction and pulls on latex gloves.

He looks over sixty years old and his beige polo shirt barley covers his hairy stomach. He takes his time settling in to the seat, taking in the of the room; art books, sketches, paintings and drawings as well as a long table with the tattoo machines; needles, grips, ink and creams.

'It reminds me of a dentist,' he quips, revealing uneven yel-low teeth while nodding at the rotary and coil tattoo machines.

'It's far more painful,' Yolanda smiles. 'I don't believe in pretending or lying. What would you like?'

'A dragon and a black skull, intertwined...'

He's specific, he's detailed and he's obviously done his homework.

I know Yolanda has done countless dragons, skulls, hearts, tribal and even more adventurous, full blown art canvases by

59

famous artists. My body is a testament to her artistic passion and I'm a walking biblical replica of fine art.

I perch against the architect's desk and fold my arms wondering what she meant. None of this is to do with you? None of what?

'Do you have any other ink? Yolanda asks the stranger.

'No, this is my first.' He sits proudly with his jacket folded on his lap.

Yolanda barely pauses. 'I will not ink anyone for the first time,' she says.

'But that's exactly why I've come to you, because it is my first time.'

'I'm sorry,' she replies and rolls the gloves off her hands. 'It's just a policy I have.'

'But I've waited months for this appointment.'

'I'm sorry, we should have asked you when you first booked.'

'I can afford it. I'll pay you...double.'

I raise my eyebrows.

'Money isn't the issue. It's the principle,' Yolanda says firmly standing up.

'But I'm not a child. I'm not underage. I'm an adult.'

'I know and I'm sorry. I should have checked with you, prior to making this appointment.'

He pulls out his wallet. 'This is a direct debit card. Tell me how much?'

'I can't. I'm sorry.' She screws up the gloves and tosses them on the table.

'This is ridiculous. I've waited more than four months.'

'I understand. I'm sorry.'

'I'll pay - anything you like just tell me how much. Name your price.'

She shakes her head and opens the door.

He stands but stays rooted to the spot beside me. His chest is heaving.

'I only want you.'

'Then you'll have to come back after you've had your first one done by someone else.'

'This is crazy. You're nuts. I certainly won't come back here. You've wasted my time.' He storms from the room pushing past me bumping my shoulder but I'm stronger than I look, for he holds his shoulder as he strides from the salon and slams the shop door.

'First timer,' she calls out to Enrique.

'Really? Then he lied to me.' Enrique appears at he door. 'You know I always ask when I make appointments.'

'Don't worry. He's not the first and he won't be the last.' Yolanda turns and says to me. 'I trust Enrique. He's been with me since I opened and I know everything there is to know about him. Every broken heart, every lover, every sexual position and just every drug he's taken...'

I stare at her. She might be talking about me and I cringe with shame.

There's a folded up copy of the SUR on the table and I pause deliberately, even though I know what it says, to read the headline.

'What do you think of this?' I ask. 'The poor boy was murdered. In broad daylight with all those people around during the Easter processions. I can't believe someone didn't see anything.'

'There's always so much going on...it's always so crowded,' Yolanda replies. 'We were standing near the Cathedral and we heard rumours someone had died. It held everything up.

61

Enrique says it's drugs. There's always some mafia turf war going on between the Russians...'

Her phone rings and I glance down at her mobile on the desk to read the caller ID.

'Do you want to get that?'

She ignores it and it goes to voicemail.

'It's only my father,' she says.

'Are you still the rebel in the family?'

She looks up and for the first time her wide, grey eyes crinkle in a genuine smile. 'Yes. Thank God.'

I walk past the Cathedral and through the narrow streets to the Picasso Museum where tourists have arrived in great hoards. Eventually, I manage to push past them and I'm shown into Carmen's office by her secretary, a blond woman with a short thick fringe, long blond hair and an enigmatic smile.

Carmen is rummaging though her desk and when she sees me she seems flustered.

'I've come to take you out for lunch,' I announce. 'It's Friday and it's the end of the week. Let's celebrate. The fresh air will do you good.'

We never had the opportunity to finish our conversation last night and I'm determined to sort out what to do with the rare manuscript. I owe it to Father Ignacio. He trusts me.

'Did you bring it with your his morning?' I ask. 'Is it safe?'

She shakes her head and silences me with a nod at the door as if I'm not to say another word.

We walk to a nearby rustic, tapas bar with giant wine caskets and walls adorned with signed photographs of well known visitors; bullfighters, singers, actors and politicians. We make small talk about the museum and staff shortages and the number of visitors while we order red wine and plates of boquerones, albondigas and pimientos de pequillo.

She bites into an olive and grins when she says.

'I told Jorge you were back in Malaga. He can't believe it.'

I stare at her.

She brushes a strand of hair from her eye and looks over her shoulder before speaking. She doesn't take her eyes from my face when she whispers. 'You know he married Isabelle last year?'

My head is a kaleidoscope of distorted and fragmented images like a Dali or Picasso painting. I sip my wine and say nothing hoping my heart will find stillness.

'He's a detective now.'

I look up sharply. Jorge had always been ambitious and he was talented and shrewd.

'I'm pleased he's doing well.' I finally find my voice.

'He's busy with the killing of that boy on Good Friday in the processions. He said there's a territorial war going on at the moment. It seems the boy was killed because he was supplying drugs and he got caught in the middle of some deal with the Russian mafia,' she pauses and then says, 'He wants to see you. He's asked me for your number. Do you want to see him?'

'I'm pleased he married Isabelle, she always liked him,' I say truthfully.

'You should meet up with him.'

I shake my head. The thought of seeing Jorge had not been part of my reconciliation with the past. As far as I was concerned Jorge and I were finished when I left Malaga - before I went crazy.

'So, what do you want to do with the manuscript?' I ask,

changing the subject.

'It's in the museum. I took it there this morning. I don't know what was wrong with me yesterday. I had no intention of taking it really, Mikky. I couldn't steal it. I certainly couldn't take it from the church or Father Ignacio.That would be the end for him - he seemed so...'

'Disillusioned?'

'Fragile. Besides, I'd never get into heaven, would I?' she laughs. 'It's only money...'

'Thank you.'

I'm relieved I can't believe the turnaround. This is the Carmen I remember; honest, sincere and sensible. I lean over and kiss her cheek. My heart is suddenly lighter and the weight from my shoulders ease. 'Will you get one of the auction houses to look at it?'

'Of course.'

'Which one?'

'I've got Madeline looking into it.'

'Madeline?'

'My secretary with the heavy fridge and square glasses.'

I bite on a green pepper and relish the bitter taste in my mouth then I swallow red wine and lean back in satisfaction, and say. 'I called Simon Fuller this morning. He's based in Canterbury now but he's delivering a paper on rare manuscripts to a University in Asia and he won't be back for least at another week.'

'It'll be too late by then.'

'What will?'

'I'll have sorted it. I'll ask another expert to come and look at it. Come on, worry-chops,' she says. 'Let's tuck in, I'm starving.' She flings her arm over my shoulder and offers me a piece of manchego cheese.

'Don't fob me off. Tell me what's really going on, Carmen.'

'Okay, I've got someone coming to look at it on Monday.'

'Really? Who?'

'An expert from Bonham's. He's flying down from Madrid.'

'Have you told the committee? Have you told Miguel Angel?' I refer to the chairman of the museum and the man responsible for the costs, funding and management of it. When I'd worked for the museum for a few months, photographing and cataloguing some of the artwork, he'd always been very kind to me. He treated me in a professional manner even though I was young and had only recently graduated.

'Yes.'

'And what did he say.'

'Stop interrogating me, Mikky. Let's just wait and see what happens. Besides there's more important things to discuss.'

'Like what?'

'Dinner tonight. Some of the old crowd want to get together. They can't believe you're back.'

I stare at her. 'I'm not ready to see anyone. Not after...'

'It was four years ago. It's time to move on. It's all in the past.'

I shake my head. 'Give me a few days, Carmen,' I say, knowing that I will leave here now that the manuscript has been sorted out. I'll avoid any chance of a reunion.

'It'll be a few drinks, nothing-'

'I went to see Yolanda this morning.'

'Why?'

'I thought of getting another ink,' I lie.

'Of what?'

I shrug. 'I haven't decided.'

Carmen frowns and tugs her hair.

'You didn't mention the book to Yolanda, did you – or about meeting Father Ignacio?'

'No.'

'Good.'

'She seems to be avoiding her father though,' I say probing.

Carmen looks up and pauses with her wine glass half way to her lips. 'What did she tell you?'

I smile and nod as if I know something.

'She told you?'

I shrug in understanding.

'He wants to sell our apartment,' she groans and puts her face in her hands.

'Yours?'

'Yes.'

'I thought you said, Yolanda owned it.'

'When he bought it he put it in her name and now he wants it back. He wants to sell it.'

'Why?'

'He says he needs the money.'

'Can't you buy it off him?'

She tugs on her hair. 'No.'

'Isn't there some connection with your family and Yolanda's? Didn't your father know her father or something?' I ask.

'My father was Steven Drummond's – Yolanda's father's chauffeur – for years until he retired but they were never really friends.'

'I remember you vaguely talking about him at Uni.'

'We weren't very wealthy and when Papa went to work for Steven our life changed. Steven helped finance my education.

He took an interest in me and my schooling. He was always very proud...'

I remember flashes of conversation from years ago.

'Did you and Yolanda grow up together?'

'No. Although we all lived in Madrid, She was sent away to boarding school in Switzerland and I was educated here in Spain. I saw them everyday – Steven and Sofia. Papa was up at their house or at Steven's office every day. After he picked me up from school, I would hang around and wait for him to finish work, sometimes I would do my homework in his office or in their kitchen at home and Steven or Sofia would come in and talk to me.'

'Sofia?'

'Steven's wife. Yolanda's Mum was a well known ballet dancer. She's Argentinian.'

'And Steven – he's English?'

Carmen laughs. 'He's Scottish. That's where Yolanda gets her red hair and olive complexion.'

'Do they know that you and Yolanda are together?'

'Of course. At first we just said we were friends but then over the last few years we stopped hiding.We decided we didn't care what they think.'

'Do you see a lot of them?'

Carmen inhales deeply.

'He's always got tickets for something; a concert, show or a special dinner. He's very well connected in Madrid and he asks us along to all the social events. That's how Yolanda's met so many famous people. We started attending all the charity functions where celebrities, you know the sort; actors, footballers, singers. Tattoos have become very popular and one by one they asked Yolanda to ink them and they began

67

recommending her. She's made a name for herself and they have to book months in advance if they want her. Steven's been very kind to invite us. We saw Glorietta Bareldo at the opera last year - and he often asks us to go to the theatre London and we meet actors backstage.'

This is a different Carmen to the one I spoke to yesterday who said Yolanda's father was a control freak.

'It's understandable that you want a place of your own. I can see how you were tempted to steal the manuscript,' I say.

'It hasn't been easy. We fly up and down to Madrid. Steven has his own plane and no expense is spared. It's hard to turn him down.'

'What does he do?'

'Importing and exporting - furniture and stuff...'

I think of all the expats immigrating to Spain and imagine the money he's made over the years.

'To all over Europe - the world.'

'Sounds lucrative.'

'Oh God, Mikky! It's all so awful having to keep going up there at a drop of a hat. I'm so fed up with these parties in Madrid.'

'And what does Yolanda say?'

Carmen shrugs. 'It's good for her business and besides, he's her father. He'd like us to move up there...'

'To Madrid?'

She sighs.

'Well at least you've done the right thing by taking the manuscript to the museum.' I raise my glass.

'Stop acting so piously.'

'I'm not. I just don't want you to get into trouble.'

'That's a first - and coming from you, it's an insult.'

'What about...'

'Stop asking so many questions,' she snarls.

'I'm not asking. The only thing I asked you - was not to steal that manuscript. You're the one who asked me to come to Malaga. In fact, I still don't know why you want me here. Why did you come to find me, Carmen? I don't understand.'

'You've gone all moralistic on me.'

'I worry about you. I-'

'You always have to be so bloody perfect. Always so bloody full of religion and doing the right thing,' her voice rises and I'm surprised at the anger in her tone.

'I'm not perfect, Carmen but-'

'I'm an adult, Mikky. I can do as I please. I don't need your permission to do anything. I'm my own person. I can do what I like; talk to who I like, say what I like and I don't need you telling me what to do or giving me a moral lecture.'

'You're the one who asked for my help, Carmen. I wouldn't be here if you hadn't come to Tarifa. I told you I didn't want to meet Father Ignacio but he was sitting on your couch when I got there. I'm the innocent party here.' I stab my Iron Maiden T-shirt with my thumb.

'No, you're not - you just think you are - you're always dishing out advice thinking you know best - just like Yolanda!'

'Don't get angry at me! I came here because you asked me and because I care about you-'

'You care about me? That's a joke! How do you think I've managed all these years without you?' She raises her voice and spits a piece of olive from her lip. 'Imagine me losing everything - my apartment - my home - I'll have nothing. After everything I've done and all my hard work, I'll have nothing left. You have no idea what it's like not to have a

69

roof over your head. It's awful when you have nothing and-'

'You don't have nothing,' I argue as if she is deaf or just not listening. 'You have Yolanda - you have all those lovely things you've collected. Your home is like a museum and you have a good career-'

'Well, maybe that just isn't enough.' She grabs her handbag and stands up.

'Where are you going?'

'I've had enough. I thought you'd changed, Mikky. I thought you'd be different but you're just the same arrogant self, the girl who knows everything. The girl who had such a terrible upbringing that she wears it as a badge of honour and no-one could ever suffer as much as you.'

'That's not true,' I shout back, ignoring the group that turn around from the nearby table.

'You're not the person I thought you were,' she says.

'Why are you so bloody-minded, Carmen?'

'I thought you of all people would understand me. I thought you'd be far more supportive and realise everything I'm going though-'

'I do understand you. Don't just ...walk out'

She turns and disappears through the crowd standing at the bar.

'Carmen?' I call, but her name bounces back at me, carried by waves of laughter from the people in the bar around me.

Chapter 5

"A book must be an ice-axe to break the seas frozen inside our soul." - Franz Kafka

All plans of a reunion with old friends fortunately seems to have been forgotten. Carmen is still at work and Yolanda and I wait for her to join us in a bar near the cathedral steps. We're sitting under an outdoor heater, and my face and neck are warm, I'm drinking beer and watching a young crowd at the table beside us.

'Don't you feel old?' Yolanda shakes her head with despair. 'Look at them. They think they know it all.'

'That's the beauty of youth, isn't it? Besides we're hardly old – early thirties.'

'It seems a long time ago that we just used to hang out without a care or worrying about stuff.'

'There was always something to worry about; money, love, security – it's just that you've forgotten what your troubles were. Troubles fade quickly when they're no longer there,' I reply.

'You had it tougher than most...' Her grey eyes fix on me like a watchful cat before it pounces on its prey. 'You lost your mother when you were young, didn't you?'

'Fourteen.'

'An accident?'

'She wrapped Papa's motorcycle around a tree.' I don't add that she was in a blind drunk and jealous rage.

'That must have been awful.'

Self consciously, although Yolanda's seen it a millions times, I hide the scar on the back of my hand under the table.

'I survived,' I reply.

I'm conscious of her heavy stare then she asks. 'How was your lunch? Was Carmen okay?'

'She seems very...nervous and uptight.' I don't mention our argument or the fact she walked out. 'Are things okay with you?'

Yolanda rubs her eyes before replying.

'She's under a lot of pressure. She's very stressed. There was a big exhibition last year and with the Pompidou in Muelle Uno opening and the Museo Thyssen, I guess it's all competition for the Picasso Museum. They've got to get the best exhibition to get people through the door.'

'Picasso was born here, I thought that would make Malaga more of an attraction for art lovers.'

'It does, but Carmen seems to think the other museums detract from the Picasso. I don't know why considering there is so much dedicated to him...' her voice trails off. 'Has she said anything to you – about anything?'

'She seems worried.'

'She's changed,' Yolanda says simply. 'When we met she was so different. She was interested and excited in everything. I took her to Argentina and we visited my aunts and uncles. We went exploring, we took busses and trains and I got to know my mother's country. The following summer we went to Dad's family in Scotland. We loved it so much that we still go back every year. We stay with my Scottish Aunt, my father's sister, near Edinburgh and we explore castles, churches, chapels and manor houses. We walk for hours across fields and hike up mountains and we forget all of this.' She waves her glass at the people in the square. 'We don't party. We have early nights. It's like getting in touch with nature and ourselves again. We spend time together and we talk/ We get our relationship back on track but this year...it's like she doesn't want to go anywhere or do anything. It's like she's lost interest-'

Yolanda breaks off and to the waiter who finishes serving the young crowd. She orders more beer.

'This year, she doesn't even want to go on holiday,' she finishes.

'Have you asked her why?'

'Papa is taking a yacht around the Greek Islands for a few months and they've asked us to join them for a few weeks but she doesn't want to go.'

'Do you?'

'We meet new people. It's good for business.'

'Maybe she just needs to be with you and not your parents. Why don't you go somewhere on your own without family?' I ask.

Yolanda stares at me. 'It's difficult.'

'Have you spoken to her about it?'

'She's been working late most evenings and she's not very talkative at the moment. She used to love her job. She would have come home and chat about everything but now, more recently, she's quieter and more withdrawn and I can't speak to her-'

'Perhaps she's under pressure.'

'Has she mentioned the apartment?'

I lie. 'No.'

Yolanda's phone rings and she checks the caller ID.

'What about the apartment?'

'Shit! Hold on,' she says and answers her phone with an exaggerated smile. 'Papa, how are you?'

I lean nearer to her ear and pretend I'm studying the Cathedral facade and the teenagers hanging around the fountain. I can hear his angry voice.

'I've been calling you. Why don't you answer your phone?' he shouts.

'Only just finished work,' she replies mildly.

'It's....' I don't hear what he says next.

'Well, you know what it's like Papa, having your own business...' she replies still smiling. 'It's like you, when you entertain your clients from abroad with dinners until the early hours - you forget to call Mama...'

The music from across the square finishes abruptly and I hear his voice.

'We have to speak about it sometime, Yolanda.'

He is still shouting.

'I'll call you,' she raises her voice. 'Sorry, it's busy here - too many people. I can't hear you.' She clicks the red button, throws it on the table and says to me. 'He's a bloody control freak.'

She rubs a hand through her auburn hair. 'I know it irritates him when I compare my business with his multi-million empire but it's still mine and the principal is the just same. It's my heart and soul, just as importing and exporting is his - he has no claim over my life. He will not control me. I'm a free spirit and I always will be.'

74

'I'm pleased it's not just me that has a difficult relationship with their father,' I smile.

She reaches for her beer and gulps quickly.

'The only thing that links me with Steven Drummond, is my auburn hair, fiery temper and successful business acumen. Drummond's Importers and Exporters; he started importing furniture for all those Brits who sold up in England and moved here. He's built up a big property portfolio-.'

She calls the waiter over and orders more beer.

'He came here when he was twenty-four all the way from Perthshire. He built a very successful business probably half of which - I know nothing about but he still wants me to sell my apartment. Carmen is really upset about it. I'm surprised she didn't tell you.'

'Why does he want you to sell it?'

She shrugs.

A teenager wobbles precariously on his moped and we watch him turn the corner, then I say.

'Perhaps that's why she's stressed? Can't you buy him out?'

'I've blown my savings going backwards and forwards to Argentina and Scotland, and Carmen collects all those antiques in the apartment - you know - all that old furniture and stuff, and old paintings. She likes all that. She's a collector and it keeps her happy. So we don't have the money.'

'Could you get a mortgage?'

She stares at me. 'That would be a commitment.'

'Well, you've been together long enough.'

'Almost seven years.'

I laugh. 'That's a commitment, isn't it?'

'He's just being a bastard,' she says. 'He's not getting it. I'm not moving out. It's our home.'

'Can he sell it?'

'He put it in my name as a tax loop-hole a few years ago when business was booming but now business is not as good. He says the recession has hit him hard and he's claiming it back. He says he needs the money. He says he needs to pay other stuff but he's a control freak. He's always wanted to manipulate me.'

'Why?'

'He doesn't want me working for myself and being success-ful. I'm an embarrassment to him.'

I think of Carmen telling me how he's invited them to all the main social events in Madrid and how she met all the famous celebrities who have become her clients. 'Surely he's proud of you?'

'The opposite. He hates what I do. He thinks tattoos are common.'

'But surely, he can't help but admire how well you've done and how talented you are?'

'He's always hated me. That's why they sent me away to school in Switzerland,' she replies. 'He wanted a boy so I've always been a disappointment. Then Carmen was much cleverer than me and he was always comparing us, the chauffeur's daughter - imagine that. She always had a better school report and grades than me. She always studied harder than me. She's on a good salary. Nothing and no-one is ever good enough unless they have lots of money. That's his measurement for success. Talent never comes into it. I don't know how my mother puts up with him.'

Yolanda resented my friendship with Carmen and it was only when I trusted her skills as an artist to use my body as a canvas that she relented and accepted me grudgingly into their life. I have a feeling that Yolanda is also controlling and I wonder if it's a family trait.

'So, what will you do about the apartment?'

'He's not getting it back without a fight. He can sell one of his other bloody properties first.'

I drain my glass and ask myself, how can a man with a private aircraft who's going to sail around the Greek islands for a few months could possibly be so hard up that he wants to sell his daughter's home?

By the time Carmen joins us I'm tired and more than a little drunk. Keeping Yolanda company had not been on my list of things to do and I'm wondering what I am doing still in Malaga. Now that the manuscript is in the museum, the experts will verify its authenticity so there's nothing for me left here. Malaga was my past. Mallorca is my present.

I'll leave in the morning. I'll say nothing. I'll simply go. Disappear.

Besides, I miss Eduardo.

Carmen looks pale and tired. 'I cancelled the reunion,' she says, pulling the collar of her jacket round her neck, she moves closer to the overhead heater.

Yolanda is brimming with indignation.

'You're late! You can't just keep us waiting here like we are not important,' she complains.

Carmen picks up a slice of jamon from the selection of cold meats and nibbles a chunk of bread. She turns away clearly uninterested in Yolanda's protestations. 'I had a meeting that went on a longer than I thought.'

'That's not much of an apology.'

77

Yolanda's not the only one who is upset with her. Carmen doesn't look at me and she doesn't mention how she stormed out at lunch time. I'm irked by her aloof behaviour and her earlier accusations.

'Mama is coming down on her own tomorrow. She's asked us to have lunch with her,' Yolanda says.

'I'm working tomorrow.'

'You never work Saturdays.'

'Ten Picasso's are on loan from the Kunstmuseum and they're arriving from Switzerland. I must be there-'

'That's ridiculous, Carmen.That's three weeks in a row you've been working-'

'So, it's alright for you, to tattoo a celebrity or a footballers wife on a Saturday but when I have to go to the museum you get annoyed,' she retorts.

Yolanda tilts her face and the light causes her deep auburn hair to catch the light. It's a pose I would like to capture with my lens but this isn't the right time to suggest that I take her photograph.

'Papa wants you to be there, he said Mama wants to speak to us both about the apartment.'

'I can't go. Take Mikky with you.'

'I can't!' I reply.

'She wants to speak to us,' Yolanda emphasises. 'Papa likes you more than me. We both know he would like you to be his daughter.'

Yolanda pours beer from a pitcher on the table into her glass. 'He thinks you're smarter, more professional and more dedicated than I am. He admires your work - and he hates me. He hates what I do for a living.'

'Don't be ridiculous-'

'It's true. Did you know, Mikky, that Carmen's Papa was the chauffeur for my father for almost fifteen years?'

'I think it has been mentioned,' I reply with as much diplomacy as I can muster without slurring my words.

'It's true. It's also true that when we grew up my father had more time for Carmen than he had for me. He took an interest in her education–'

'You're speaking rubbish...' Carmen interrupts.

'I'm not. He took more interest in your career and what you were doing. He was always comparing me with you and what you were doing and how clever you were. He even put you through the best school in Madrid and paid for you to go to University, didn't he? Have you told, Mikky?'

'Please, let's leave it. Stop!' I hold up my palm.

'It was a business arrangement between him and my father.' Carmen pours more wine into her glass. 'I had no choice where I went to school. Do you think I want him interfering in our life now?' She diligently picks at pulpo a la gaiga and wipes garlic juices from her chin.

'He even went to your Graduation.'

'I didn't ask him. It wasn't up to me. I barely got through the course, as you know.' Carmen looks at me. Her irises are deep brown and as our eyes meet we share a complicit look.

I'd returned from a summer course, studying with Raffaella Pavelli the renowned Italian artist. I arrived at Carmen's flat and found her lying in the bath, so I carried her to a taxi and got her to the hospital where they pumped her stomach and bandaged her wrists. She'd always said it was a miracle that she had survived, let alone Graduated and I'd always replied, that it wasn't her time to die.

'He hates me.' Yolanda slurs.

'He doesn't hate you. You made him angry, that's all. You trained to become a tattoo artist and he wanted a business woman,' Carmen replies. 'Besides, whatever you do will never be enough. He's driven by money and motivated by greed. He's a selfish and controlling.'

Yolanda stumbles over her words. 'He wanted me to study Economics, did you know that, Mikky?'

'None of this matters now, does it? You're happy doing what you do,' I reply.

Yolanda glances at Carmen and her eyes soften when she says.

'He always talked about this girl; his chauffeur's daughter and how clever she was and how she was going to University in Madrid and how she was an artist and so talented and wonderful...I think I fell in love with her then.'

Carmen giggles. 'You thought I was wonderful...'

'I still do.'

Yolanda reaches for Carmen's fingers and they hold hands across the table.

'It's just that life sometimes gets complicated.' Then she turns to me and says. 'I've asked Carmen to leave her job and run away with me. I can work anywhere. We could live beside the sea. We could go to Morocco or Greece and in the winter we could go to the mountains...'

Carmen laughs and pulls her hand away. 'And what would I do in this dream?'

'Do you like being a Curator?' I ask.

'Jobs like mine don't come along that often. I'm lucky to have been offered it. I can't just walk away - even if I wanted to.'

Yolanda bangs the table sending her beer glass flying across

80

the table.

'We need to be independent and buy our own place. Then I can get rid of Papa from constantly hanging around my neck. He's a weight dragging us down-'

'That's the best thing you can do,' I agree. 'Be independent - together.'

'That's rich coming from you,' Yolanda laughs. 'I don't see you settling down.'

'What would you invest in, Mikky?' Carmen asks me but it's Yolanda who replies.

'Don't bother with property,' she says. 'Papa has hit a brick wall. He will have to sell his properties cheaper than he bought them-'

Carmen interrupts. 'Selling the apartment has nothing to do with the property market or because he wants the money. It's because he wants to control us. He wants us to go to Madrid and meet his important clients. He wants to impress them. Do you remember the Chinese investor, a few weeks ago? I was stuck to him talking about investment opportunities in the art world. When it suits him, he introduces us to people he thinks he can get something out of - Steven's only kind to us when other people are around and he wants something.'

'We give him credibility when he wheels us out; the prodigal daughter and her girlfriend-'

'It shows the world that he's a tolerant, loving and understanding father but deep down he's misogynistic and homophobic.'

'He's a controlling and vile little shit,' says Yolanda.

'He's evil.' Carmen says with harsh severity and bitterness that makes my skin tickle.

I realise then, sitting under the heater, near the illuminated

81

entrance of the cathedral that I don't want to be involved with all this hate and negativity.

I cannot wait to leave this city. Palma is calling me. I need Eduardo.

And, I shouldn't drink any more beer.

The bedroom is dark when I wake. My mouth is dry and my head thumps dully against my temple. I open the shutters where the sky in the east is growing lighter and the beginning of a beautiful orange sunrise - too colourful to miss - is illuminating the new day.

I pull on my jogging gear, hook my rucksack onto my shoulders and open my bedroom door. I take a few steps into the hallway and hear angry voices from the kitchen so I pause. It's the tone rather than the muffled words that makes me strain to listen and although I am like an intruder, I'm unable to help myself and I inch forward to eavesdrop.

'It's for one bloody lunch,' Yolanda shouts. 'You can't work your whole life. It's about having fun - something that you've forgotten about recently.'

'Why do you have to wind me up all the time?'

'It's because you're so bloody sensitive, Carmen. I don't know what's wrong with you any more.'

'I want to spend time with Mikky.'

I stiffen my shoulders at the mention of my name.

What's this got to do with me?

I'm torn between retreating back into my room and exiting again loudly to warn them of my presence but I'm trapped in the web of my own curiosity.

Yolanda explodes. 'Chrisake, Carmen. How come everyone

else come first – before me – before us? If I hear another word about Mikky and how she's changed and how wonderful she is – I'll go mad. She's not a saint. She's a mixed up, screwed up kid pretending she's an adult. She never tells you about herself or what she's doing. Do you know what happened to her last year when Josephine Lavelle came over to collect that package? We never heard after that. It was Dolores who told you, she'd been in a fire and how she was having to rebuild the studio. She said, Mikky nearly died and was lucky to escape with her life but there's not a scratch on her. She looks bloody amazing.'

'She was hurt. It's taken her this long to recover–' Carmen doesn't sound convinced and I remember the way she looked at me in my wet suit on the beach.

'She's kitesurfing again. There's nothing wrong with her!' Yolanda shouts. 'It's all a game – a pretence – all this business that she's here because she wants our friendship and she wants to put the past ghosts to rest – she doesn't. I don't know what she wants or why she's here–'

'She's our friend–'

'She's no friend of mine–'

'Stop!' Carmen shouts. 'I've had enough. She might hear us and I'm not having you upsetting her with your jealousy and your angry Scottish temper. I'm going back to bed.'

I run into my room.

My heart is thumping as Carmen's footsteps echo across the tiles and her bedroom door slams shut.

I wait, then guessing Yolanda has followed Carmen to bed, I open my bedroom door and venture into the hallway.

The kitchen is empty but I hear a sound and I call out softly, 'Morning.' I peer into the lounge 'I'm going out to photograph

83

the sunrise.'

Yolanda has her back to me. She has moved aside the Flamenco en Llamas painting and her finger is on the dial of the safe. She turns at the sound of my voice and her grey eyes stalk me as I stand in the doorway.

'It's okay, Mikky. Come in. I've an early appointment. Someone phoned last night and left a message. They're a good client and I won't be working for long...' She nods at the safe. 'I'm just getting some cash.'

'On a Saturday?'

'I'll be finished by lunchtime. Carmen is waiting for paintings to arrive for a summer exhibition, so we can all have lunch together. Mama was talking about getting some professional photographs taken. She's writing a memoir.' Yolanda turns her attention back to the safe and I watch her move the dials. It's an old fashioned safe with numbers - and no key. 'Carmen knows what buttons to press to start me off. It's what amazes me about our relationship. When you meet someone you tell them your weaknesses and the things that upset you. You're honest and open, and you build trust by sharing your fears and your secrets but when you have an argument they use it against you. They turn your weakness into their weapon.'

'Sorry?'

She pulls open the safe door then she turns to glare at me. Her cold grey eyes like slate. 'I know that Papa bought me this apartment. But I'm not spoilt. They sent me away to school and I had to learn to be independent. He encouraged me to be tough. He made me strong, mentally and physically. He did it because he wanted a son. But he tested me. He pushed me further and further - when we went skiing he sent me on black runs, off piste, in deep powder snow, and mist and fog.

When we went deep sea diving I wasn't allowed to surface until there was the minimum amount of oxygen left in the tanks so I would learn not to panic. When we took out his speed boat in Marbella, he went fast on choppy seas tempting fate, and waves grew larger and swells rose and sank, and I learned what fear was. I tried to conquer my fears and I hate him for it. For putting me through it all-'

'Yolanda, I-'

'Why are you here, Mikky? Did Carmen ask you to come?'

I shake my head but she doesn't give me chance to reply.

'Let me tell you something - since becoming an adult and having my own business, I pay for everything - and that's something that annoys Carmen. Like most people with their own business, I don't declare all my earnings. Papa taught me that too. So any cash I put in an envelope and keep at home. Look! That's another reason I can't get a mortgage.'

She pulls out of the safe a large padded envelope.

'See this? Sometimes I covert it to dollars - just before an election like in America - that's when it usually drops or I buy Swedish Krona or Chinese Yuan or Indian Rupees. Again, my father being an importer and exported, taught me well.'

She taps the envelope on the palm of her hand.

'Are you shocked?'

I shake my head. 'Why would I be?'

'Because you're so holier than thou - I think the ink drawings I did on your body have turned you into some sort of religious person. A walking bible, a freak-'

'Why do you think that?'

'Because you haven't got pissed or stoned, since you've been here and the last time I saw you, you couldn't even string a sentence together.'

85

'That was four years ago and besides I do have a hangover this morning.' I rub my temple.

She extracts a wad of euros from the envelope and waves them at me before returning the envelope to the safe.

Whatever I say will be dismissed but I'm tired enough to want to justify who I am, so I say.

'I'm sorry if my behaviour offends you, Yolanda. I have no ulterior motive. I'm going back to Mallorca. I think Eduardo has helped me and for the first time I have some sort of balance – some sort of equilibrium back in my life – thanks to him.'

I want to tell her Josephine is my birth mother or about the events that almost led to my death last year but this isn't the time or the place. I also realise Yolanda isn't listening, so I turn to go.

'What's this?' She turns from the safe holding a familiar hessian bag. 'Oh my God! What is it?'

She lays the book on the dining table.

I stare as she unfolds the cloth. I know it's the manuscript that Carmen said she had taken back to the museum but I still reach out and touch the calf brown, book cover.

'Do you know about this?' Yolanda levels a grey stare at me and I'm trapped in the sun's rays of her hot gaze.

'No,' I lie.

She turns a few pages just as I did, barely two days ago, and I gaze at the vellum pages reassured that it's the same book with the same Gothic writing.

'Why does she have it here and not at the museum?' she whispers. 'Is it worth a fortune?'

'I don't know.'

In the hallway the bedroom door opens.

'Yolanda?' Carmen calls softly.

'Don't breathe a word. Don't tell Carmen we've seen it.'

Yolanda wraps it quickly in the hessian and I turn away and walk toward the hallway, to block Carmen's path, feeling anger rising inside me.

I stand with a ready smile on my lips, aware of Yolanda behind my back, closing the safe and replacing the painting on the wall.

Father Ignacio trusted me and in turn I trusted Carmen to take it to the museum and have it authenticated by specialists. She lied. She has deliberately misled me and I intend to find out why before I call the police but I can't tackle her about it now without admitting to Yolanda, I know about it and betraying Father Ignacio's trust.

'I'm going to photograph the sunrise,' I say to Carmen but I can't look her in the eye. 'Eduardo will love it.'

'Sorry about the arguing yesterday.' She stands on tiptoe in bare feet to kiss my cheek. 'Let's have a coffee later?'

I nod but I cannot speak.

'I'm sorry,' she whispers. 'I'm sorry, I ever dragged you into this mess, Mikky.'

Chapter 6

"Books are like mirrors: if a fool looks in, you cannot expect a genius to look out." - J.K. Rowling

I jog to get rid of my mounting anger and frustration. I run past the Plaza de Toros, La Malagueta, the Pompidou Centre and along the Paseo del Muelle Uno. It's still early and I'm working up a good sweat by the time I'm on the deserted boulevard, passing designers shops, restaurants and bars on my left and a neat row of expensive sail boats in the marina on my right.

I suck the air into my lungs, gulping like a man who's crossed the desert and found an oasis. The sun and breeze on my cheeks invigorates me and my anger dissipates with the rising sun.

There's a reason for everything, I tell myself.

Why has Carmen lied?

At the lighthouse, I remove my rucksack and drink from my water bottle. The sunrise is beautiful and I pace backwards and forwards, sipping water, regulating my breath gazing at the backdrop of the harbour; the magnificent old city; the cathedral; the old walls of the Alcazaba and the Parador nestled on the hillside. It's a stunning view and by the time the orange and yellow fingers of the sun's rays have reached out like giant tentacles of brilliant light across the pink and purple sky, I've removed the drone from my back pack and fly it over the sea.

Aware of the flight path of Malaga airport, I manipulate the Phantom 4 along the coastline, across the dazzling Mediter-ranean and watch the images relayed back to me on the controller in my hands. I navigate the drone through the rigging of the yachts berthed in the marina and it hovers over the cathedral before I bring it back to the Moorish wall of the Alcazaba and the Parador on the hill where guests are still sleeping.

The city looks resplendent in the early light and conscious the battery life is ebbing I bring the drone slowly back, filming one last glimpse of the rising sun before it settles at my feet, and I'm thinking how happy Eduardo will be when a man behind me says.

'Do you know that's illegal?'

He has a thin trimmed beard, a stocky frame and a green baseball cap shading his serious deep-set brown eyes. He's dressed in a polo shirt and cargo pants - the uniform of the Guardia Civil.

'Like I care,' I reply.

'Hola, Mikky.'

I stare at him until he leans forward to kiss me on both cheeks, and I remember the familiar warmth of his embrace. He smells of toothpaste and shower gel and a flood of memo-ries and emotions collide in the pit of my stomach.

'Hello Jorge. How did you-?'

'Carmen told me you were here.' He smiles and holds up the palm of his hand. 'Don't blame her. I forced her. I wanted to see you before you took off again.'

89

I can't move. I don't even blink.

'You look great. Carmen said, you were looking good but I had to see for myself... I heard about the fire.'

'Oh?'

'Short hair suits you. It shows off your lovely cheek bones.'

'You look well,' I lie.

His eyes are bloodshot and there are black circles around his dark eyelashes. He puts his hands in his pockets. A gun hangs ominously in a black holster on his waist.

'How long are you here?'

My mouth is dry and I don't trust myself to speak so I bend to pick up the Phantom and pack it away.

'You've got to be careful with those things,' he says. 'They're used for spying and in the Netherlands the police are training hawks to take them out.'

'This is the new Phantom 4.'

'It's amazing.' He takes the drone from me and examines it carefully. 'Its really sleek. It's got a three axis gimbal...'

I laugh. 'You're an expert?'

'Greater stability,' he replies. 'It has Visual Positioning to give you precise hovering.'

'It has a good camera,' I agree.

'Yes, and collision avoidance.' He points to the two black dots at the front. 'It can recognise an obstruction forty metres away and can avoid bashing into things. It's really cool.' He hands it back to me. 'What were you filming?'

'The sunrise'

'Really?'

'I've also used it for sport. It has TapFly function, so I can send it anywhere and AutoTrack to follow or circle around a subject, like a kitesurfer or skier so I can film them.'

'I'm impressed.'

'I'd show you but the battery needs charging.'

'How long does it last?'

'About twenty minutes, depending on the weather.'

I place it in the bag and without looking up I say.

'I heard you married, Isabelle.'

'Last year.'

'She always had a soft spot for you.'

'I didn't think you noticed.' His laugh is a throaty rumble that I remember well, and when I don't reply he adds. 'Those drones are illegal this close to the airport.'

'So? Arrest me?'

'Perhaps, maybe next time.'

'There won't be a next time.' I pick up the bag but he takes it from me.

'Let me help you. Coffee? Breakfast?'

'Aren't you on duty?'

'I start later. There's a cafe open in the marina. They do a good expresso.'

We walk together in companionable silence and I wonder what he's thinking. It's awkward yet familiar being with him and when we both start talking at the same time, I laugh.

'I believe you're a detective now?'

'Teniente.'

'You've done well. It must be a tough job keeping law and order around here. Is there still a lot of crime...shoplifting and things like that?'

'It used to be money laundering and black money investments in property now it's gang warfare, drugs, human trafficking and illegal immigration.'

I remember the headlines of the SUR and what I've heard

about the increasing presence of the mafia along the coast.

'You still enjoy it?'

'Here let's sit in the sunshine.'

He places the drone on the floor and pulls out a wooden chair for me.

The cafe is opening and the waiter appears and greets Jorge with a handshake and a backslap. It reminds me of how it had been when we were together. Jorge was greeted with affection in the bars and Clubs and being with him had made me feel good. I'd felt important. He was known, recognised and popular and I'm pleased this hasn't changed.

After the waiter disappears Jorge removes his cap. His hair has been shaved and there are grey flecks above his ears making him look older and more serious than the youthful man he had been only four years ago and I'm reminded once again of Father Ignacio and how the years haven't been kind to him either.

'So, how have you been?' he asks leaning his elbows on the table.

'Good.'

I stare at the view before us; the marina with the expensive yachts and the cathedral behind. It's a beautiful view and I would like to take photographs. I would even like to take a photograph of Jorge and capture the expression in his tired eyes and the spark of curiosity when he says to me.

'Still painting?'

'Not so much. More photography now,' I reply.

'It seems a long time since you were here,' he says softly.

We watch a sail boat glide from its moorings with a family on board toward the open sea and Jorge turns away and nods at the drone beside us on the floor.

'Are you filming with that?'

'Maybe in the future – it would make a change from pho-tographing artwork in museums and art galleries.'

He smiles and scratches his beard. 'Are you coming back here to live?'

'Here? No.'

We wait while the waiter places ham filled mollettes and hot coffee on the table.

'I saw your father a few months ago,' he says.

I don't reply.

'He wasn't very well.'

I eat slowly and chew thoroughly.

'He said he saw you in hospital in Palma, last year.'

'Yes.'

'Your forehead has healed.'

'Don't play the detective with me, Jorge. I know you too well.'

'I wish I knew you, Mikky. What happened? I couldn't believe it when you just disappeared without saying a word to me.' His voice is low and he doesn't take his eyes from me. 'I tried to find you. I wanted to help.'

'I wanted to be alone. I needed to sort myself out. Besides, it was a long time ago and we've both changed. We've both move on. You're married now...'

'Are you with anyone?'

'It's early days yet,' I reply, 'just a few months.'

'Who is he?' asks Jorge.

'His name's Eduardo. He's in Mallorca. He's an Intensive Care nurse.' I don't say that he was upset at being despatched back to Palma or that I didn't want him to come with me to Malaga, because I wasn't ready for my present to meet my past.

'Is it love?'

I shrug and smile. 'So far, so good. He's uncomplicated and I like that.'

'Not many of us around.'

'Keep it simple. It's the best way. No ties–'

'Marriage doesn't mean you complicate things,' Jorge says. 'We're happy and it makes the children feel secure.'

'Children?'

'Twins. Last year. Didn't Carmen tell you?'

The ham is lodged in my throat and I swallow repeatedly. It's no wonder he looks tired.

He lays his hand on top of mine. 'I'm sorry. I waited for you to come back,' he whispers.

I pull my hand reluctantly away.

'I'm pleased for you. I really am. Isabelle is a lovely person.'

He turns and stares at a couple wandering hand in hand along the quay.

'Do you see much of Carmen and Yolanda?' I ask.

'Sometimes. Carmen and Isabelle hang out together. She's godmother to the twins.'

That's something else Carmen hasn't told me and I wonder why.

'She seems very tired,' I probe. 'Preoccupied. Not at all carefree like before.'

'We're all tired,' he grins. 'We all work hard.'

'Do you still kitesurf?'

'Not like we used to – and you?'

'I've taken it up again. I spent a few months in Tarifa.'

'Do you remember how I taught you? All the times we went–'

'Yes.'

'And ski-ing? Do you still...?'

'Sometimes.'

'You had a good sense of balance, Mikky. You picked it all up really quickly. You were a great student.'

'You were a better teacher.'

'Why are you here?' His gaze is penetrating and so I glance at the moored yachts to avoid his persistent and hypnotic gaze.

'I wanted to see Carmen.' It's not a complete lie. 'I'm worried about her.'

'Why?'

'I think they've problems with the apartment.'

'Um, I heard Yolanda's father wants it back.'

'Did she tell you?'

'Isabelle told me.'

'Didn't you do some work with Carmen at the museum when it opened?'

He finishes his roll, wipes his mouth and screws up the serviette and then he looks up. 'I'm surprised you remember. I just advised them on finding the right security company that was a while ago now.'

'Yolanda's done well. She seems to have a successful business - lots of celebrity clients.'

'Like father, like daughter.'

'What do you mean?'

'He's a wealthy man and by all accounts not someone you'd like to deal with. Yolanda has been given everything on a plate. She's spoilt and she thinks Daddy owes her big time because he sent her away to school and favoured the chauffeur's daughter.'

He seems very well informed and I drain my coffee.

'I wonder where they'll go if they have to move...'

95

'Carmen was looking at a villa near ours. I thought she was quite happy moving into somewhere with a garden...'

'Really?'

'That's what Isabelle said. I think she was hoping that Carmen would be around to see the twins more because she's been working a lot recently and we've hardly seen her.' He rubs his eyes and I imagine his sleepless nights, rocking the twins to sleep and humming to them in the darkness.

'What are you thinking?' he asks.

I blink. 'I'm worried Carmen is working so hard.'

'We all have to make a living. Don't you put in the hours?'

'I do,' I answer truthfully.

He shrugs. 'It's life.'

'Thanks for breakfast,' I say, about to stand up.

He clutches my hand. 'Are you happy, Mikky?'

'Yes. I am.'

He releases my fingers.

'Not the tortured soul you were?' He traces the anguished scream running down my arm with his finger and I shiver.

'No,' I lie.

'No drugs?'

'Rarely.'

'Good.'

'I'd better get back.'

'What are you plans?' he asks.

'We're having lunch with Sofia - Yolanda's mother.'

'I haven't seen her for years. She was a beautiful looking woman. Wasn't she a dancer?'

'She's writing a memoir of her life in the ballet in Argentina and she wants me to take some photographs.'

We walk companionably to the Boulevard and he hands me

the drone in my rucksack.

'When are you leaving Malaga?'

'Not sure - probably the end of the week.' I lie.

'Come for dinner? Isabelle would love to see you.'

I doubt that but I lie and say. 'That would be lovely.'

We kiss cheeks and he continues to hold my shoulders even though I pull away from him.

'It's good to see you,' he whispers.

'Goodbye, Jorge.'

I skip across the road and back to the safety of Carmen's apartment. I don't turn around and I don't look back but I feel his penetrating stare as if he is an X-Ray machine at the airport and it sends a shiver through me as I remember our past together and what our future might have been.

A few hours later I'm sitting in a seafood restaurant on the beach with Yolanda overlooking the bay of Malaga waiting for Sofia and Carmen to arrive. The mediterranean shimmers and dances and out at sea a charter plane turns and banks before making its way to land at the airport.

My mind is made up.

After seeing Jorge this morning it has only reinforced my plan. I will leave first thing in the morning. I will drive back to Palma. Malaga is no longer my home and there's no point in me staying and wallowing in the past. Jorge has moved on and so have I.

All my ghosts are laid to rest.

All I need to do now is to find out what Carmen is planning with the book - and if she won't tell me the truth, I'll get her to open the safe and I will frog march her round to the Picasso

Museum and register it officially under Father Ignacio's name this afternoon.

Opposite me, Yolanda is staring at sunbathers on the beach. She's lost in thought and when she feels me looking at her she picks up the menu.

'Did you ask Carmen about the book in the safe?' I ask.

She pretends she's reading the list of hors d'ouvres.

'Will you tell her, what you found?' I insist.

Her grey eyes reluctantly leave the menu and she hard stares me.

'What's it to do with you, Mikky? This is between me and Carmen. The sooner you leave Malaga the better.'

'Why do you say that?'

'Things have a funny way of going wrong when you're around.'

'What's gone wrong?'

'What's gone right? There's no reason for you to be here, is there?'

As she speaks she suddenly isn't looking at me, she's looking over my shoulder and I turn to see her mother walk toward us.

Sofia Drummond is tall, slim, and still elegant from her years of ballet training. She has the refinement, confidence and elegance of someone used to money and fame and I can't help but compare her to Josephine Lavelle. They create an aura as they walk, heads turn and people around us pause their conversation to stare.

She greets us with air kisses on both cheeks and within seconds she summons a waiter with a purple painted nail and orders an expensive Rueda. While she's waiting for the wine she makes small talk with Yolanda, sips chilled water, eats an olive and her eyes flick over the other diners.

The mother and daughter ignore me, so I compare their features and the way their almond grey eyes hold the same expression of distain; an expression I would like to capture with my lens. I look forward to taking this woman's photograph and I wonder what she would look like if she smiled.

'Carmen's not answering her mobile. She should be here by now. She's waiting for some bloody paintings to arrive. She's probably still at the museum.'

Yolanda taps another message into her phone.

'We'll have to order without her. I haven't got long before I have to get back to the airport,' Sofia says.

'She'll probably join us for coffee,' Yolanda adds, tossing the phone to one side.

'Let's have fish baked in salt?' Sofia announces and closes the menu decisively.

'Perfect, with a salad?' I decline wine from the waiter. My head is still tender from the beer last night and besides, I want to speak to Carmen and get the manuscript registered in the museum.

'Did Yolanda do that?' Sofia nods at my arm.

'Yes.' I hold it out for her inspection.

'I don't like tattoos. I can't see the point of them but it's very unusual.'

'It's very artistic.'

Sofia frowns. 'It's an amazing replica, the ghostly scream is haunting. How do you live with it on your arm?' she asks.

'It reminds me of how far I've come.'

'Mikky has other masterpieces on her body,' Yolanda adds.

'I don't want to see any more.' Sofia holds up a hand and, once again, I'm forced to listen to their stilted conversation.

'Mikky is a friend of Josephine Lavelle's.' Yolanda drums

her fingers on the crisp cotton table cloth. 'Do you know her, Mama? I met her last year, did I tell you? Carmen and I had lunch with her–'

'We were on a yacht together, many years ago,' Sofia recalls. 'Somewhere in the Mediterranean. We were touring on a friend's yacht around the Greek islands. I think she was on another yacht – it might have belonged to Dino Scrugli – you know the Italian billionaire – the philanthropist who owns all the art work? He opened that new Theatre Il Domo on Lake Como. That was before she was shot on stage but I do remember her singing. She had a beautiful voice. It was a long time ago, before… before her fall from the public arena – so it must be over five or six years ago. I never knew she took cocaine although, I suspect a lot of people did at that time…'

The waiter arrives with our fish in a large steel tray and peels back the thick crusted salt. He fillets it with skill and while we watch him our conversation pauses.

Sofia will be an interesting model to photograph; high cheek bones, flared nostrils and brown eyes that dance when she speaks. Her manner is formal but when off guard there's a sad expression that swells from her soul. It only lasts a nano second; when she unfolds her cotton serviette to place it in her lap, when she watches the waiter top up her glass or when she adds black pepper to her fish, she is preoccupied, and I decide that is the expression I will capture with my lens. That is the image for her memoir.

What makes her so sad?

'How do you know her?' Sophie looks at me.

'We met last year. My flatmate was commissioned to paint her portrait,' I answer truthfully.

The fish is soft, delicate and juicy. I pour oil and garlic

dressing onto my boiled potatoes and over the mixed salad.

I have no intention of telling either of them that Josephine is my birth mother.

Sofia pushes her food around the plate and when the conversation stalls for the third time, I say.

'I believe you're writing a memoir.'

She blinks then nods dismissively.

'It's under negotiation with the publishers. My agent is dealing with it.'

I'm about to ask about photographing her but she turns to Yolanda.

'Your father is determined to sell the apartment. There's no point in arguing with him. You know what he's like.'

'It's my home. Why doesn't he sell the other apartments?' She wipes her mouth leaving a smear of lipstick across the white linen napkin. 'This is where I live. My business is around the corner. I can walk there and Carmen can walk to the Picasso.'

'Don't upset him, Yolanda. This has been going on for too long.'

'It's in my name – I don't have to sell it. He's in the wrong, Mama. He can't do this and you're wrong to support him.'

Sofia takes a small bite of fish and her face is impassive. She has been sent to do her husband's dirty work and I begin to believe that my taking photographs of her for this fictions memoir is just a ruse to have another guest at the table so that Yolanda won't make a fuss.

'He always gets what he wants–'

'I know, and I'm still angry with him for taking that painting–'

Sofia blinks and concentrates on the table cloth.

'It wasn't his, Mama. Sasha gave it to me,' Yolanda cries. 'He thinks he can just walk into my apartment and take what he likes.'

'He did it for me. He though it would remind me of Buenos Aires.'

'But it's mine. He's not getting, Flamenco en Llamas. He's not taking that off my wall.'

They are talking about Sasha McBride a well known artist and the painting covering their safe.

'Sasha is my niece.'

'She's my cousin.'

'Don't upset him-'

'He's a control freak, Mama. You know that,' Yolanda raises her voice. 'He bullies you and he controls me - through money. He takes what he wants. He pretends he's generous and kind and that's how strangers see him but he's manipulative. I'm like a dog on a lead. He pulls me and I have to sit when I'm told, run here, go there... and he's just the same with you. He pats and strokes us when we're good and rewards us with theatre tickets or exotic holidays but he's rude and insulting. '

Sofia blinks quickly and I watch their exchange with curios-ity.

'It's because he cares about you.'

'Bullshit!'

'He loves you very much-'

'That's not true.'

'He wants what's best for you-'

'That's another lie. He always wants what's best for him...'

I place my knife and fork together and make an excuse to visit the bathroom but they don't even bother to look at me. I take a detour and sit outside on the promenade wall pleased to be away from their angry exchange. I raise my cheeks to the sun and close my eyes.

What is Yolanda not doing that makes him want to sell the apartment?

The thought of leaving here fills me with relief and happiness. I check my watch. Eduardo is working his shift but I will call him after six. I need to hear his voice. The thought of him waiting for me in Palma fills my heart and it skips a little. I'm so lucky to have met him. Perhaps I did need to confront my past before I move forward but now I'm ready to move on - back to Palma - back to Eduardo. I need a simple life not like Sofia and Yolanda's materialistic world that revolves around money, possessions and status. Although it's a world that I wanted to be a part of until last year, I thought money would bring me the security I craved or would give me power to do and say what I like but there is so much more to life.

I know from my adopted mother about jealousy, anger and hate but it is Josephine, my birth mother who, during the winter, taught me the power of love. Her acts of kindness are invaluable, worth more than any money. Life is so much more than possessions.

I walk slowly back inside playing air guitar and humming to Queens of the Stone Age, No-One Knows, and I'm so lost in the music that I bump into a man with a salt and pepper beard.

'Oops, sorry,' I apologise but he doesn't smile so I poke my tongue out at his back.

I return to the table, slide into my seat and they ignore me.

'I'd be just as happy in a caravan on the beach...' Yolanda is saying. 'Maybe I'll move back to Switzerland, I spent enough time there as a child...'

'Don't be ridiculous. What about your business?' Sofia looks flustered.

'My clients will pay to come to me. I'll set up a studio-'

'That's ridiculous, Yolanda. Look for somewhere smaller - somewhere not quite so expensive or move back to Madrid. Papa thinks that would be better for you if you...'

The waiter removes the plates.

'Papa is not going to control me,' Yolanda whispers.

'Yolanda, please-'

'Mama, you have to please him. You're his wife but I don't. I hate him.'

'Don't fall out with him. You know what he can be like-'

'I don't know why he's doing it. He doesn't need the money. He can sell his private jet or he can stay at home this summer instead of renting a yacht and sailing round the mediterranean. Why does it have to be my apartment - my home that he wants?'

I smile, pleased that Yolanda is asking the question on my mind. My chest swells with pleasure and I lean forward interested in the answer.

'You know what he's like when he's made his mind up...'

'Yes - I do. I only wish I knew what I'd done to upset him.'

'You'd better call me a taxi. I can't wait any longer for Carmen to turn up.'

My balloon is deflated. Sofia doesn't have the answer.

'Where the bloody hell is she?' Yolanda says checking her mobile. She throws it back on the table. 'She's not picking up.'

I check my watch wondering how quickly I can book my plane ticket back to Palma.

The front door is unlocked and Yolanda sighs.

104

'Bloody hell, she's at home. I bet she didn't want to face Mama. Carmen?' Yolanda dumps her bag on the floor in the hallway and heads down the corridor calling out. 'Carmen. She's probably in the shower,' she says to me over her shoulder.

I head to my bedroom, throw my bag onto the bed and fumble for my mobile wishing we hadn't stopped for another drink.

I check my watch. Six fifteen. I'll call Eduardo.

'Carmen?' Yolanda screams.

It's not a normal sound. It's primeval and filled with fear. I follow the sound of Yolanda's piercing, guttural, shriek then sobbing.

'Oh my God, Carmen!'

In the lounge I think Yolanda has fallen but she is on her knees. Carmen is on the sofa, where Father Ignacio sat, her head lolls forward onto her chest. She's asleep. Her mouth has fallen open but she's not snoring. She's not moving.

It's then I see blood seeping though her navy jacket and it drips slowly onto the wooden floor.

Fear fills Yolanda's voice and a tremor of alarm shudders through my body.

'She's dead,' she whispers.

Chapter 7

"You know you've read a good book when you turn the last page and feel a little as if you have lost a friend." - Paul Sweeney

I pull Yolanda into my arms and away from Carmen's motionless body. She leans against me for support while I fumble for my mobile. I can't take my eyes from my friend's dead face. My fingers are slippery, Carmen's blood covers the screen.

'We mustn't touch anything,' I whisper pressing Yolanda's head against my chest, trying to cover her eyes. 'The police are on their way.'

The breeze from the half open window causes giant sunflowers in a maroon vase to flutter and a yellow petal falls to the floor.

Yolanda sobs. 'Carmen, my God. What's...? Oh, no. She can't be dead, Mikky? ...What the fuck?...Oh my God...' she wails. She shuffles away from me and her hands are shaking when she dials a number on her mobile.

'Jorge? Shit. It's an answer phone. Jorge, CALL ME. URGENTLY. It's Carmen, she's...'

She hangs up.

Carmen is sitting on the sofa, where I sat just three days ago talking to Father Ignacio. Her head moves and her arm falls off the chair. Her eyes are slightly open and she's staring at me and for a second my heart beats rapidly and I'm filled with relief.

She's not dead.

I lean forward to feel her pulse. 'Carmen?'

Her eyes are open and she is unmoving, unblinking and vacant. The back of her head is covered in a matted crimson tide. I'm no expert but it looks like a gunshot wound.

Yolanda holds my arm.

'She's dead - gone.'

Her phone rings and when she ignores it, I snatch it from her hand.

'Yolanda? What's wrong?' Jorge asks.

'Jorge - it's me, Mikky. We've just got back to the apartment. It's Carmen....she's... she's dead....'

'Mikky? Where are you?'

'In their apartment,' I repeat.

'I'm on my way. Don't touch anything.'

I crouch down beside Yolanda.

'Come on, Yolanda. We mustn't touch anything. The police are on their way. Jorge is coming...'

'I should never have have left her-'

'Shush.' I pull her into my arms and lift her to her feet. 'Come on, let's wait in the hall.'

'I can't leave her.'

'Come on,' I insist.

'I should never have...' Snot and tears fall down her cheeks and she hiccups, speaking in short bursts. 'I should never have... who could have done this? Mikky?'

I don't answer, I'm looking over her shoulder at the Flamenco en Llamas painting. It's been pulled to one side and the safe door is hanging wide open.

'Yolanda, look! The safe is open.'

I turn her around by the shoulders and she wipes her tears and nose on the back of her arm.

I take a tentative step forward and place my hand inside the empty safe.

'It's gone.'

She stares at me. Her face is ashen, her eyes are swollen with tears and her nose is dotted with a shower of freckles that I've never noticed before.

'The money?'

'Everything.'

'Say nothing,' she hisses as the doorbell buzzes. She wipes her nose on her hand. 'Don't mention the manuscript, Mikky. Pretend you know nothing about it.'

'But we have to - it could be why they - why someone has-'

She grips my arm, her nails bruise my skin and she hisses.

'If you love Carmen, then trust me. Don't utter a fucking word about the book. Don't even tell Jorge.'

Everything happens quickly and yet in slow motion. I'm moving behind a thick web, trapped and sluggish. My body is on auto-pilot, functioning like a programmed machine and I want to escape. I don't want to be here. I want to rewind what happened. I want to change everything.

The apartment is suddenly crowded. We're ushered from the living room and I sit in the kitchen, answering questions. I try to concentrate but all I can see is Carmen's dead face swimming on my retina. I'm interviewed by Inspector Miguel

Barcos-Lozano. He has a thick moustache that covers his uneven discoloured teeth. He leaves the room periodically and I'm left with a police officer; a silent woman with thick dyed black hair and I wonder how often she has seen scenes like this.

Sometime later, Jorge appears looking hollow-eyed and tired. The purple circles under his eyes are more pronounced as if he's been up all night, and he yawns and takes off his cap. He whispers to the police woman but I can't hear him. When he comes over to me I stand up automatically and he pulls me to his chest. He kisses my forehead.

'I thought I'd seen it all,' he says, 'but nothing could prepare me for...this.'

I hold him reassured by the strength of his strong body and beating heart. 'I can't believe it.'

Fresh tears fall down my cheeks and I pull away from his hold wiping them with the back of my hand.

'Is Yolanda okay?'

'She's shocked....do you have any idea - who?'

Wiping my eyes I move away from him and circle the room, prowling and caged. I tell him how we'd lunch with Sofia and how Carmen was supposed to join us but hadn't answered her phone. We'd stopped for a drink on the walk home. I tell him where and give him approximate timings. Then I say.

'I can't believe it, Jorge. Who would do such a thing?'

'We're looking at everything - was there anything out of the normal?'

I shake my head and shrug. 'I've only been here a few days.'

'You spoke to Inspector Barcos and made your statement?'

'Yes.'

'Did you tell him everything?'

'Yes. It all seems surreal, Jorge as if I'm having an out of body experience and this isn't happening.'

He holds me in his arms and once again I'm reassured by the warmth of his touch but the faint smell of his aftershave makes me pull suddenly away.

'The safe door was open,' he says. 'Do you know what was in there?'

'No.'

'But it was definitely open when you and Yolanda arrived home?'

'Yes.'

I have a feeling that although I have given my statement he's been sent to double check my story.

'They stole money that Yolanda kept in the safe - black money - it's illegal but quite common place when you have a cash business but it was a considerable sum...'

I shrug as if I have no idea.

'Over twenty-five thousand euro.'

'Wow, that is a lot.'

'Do you know if Carmen or Yolanda kept anything else in the safe?'

'No, Yolanda would know better than me.'

'I just wondered if Carmen had shared anything with you - you know - when Yolanda wasn't around.'

'No.'

'Do you think she might have kept other things in there?'

'Like what?'

'She didn't mention anything to you?' he persists.

I shake my head.

'Nothing at all?'

I think of Father Ignacio sitting on the sofa and realise that my lie might soon be discovered and what will happen when he finds out that Carmen has been killed?

'You look exhausted, Mikky. You're coming home with me tonight. Inspector Barcos has agreed that you and Yolanda can stay with us. Isabelle has prepared the spare room for you both.'

It's not my first choice and I certainly don't want to see Jorge's cozy set up with his wife but I'm relieved to leave the apartment. When Jorge escorts me from the kitchen I catch a glimpse of the lounge where a few white-suited and gloved-up people look like aliens in this pristine home. I recognise the camera cases of the forensic specialist and morbidly wonder what angle and shots they would have taken of Carmen's murdered body. It's all so final. My step falters and Jorge grabs my arm. He links his arm through mine and pulls me out into the corridor.

'Who will tell her family?' I ask him.

'A detective in Madrid has informed them.' Jorge replaces his cap. His eyes are serious and I risk a glance down the stairwell and shudder.

'Where's Yolanda?'

'They've taken her back to my villa.'

'Is she okay?'

'She's sedated.'

He escorts me into the lift and I'm surprised that outside it is already dark and the street lamps illuminate our path and a chilled wind from the Sierra Nevada hits my cheeks. We're in his Land Cruiser and my head rests against the leather seat when he asks.

'They've been arguing a lot recently. I wondered if that's why you came back here?'

He drives through the quiet streets of Pedregaleco, an old fishing village and now a trendy area with expensive restaurants, and when he pulls to a stop at a red light his gazes rests on me.

'I'm sorry I have to ask, Mikky but we have to eliminate everyone, including you.'

I nod and sigh. 'Of course, you must but you can't suspect Yolanda. She was with me the whole time. I told that other detective where we were and the time we left. He can check it out. There should be phone records too. Yolanda tried to call Carmen loads of times but she didn't pick up...' I wipe away a tear.

'I'm sorry but I–'

'It's okay, Jorge. Do you know what time – it happened?'

He shakes his head. 'We're waiting for confirmation but not very long before you got back to the apartment.'

'We might have caught him. We might have saved her – if only we'd got home earlier.'

'Why did you say him?'

I glance at Jorge and in the darkness he turns to look at me.

'Him?' I repeat.

'You said, you might have caught, him – a man?'

I shrug and frown. ' I don't know. I guess it's just a figure of speech.'

'Did Carmen mention anything else at all to you – anything that might be important or related to anything.'

'No.'

'When did you arrive?'

'Thursday.'

He knows this and I wonder if he's testing me.

'And today is Saturday – barely three days.'

'What are you saying?'

'Did Carmen mention the museum or anything about her work?'

I shake my head and close my eyes and feel the power of the Land Cruiser as we accelerate. 'No.'

'Nothing?'

'She had to work today. She was very busy. She didn't meet us for lunch but I think that was something to do with a painting arriving for a summer exhibition from Switzerland.'

He nods as if I'm confirming it was something he heard already and as we pull into the driveway of his villa, I know that my lies won't stand up to scrutiny, especially if Father Ignacio hears about her death and the loss of the priceless book that he had entrusted into my care.

I open the car door and stumble out into the illuminated driveway and a beautifully manicured garden. Above me, the silver fingernail moon ducks behind a cloud and a cat miaows from the bushes. I slam the car door and look at Jorge over the bonnet.

'I said Him, because I thought it was a man who did it. It was such a bloody scene, I couldn't imagine a woman doing something so heinous and brutal.'

My head is thumping. My neck and shoulders ache and my eyes are raw. I lay in bed with my arms above my head watching the new dawn spreading across the ceiling and listening to Yolanda's soft breathing beside me.

Last night after arriving back at Jorge's villa, I called Eduardo and Josephine both of them had offered to fly to Malaga but I had said not at the moment - there was still too much to sort out and too many unanswered questions. Their shock had been palpable and I'd taken refuge in the comfort of their loving words and understanding compassion.

Six years ago Isabelle worked for the tourist board and I was working on archiving and photographing museum pieces. We'd become friends and we all hung out together, surfing and later kite surfing and ski-ing. We'd shared barbecues on the beach, roasted horse chestnuts, cooked meals and drank copious amounts of alcohol. At first she had been shy and withdrawn but once I knew she had a crush on Jorge, I had tried to avoid her and our friendship had dwindled.

Last night Isabelle welcomed us warmly. She was serene but composed and although she'd been crying she was controlled and when Jorge suggested a whiskey nightcap she shook her head. She would have to be up early for the babies. I also declined his offer.

They will miss Carmen and the children would grow up not knowing their godmother. Why hadn't she told me?

I lay listening to the sounds in the villa; the twins crying upstairs and Isabelle's footfall on the tiled floor as she carries them down into the kitchen trying to make sense of my situation. Yolanda has made me complicit in her deceit but there was something in the way she had urged me to stay silent and why she specifically said not to tell Jorge that has made me keep quiet, but the more I say, the more lies I tell and it could make me look like I am involved in Carmen's death. I didn't want to complicate the situation by having to explain about Father Ignacio or the missing manuscript. If he's gone on a retreat, he would be out of contact with the outside world and no access to the news or newspapersI reason. I might have some time to find out why she wanted me to lie.

Last night Yolanda had been sedated. She'd been tormented but the doctor had been kind and gentle and she had eventually succumbed to sleep. Now her face is pressed against the pillow and her breathing is calm and regular and I'm waiting for her to stir beside me. I'd been unable to lose myself or switch off. My mind has been a whirl of activity as I lay trying to piece things together. I'm wired and tense but my body is heavy and sluggish.

I need to speak to her.

My phone bleeps. It's another text from Eduardo: Call me - if you need me.

I sigh, throw the covers off my legs and climb out of bed. I stand at the window and even in the midst of my sadness and heartbreak I can see it's a pretty villa with a beautiful gated garden, trimmed grass and neat borders. Beside the garage is a sleek, powerful motorbike another of Jorge's hobbies. He's been very successful but something in my subconscious reminds me that Isabelle's father owns a few hotels along the coast and she's from a wealthy family.

Yolanda stirs and stretches. She opens her eyes and they fix on me. She appears to focus and then she groans and like a feline she is motionless and eerily quiet, staring at the ceiling.

'It wasn't a dream, was it?' she whispers.

'No.'

The front door slams.

Yolanda leans up on her elbow. Her eyes are swollen and red. 'I feel sick.'

'Do you need the bathroom?'

'I can't believe it - I can't believe, Carmen's...' She slumps back against the pillow.

I sit beside her and she stares up at me.

'Will this pain go?' she asks.

'Eventually.'

We sit in silence.

'Jorge said, she didn't suffer.' I don't tell her I'm haunted by the way Carmen's mouth hung open on her chest or the puddle of blood at her feet.

'Why didn't she struggle?' she asks.

'I don't know.'

'She was shot for fuck's sake. Shot in the back of the head – like an execution. Who would have done that, Mikky?'

'I don't know.' I shake my head and trace the wound on the back of my hand. A ragged scar. A souvenir from Mama. I think of the people who may know about the manuscript and the priest sent to a Mission in Africa.

'I wanted us to run away. I wanted to get away from all this and lead a hippy life on a beach somewhere. I laughed at the incongruity of our situation. She thought I had everything. Yet I only ever wanted her. Do you know Mikky, she was convinced I had it all? A good business, an apartment, a supportive family but I have nothing. I don't have anything without her. She's not here to share things with me...' She wipes her eyes with the back of her wrist and I pass her a tissue.

'I know,' I whisper.

She blows her nose.

'Why did she do it?'

Her question takes me by surprise.

'Why did she steal that fucking book?' Yolanda cries. 'It should have been in the museum.'

'Do you think that's what all this is about?'

'They were after something...'

'She wouldn't steal it. Carmen wasn't like that.'

116

'She must have done. It was in the safe - in our home - and someone came after it.'

'Maybe she kept it there for - safe keeping?'

'She never bought anything home. Never - nothing of any value. The museum is geared up with alarms and security. Everything is logged and recorded and monitored. It should have been there. Did you tell the police about it?'

I shake my head. 'You told me not to.'

'And Jorge? Did you tell him?'

'No.' I take a deep sigh and decide to tell the truth. 'But it won't be long until he finds out that I lied.'

'What?'

I stand up and pull on my jeans. 'Because Father Ignacio will soon tell him the truth.'

'Who?'

'Father Ignacio brought the book of hours to Carmen. I met him with her on Thursday. I walked into the apartment and they were sitting there with the manuscript.'

Yolanda sits up and watches me buckle my black jeans. I step into my biker's boots and continue speaking.

'It won't be long until someone puts two and two together and wonders why I'm back on the coast - if they haven't done that already. It's hardly a coincidence that I'm here and three days later Carmen is dead.'

'What do you mean?'

'Carmen was going to do a deal - without the museum being involved.'

'What?'

'She was going to sell it privately. She wanted to get it authenticated and valued.' I pull my Foo Fighter's T-shirt over my head and push my hair into some sort of shape but it

117

still looks as if I've just crawled out of bed so I give up.

'She didn't tell me. You said, you knew nothing about the book,' Yolanda whines.

I shrug. 'Carmen told me not to tell you. Maybe it was going to be a surprise for you – I don't know. She wanted money of her own – probably to buy you an apartment.' Looking in the mirror I apply purple lipstick, adding colour to my tired and drawn face.

'What are you going to do?' Yolanda sits up.

'I'm going to tell Jorge the truth.'

She watches me sling on my black leather jacket.

'Wait!'

I pause with my fingers on the door handle. It wouldn't be easy telling Jorge or Inspector Barcos the truth but this was serious I had to work with them.

'Carmen's work always came first. She was dedicated to her job. She wouldn't have taken it – would she?' Yolanda throws off the duvet and I realise she's still full dressed. 'Did she steal it?'

'She was murdered, Yolanda, and I think she was killed by someone who wanted that manuscript.'

'But they didn't get it,' she says.

'Carmen's dead,' I say trying to control my voice so that Isabelle and the twins won't hear me. They're playing in the kitchen and when one of them screams, I shudder. 'They killed her and stole the manuscript,' I hiss.

She kneels on the bed and without speaking she begins to unbutton her checkered shirt, revealing large rounded breasts and a deep cleavage. She pulls out a white vest tucked into her jeans, and underneath, attached to her skin, a package is strapped to her torso. She rips it free from the velcro and lays it before me on the bed.

'I'm trusting you,' she whispers.

My heart is gathering momentum as she unfolds the parcel and when a familiar hessian cover falls onto the duvet, I gasp. I sit down on the side of the bed conscious of Yolanda's shallow, stale morning breath over my shoulder and invading my senses. I pick up the manuscript and unwrap the tome, turning the pages carefully, marvelling at the delicately hand-drawn images hardly daring to believe it's the same one.

'I guessed you knew about it,' she says. 'I knew when you saw it in the safe that you weren't surprised - you only pretended to be.'

'When did you take this?'

'Yesterday.'

'You went back to the safe?'

'When you met Carmen in the hallway, I tucked it into the back of my jeans,'

I remember; the safe was open; Carmen called out; I told her I was going to photograph the sunrise. Let's have a coffee later? Then she said, 'I'm sorry, Mikky. I'm sorry, I ever dragged you into this mess.'

They were the last words she ever said to me.

'You never put it back?'

Yolanda shakes her head. 'I thought I'd play her game and wait and see if she'd tell me once she realised it had gone missing from the safe. Crissake, Mikky, I wanted her to trust me.'

'You've had it all this time - since yesterday morning?'

'Yes.'

'Strapped to you?'

'I often carry cash like this.'

119

'It was round your waist when we had lunch with your mother?'

'Yes.'

I shake my head in disbelief and she continues speaking.

'Don't you understand, Mikky? Someone killed her for this manuscript but they didn't get it. It wasn't in the safe. If she had given it to them, she might still be alive.'

'They might have been after your black money...'

Yolanda's red-rimmed grey eyes fill with tears.

'Even Carmen didn't know I kept that amount of money in there. They were definitely after the book and I'll never forgive myself for taking it. It's all my fault...'

We both gaze down at the book.

I don't know what to say.

'I killed her,' she sobs.

'You didn't kill her, Yolanda.' I place my arm awkwardly on her shoulder.

'If I hadn't taken the book, she could have given it to them and if she'd given them this bloody book then she would still be alive.'

'Not necessarily. Be kind to yourself, Yolanda.'

'Why did she contact you - was it about this?'

'On Wednesday I was in Tarifa - kitesurfing.'

'How did she find you?'

'She phoned Dolores and she drove down to the hippy camp and found me.'

'She never told me. I was in Madrid and I thought she was at work on Wednesday.'

'This is why I have to tell the truth. Yolanda. The Guardia Civil will retrace her steps and they will find out that I came here and they will know I met Father Ignacio.'

'Who's he?'

'A priest I knew a while ago.'

'The same one that you fell in love with when you were renovating that church?'

'He asked Carmen to find me.'

I tell her how he listened to Father Benedict's confession and the conversation we had only three days ago that now seems another life time away.

'And Carmen put the Book of Hours in our safe?'

'She knew that if it was authentic it could be worth millions. She asked me to contact my friend Simon Fuller to examine its authenticity.'

'So, that's why she contacted you...'

There's a quick rap on the door.

'Girls? Are you awake?' Jorge calls.

I put a finger to my lips, silencing Yolanda - then call out. 'Yes - just getting up.'

'Good. I've some news I want to share with you. I'll put some coffee on.'

And as I open the door, Yolanda hisses, 'Don't say a bloody word.'

Jorge's deep set eyes are rimmed with deep, dark shadows. His beard looks unkempt and each time he scratches his chin or his cheek, his bristles crackle huskily under his nails. Like me, he looks as if he's been awake most of the night.

Isabelle is upstairs coping with the twins and the death of her best friend. She moves around silently with only an occasional murmur. Life is for the living and the twins must be cared for, routines still exits and life goes on - Carmen is no longer a part of this life and I brush my eyes with my sleeve.

Yolanda and I sit with Jorge at the pine kitchen table drinking coffee. There's croissants and bread but I can't eat so I peel a orange and suck the juice from its bitter skin. It balms my raw throat while I listen to Jorge and the research he's already done.

'Viktor Gruzinsky is Russian mafia. He came here to Malaga in the late nineties and started a protection racket down near Algeciras. He's a thug but a clever one. He's been involved in stealing cars, mostly Mercedes and Audis and transporting them to the eastern block to sell for a significant profit. Hundreds of cars get stolen each year and end up in Siberia or Moscow with their numberplate changed and the chassis number burnt off.' He scratches his cheek and sips coffee. 'But more recently stolen property has become more his thing. His crews steals to order. They mainly target big houses along this coast; the villas that are left empty for months by owners who live in Madrid, London or New York...'

'So what's this got to do with Carmen?' I ask but at the mention of her name Yolanda's eyes fill with tears and Jorge slides a box of tissues across the table. When I reach out and take one, Jorge's fingers accidentally brush mine but he continues.

'Sometimes stolen paintings, sculptures or jewellery have turned up in the city and he's asked Carmen to help him sell the stuff on the black market.'

'Isn't that illegal?'

He places his hand on mine to stop me from speaking.

'She refused to help him but a few months ago but he threatened her.'

Yolanda gasps. 'She never told me.'

I sit up and move my hand away from his touch.

'He threatened, Carmen?'

'According to Madeline, her secretary, he approached Carmen back in October last year. He had a Bust of Stalin and although it's not her area of expertise he asked Carmen to get it valued for him. So, she called in an expert and although it was thought to be valuable - the expert realised it had been stolen and alerted the police.'

'But Viktor didn't get caught?' I ask.

'No.'

'Did Carmen know it was stolen?'

'Not when she agreed to help him.'

'Carmen wouldn't help a crook.' Yolanda sniffs and tosses the dirty tissue in the middle of the table.

'Madeline made a statement saying, Carmen agreed to get it valued. She didn't report the Stalin Bust as missing but Madeline says she would have done, had she have known it was stolen. This wasn't her area of interest-'

'Her specialist area is artwork - paintings.' Yolanda coughs and clears her throat then bunches up another tissue in her hand.

I think about Carmen's secretary with blond hair and thick fringe showing me into Carmen's office only last Friday. The day we had lunch or didn't have lunch because we argued - and how Carmen stormed off.

How long will it be until the Guardia Civil find that out?

Jorge continues. 'According to another member of staff, Viktor came to Carmen's office a few months ago and threatened her. They had a shouting match and Madeline was summoned. Carmen told her she would lose her job if she insisted on staying with Viktor.'

'Oh my God, is Madeline dating this guy?' Yolanda's asks.

'Madeline said, she had no idea who he was. She doesn't believe he's mafia.'

'And you think he killed Carmen?' I ask.

'He's killed that way before. We're searching for finger-prints, the murder weapon...you know the usual things...'

'He's killed before?' Yolanda's mouth falls open. 'Why hasn't he been put away?'

'It's easier for us to keep an eye on him-.'

'You should be ashamed of yourself - is this what the police do now?'

'We watch and we monitor.' Jorge rubs his bloodshot eyes.

'Well you didn't do a very good job, did you?' Yolanda hisses. I think she might lean across the table and claw his face.

'So Madeline's broken up with Viktor?' I prompt.

Jorge shakes his head. 'She got engaged to him.'

'What?' Yolanda stands up. 'How could she? Carmen never told me any of this.'

I watch her as she paces the room, walking from the sink to the fridge and back to the table and my eyes are fixed firmly on her waist. The book is well padded and protected, hidden by her thick shirt.

What would Jorge do, if he knew?

Did Viktor want the manuscript? Could the have known about it?

'So what has this got to do with what happened to...?' The sentence hangs in the air suspended and swaying like a dead fish on the end of a fishing line.

'There are witnesses who saw them together.'

'Who? Madeline and Viktor?' Yolanda rubs her forehead as if trying to make sense of it all.

'Carmen and Viktor. They were seen together yesterday afternoon.'

Yolanda slides back into her seat and we both stare at Jorge.

'She was working. She didn't even come and meet us for lunch,' she whispers.

'They were arguing about five o'clock up in the Parador, in the hotel car park,' he replies.

The old hotel is perched on the hill beside the Alcazaba, the old Moorish castle, overlooking Malaga harbour. I'd taken the drone over it yesterday morning and I imagine them together at the busiest time on a Saturday, at a hotspot for one of the most famous views of the coastline, a great vantage point to look down onto the city, the bullring and the port.

'And you think he killed her?' I ask.

I imagine how he followed her. She knew him. She would have let him in to the apartment. He stood behind her. A gun with a silencer? I remember the pain of my own wounds and scars that had been neatly removed by cosmetic surgery.

What had Viktor said to her?

Had he wanted the manuscript?

'We want to know what they were arguing about,' Jorge adds.

'Have you asked him?' I tap the table with my fingernails.

'He's gone into hiding. We think he might have gone back to Siberia.'

We sit silently at the kitchen table.

At least I could tell Father Ignacio that his book was safe. I will call him at the first opportunity.

I've been implicated in the theft of the manuscript by Carmen and Yolanda's actions. Just as Carmen had assumed control of the book, now Yolanda had it and it wasn't hers to keep.

125

I must get it back. My continuing silence over Father Ignacio's involvement might only make things worse. Wouldn't it be much simpler just to tell Jorge the truth?

Chapter 8

*"There are worse crimes than burning books. One of them is
not reading them." - Joseph Brodsky*

The following day Yolanda and I are interviewed
separately again. We travel to the police station for -
standard procedure - a run through of our statements,
to make sure we haven't forgotten anything or to see if we have
remembered something.

Father Ignacio's presence in Carmen's apartment is not
mentioned so I stay quiet. They also don't know that Carmen
came to find me in Tarifa, so I stick to my story and tell them I
decided to come and see Carmen to lay some past ghosts to rest.
I don't tell Inspector Barcos why my life was traumatised four
years ago and that I blocked the nightmare from my mind or
how I locked away the events that changed my destiny because
it was too painful in case he asked me the inevitable question.

Had I laid the ghosts to rest?

After meeting Jorge in the port the morning I flew the drone
- yesterday? I believed I had but now it was worse than ever.
My ghosts seem to have disintegrated now my friend is dead.

We return to the villa. Jorge doesn't question me or ask me
about the past. He must know that by going over the details

would open old wounds, so by tacit and silent agreement we say nothing about the past and instead I help with the twins. I change them and bathe them. I place their small fingers against my big hand and gentle comb their dark locks. I marvel at the creation of something so small and vulnerable and wonder how someone could possibly give their baby away.

Josephine told me she gave me away so I would have a better life than the one she could provide.

She must have been desperate, falling in love with her father-in-law, she became pregnant and on the verge of becoming a world famous diva. They knew their relationship would never survive the scandal. She had reluctantly given me away and my biological father, a doctor from Dublin, had arranged for my illegal adoption. My adopted parents registered me as their own and had Josephine not come looking for me, I would never have known my true identity.

Little did she know.

We were duped.

I'm claustrophobic with the domesticity of another couple's family life, so late afternoon Yolanda and I venture out for some fresh air, away from bleating children, nappies and mulched food. In the distance snow glistens on the pink mountains in the fading sunlight. The cold wind from the Sierra Nevada whips around my ears and I tuck my nose into my jacket. Here the promenade of Muelle Uno is wet and I skip over puddles before finding a low wall, that looks reasonably dry, overlooking the beach.

'Let me take the book back to Father Ignacio,' I plead as Yolanda sits beside me.

'Not yet.'

'It belongs to him,' I say.

'A book like this doesn't belong to any one person.'

'I mean, it belongs to the church, it was entrusted to them during the Spanish Civil War.'

'Don't make me laugh,' she says. 'The church is the most corrupt institution going - with all their wealth I'm sure they're not going to miss this little book that's been gathering dust in their old archives.'

'It's dangerous, Yolanda. Maybe someone in the church knows about it? Maybe it isn't Viktor-'

'They know it's him. Jorge told us that. It's just a matter of time until they do a deal with the Russian Government and he's extradited.'

'They don't even know where he is.'

'They'll find him.'

'Why don't we just give the book to the police?'

'No.'

'I'm worried, Yolanda. If someone knows about the book, like Viktor and was prepared to Kill Carmen to get it, they won't stop looking. Once they realise you have it, they will come after you.'

'Viktor's in Siberia.'

'What if he isn't? There are too many unanswered questions - why was Carmen arguing with him up in the Parador car park?

She shakes her head.

'What if it isn't Viktor? Father Ignacio is blind and who knows - he could have been followed or may be the priest who helped him find it, said something to someone.'

'You're trying to tell me priest's are murderers.'

'I'm trying to tell you it's dangerous, Yolanda.'

'What is it with you, Mikky? You're such a coward. You don't want to see this through, do you?' she shouts.

'It's not worth dying over,' I raise my voice and cast my arms aside, wanting to pin her to the ground and pull the book from her waist.

'If you can't handle this, then fuck off, Mikky. I don't need you.' She walks ahead of me but I run after her, ignoring the people near us who hear our raised voices.

'What do you plan on doing with it?'

She carries on walking and says. 'Carmen stole it for a reason. She stole it so it would give us security. Think about it, Mikky. She thought we had nothing. Papa wants to sell our apartment. Don't you understand? It all makes sense.' She stops and faces me. Her grey eyes are filled with sadness; harrowing and painful and to my shame I realise it would make an amazing photograph.

'She was doing it for us - for me. She loved me.'

'You really believe that she stole it for you?'

'Of course, she loved me.'

'It's so out of character, Yolanda. Carmen is... was more honest than that.'

'Was she? You might have been at University together and she told me you once saved her life but you didn't really know her, did you? You haven't been much of a friend, have you? You haven't been here-' She waves her arms and I think she might punch me instead she walks away and stands on the edge of the quay staring down at the murky oily water.

'I thought, I-'

'You didn't think, Mikky!' She turns on me. 'You left here four years ago in a blaze of anger and destruction. You left her devastated. She couldn't believe you would turn your back on her. Jorge was beside himself. He looked everywhere for you. I'm surprised he even speaks to you. I couldn't believe it when I saw you standing in my apartment. I couldn't believe the cheek of you, to turn up as if you didn't have a care in the world, as if nothing mattered-'

'Carmen wanted to get it valued,' I say quietly. 'And I know a guy who can do that.'

She walks slowly toward me. 'That guy you mentioned, Simon Fuller?'

'No he's in Asia - but there is another guy I know in Bruges-'

'Is he legit? I mean he won't tell anyone?'

'Theo has made his living by being discreet,' I say.

I don't add that he's probably the most corrupt man I know and has made a fortune by selling stolen art on the blackmarket. He might not be an expert on medieval manuscripts but he will know if he can sell it.

'How can we get to Belgium?' she asks.

'We can't risk carrying the manuscript through the airport. We'll have to drive.'

'They told us not to go anywhere.'

'Only while they check our alibi's. They can't hold us here forever.'

'I suppose we could tell them we're taking a few days holiday - you know - after - after Carmen's funeral,' she says.

'And what about Father Ignacio?'

'Tell him we're doing it for him,' she says. 'Maybe we can give a donation to the church.'

I follow her gaze up to the Parador on the hill.

I imagine Carmen with Viktor in the car park having only hours to live.

Why did she meet him and why were they arguing?

The Iglesia de Santiago Apóstol is an ideal example of Christian and Islamic architecture. Situated in the narrow and winding Calle Granada, it's historical value is linked with the Christian Conquest of 1487 when the Catholic Kings defeated the Moors after nine hundreds years of rule. The church is a basilica with three naves and the bell tower's thick brick is a tribute to the Moorish culture that once dominated this land.

I duck in to the doorway, into the dark silence and the heavy door bangs behind me like a sealed vault. I'm familiar with the reformation of Baroque architecture from the eighteenth century and I know it covers the original wooden frame structure and decorated plasterwork. My boots echo under the scalloped dome and I move toward the the chapels of the ship of the Epistle to light a candle under the image of the Virgin of the Rosary.

Carmen is gone.

I say a prayer.

She is gone forever. Only snapshot images in my mind and her voice resonating in my ears reminds me she was my friend. How long will I continue to hear her voice?

Watching the candle flare, makes me think of Mama and the thousands of candle I have lit for her. I don't hear her voice any more.

Once when I was a child she had given me a tattered bible belonging to her great grandfather from Ireland. It had colourful drawings of the Virgin and pictures of animals. 'You like this rubbish, you can have it,' she'd said. At first I'd studied the pictures with interest; animals, trees and religious images but without having it explained I found it full of bloody images and night after night when I was left alone in the caravan, sometimes with rain and wind pelting the grimy window, the bible drawings haunted me and I thought the devil might grab me.

I had nowhere to run.

How could something so Godly be so frightening?

I was only a child but I shouted at God in the dark. I tempted him. I challenged him and I told him to do his worst. I blamed Him, but how could he take the blame for everything that went wrong in my life?

I cannot blame him for the actions of others, any more than He can take the blame for my mistakes and the bad things I've done. I worked it all out; belief, atonement, sacrifice, redemption, salvation everything – it's guilt.

Once, when I was very young and Papa was sleeping in a drunken haze, I stole money from his wallet. I went to the church and dropped it in the box for candles but when I looked up at the altar, the Virgin frowned down on me, showing her displeasure. I never stole again – well – not on such a petty level.

For many years I was never sure if I imagined things or if they were real and actually happened; fact and fiction, drink and drugs, truth and lies.

I block out unwelcome memories and squeeze into a pew, shuffling along the narrow space to sit beside Father Ignacio who waits for me in the darkness of his own world.

'Hello, Father. Thank you for meeting me,' I whisper.

He reaches out and when I take his hand he squeezes my fingers.

I look sideways at him. His eyes have shrunk into his skull. His head has recently been shaved giving him the air of an older man who is tired and weary of the path he has chosen. The days of finding him attractive are over and like a disillusioned lover I'm already keen to leave but first, I must ensure his silence.

'It's still an enormous shock,' he sighs.

'Yes.'

We sit quietly for a few minutes while I regain my composure. He clasps his hands around my fingers as he used to do and I return the pressure of his fingers. I whisper quietly, telling him again, but this time in person, how we found Carmen's body and now Yolanda and I are staying with Jorge, a member of the Guardia Civil. I explain that he hasn't been appointed to this specific case but is keeping us informed, off the record, of its progress. Then I tell him about the Russian mafia and Viktor who has left the country. I also reassure him that the book is safe.

As we speak with our heads bent close together, I'm reminded of how we used to sit, and in particular on one day we left the confines of the church and slipped away unnoticed, spending the afternoon in a bar. After several liquors I offered myself to him - in the name of God - forever. He declined my offer, politely but firmly and his kindness had only added to my insecurity and my emotional weakness.

I had been rejected as a child. Mama had been more ruthless than I could describe. But his rejection had been more profound. I had been - for the first time in my life - in love. It had been unrequited love and I felt it with all its pain and shame like a giant sledgehammer in the cavity of my chest. In retrospect I think Father Ignacio knew this because although we remained friends, we were never alone again. There was always another Priest or visitors in the church and this made me more frustrated until, one day, I accused him of leading me on, of teasing me. He had been horrified. It never dawned on me that his career could be ruined - until he left. He simply disappeared but this time to a Monastery outside of Cordoba and to a new life dedicated only to God.

'You haven't told the police you have the book?' he whispers.

'No. I thought it best not to.'

'But they will be looking for a motive, won't they?'

'No-one knows about your visit to Carmen or about the book.'

'The truth will come out, Mikky. I cannot lie.'

'I'm not asking you to lie, Father. I'm asking you to say nothing.'

'But to what end? This is dangerous. I think we should tell the Inspector the truth,' he says.

'I want to help you, Father. Please give me the chance to carry on what Carmen and I wanted to do. Let me get it authenticated. I have a contact-'

'You have?'

'I know an expert...' I stare at the stained window above the altar and blink at the golden sunlight radiating onto the stone floor and I wipe away a tear.

'Don't feel responsible. It wasn't your fault.' His grip is reassuring and comforting.

'Thank you...for not blaming me.'

'I know you, Mikky. I know who you are and I don't think you've changed. Have you?'

I smile. 'Perhaps a little - I grew up - I had to.' I look away. A lump is blocking my throat and the liquid golden light streaming through the window suddenly fades. I won't look at him but then he squeezes my fingers.

'I'm sorry. I didn't want to hurt you...'

I could rip open my shirt and show him the colourful ink

drawings on my body; the Betrayal of Christ, The Last Supper but the most shocking of all, across my chest and breasts is the severed bloody head of St John the Baptist and Salome's gloating smile. All done to remind me of my past. I didn't think I would ever love again. I didn't think my body mattered.

I pull my hand from his.

'I survived.'

'I could never have been ordained if... if...'

'It's okay,' I say truthfully because now it is. Now it's easy for me to forgive.

'I've thought about you everyday and I've prayed that God would care for you. Did he?'

'Not especially.'

'I remember how difficult your life had been but you found a way though it with your artwork. Do you still paint?'

'Sometimes.'

'I often think of the painting you gave to the church. Christ going into Heaven,' he whispers. 'I remember you explaining it to me. It's still on the wall. Many tourists are convinced it's an original.' His chuckle is deep and warm like the amber liquid sunlight now flooding though the window.

We sit quietly for a few minutes and then he says. 'We must tell the police. It might help them find who-'

'Please, Father,' I plead with him thinking how incongruous it is that this man I once loved I now call Father. 'We don't even know if it's the manuscript that he or they wanted. It might be something else. Presumably Viktor wanted Carmen to fence stolen property for him but she refused, so he may know nothing about the manuscript. If we tell the police then they will come to the Monastery and the Bishop and everyone will find out and they will wonder why you didn't take it to

136

them in the first place.'

'I wanted to be sure. I wanted to tell them the good news...'

'They may not believe you, Father. They may think that you were stealing the book...'

It's not a kind suggestion but I'm desperate to keep the manuscript, to follow this through, one way or the other. It's what Carmen would have wanted and although I haven't worked out what to do with it, I know we must first establish its authenticity and trace its provenance.

'I have a responsibility to the church and to Father Benedict,' he says referring to the confession of the dead priest. 'Although I am in two minds what to do. Life isn't easy, Mikky and sometimes my faith also wavers. The weight of responsibility is sometimes too much to bare and I understand what you went through when you were a child and had no help. I often think we have let too many people down-'

'We?'

'The church. I'm not solely responsible but in this case I feel that I've let Carmen down. I placed her life in jeopardy and it is something I will have to live with-'

'What about your confession? Who will you tell?'

'And burden another - as I have been burdened?'

'But that's what you do, isn't it? Blame and burden the foundations of religion-'

'It's like a stained-glass window - the absolute beauty is in the sun's rays that illuminates the colours and the ink drawings.'

'What is?'

'Belief - it's like the sunlight - warm and comforting and beautiful and wondrous but when you no longer-'

'Believe?'

'Trust – in your judgement – then you are cold and isolated.'

'Don't be too disillusioned, Father.'

I have no allegiance to the church. It once took Antonio away from me and turned him into Father Ignacio and although that was a decision that he made, I'm now relying on his fear of the church to see things my way and I don't feel a glimmer of guilt.

'This is a very difficult situation,' he whispers. 'I am responsible.'

'Don't be too hard on yourself. Pretend it is safely in the monastery archives.'

'I should never have taken the book to her. It's my fault, Mikky.'

'We've lost a good friend and now we must honour her wishes. I'll help you.'

'I don't think it's as simple as that. Let me think about it.'

'Go on a Retreat, Father – have some peace and quiet – give me a week,' I plead.

'When is the funeral?'

'Friday.'

'I'll be there.'

I stand up and place my hand on his shoulder.

'Goodbye, Father,' I say, realising the irony of my words.

He's only three years older than me, less than forty, but a world away in age and spirit.

The crematorium is in the hills behind Fuengirola. It's bare white walls and mahogany pews are simplistic and packed with friends and relatives. I'd thought Carmen's parents would want the funeral service in Madrid but instead it takes place here on the coast and it appears that her family and a few friends from Madrid have travelled down.

I recognise very few people and although I concentrate on the service, my mind wanders and I'm filled with grief, tormented to the depths of my soul and I'm reminded of Mama's funeral when I was fourteen and the cascading tears down my father's dishevelled face.

Josephine Lavelle, once a world famous opera star and my birth mother, stands beside me clutching her prayerbook. She opens her palm to show me a small golden icon of the Virgin Mary. It's a symbol for us both and I smile, watching how her lips move in silent prayer. She kisses the small face of her talisman that she believes has, on two separate occasions, saved our lives and she reaches out for my hand.

Eduardo stands on my left and I grip his fingers. His bleached blond hair and weather beaten tan make him look more like a surfer than a skilled UVI nurse. I lean against him for support, feeling the reassuring strength of his strong shoulders. He's like a silent shadow, guarding me, not intrusive nor annoying. He's simply kind and attentive and he knows when to distance himself and to give me time to think and I find myself wondering what he sees in me.

What do I give him in return?

Afterwards when we stream outside into the sunshine we hide our tears behind dark glasses, gathering near a water fountain on neatly trimmed grass under a colourful purple bougainvillaea pergola. It seems incongruous that we're holding a service for a girl of my age, on such a warm spring day. It's a day to be on the beach or to enjoy tapas in the sunshine or even to walk in the hills and enjoy the cherry blossom that casts a blanket of white across the fields like snow. It reminds me of an old tale of a Moroccan Prince who brought his bride from the North to live in Malaga but she grows very sad. Although she loves him, she misses the pretty white snow of her homeland. The Prince watches her day after day, crying and staring out over the barren hills of the south. Then, he has an idea and he sets to work. The following spring the Princess wakes to a land covered in white, far prettier than the snow and far more pleasing than her cold homeland. The Prince had thoughtfully planted rows of cherry trees knowing that when they blossom they would provide beauty for his wife's eyes unlike anything she has ever seen before. After that spring she stops wishing to go home. This is her home and she's happy here with her prince and her newborn child.

When I was growing up, I'd not been happy. We travelled like gypsies crossing the country, my parents looking for work so they could get money to drink and gamble, and I had wished for a loving family and craved for a homeland that I could mourn and call mine.

Carmen's family, dressed in black, look destroyed. Her father's shoulders are hunched and he barely raises his eyes from the ground. He's surrounded and protected by Carmen's two older brothers and I join the queue, greet them briefly and mutter my condolences then I walk on, knowing there is a stream of people who come after me. Carmen's mother, a small woman, looks crushed but stalwart. She kisses Yolanda and holds her in a tight embrace whispering that she will arrange for Carmen's 'things' to be collected.

'Carmen is with us in spirit,' she says, again and again and I admire her bravery as she speaks to the line of people paying their respects.

How can they remember everyone?

People file passed where we are standing in the shade beside rows of niches. I'm on auto pilot as I inhale the scent of cherry blossom that provides a welcome respite from the clinical air inside the chapel. I'm floating on an invisible pathway and it's Josephine who steers me, gently holding my elbow and Eduardo who rests his hand in the middle of my back.

Our small group stands together under the shade of a Tamarind tree.

'I won't see any of them again,' Yolanda whispers, wiping her eyes. 'Did you know they never liked me? They never approved of her living with the boss's rebel daughter. They thought I wasn't good enough for her...'

Enrique places his tattooed arm protectively around her shoulder. His brown eyes are filled with tears and I wonder if they will work in the tattoo studio or what she will do with her business.

'Hello, Yolanda.'

I turn at the sound of a deep Scottish voice. It belongs to a short, overweight, red-headed Scotsman.

'Hola Papa.'

Yolanda kisses his cheek.

'I thought you'd have put makeup on,' he says.

'It's come off.' She rubs at her cheek.

Sofia stands beside him in a black designer dress. She greets us both with an air kiss to the side of our cheeks. It's almost a week ago that we met for lunch in Malaga and we waited for Carmen to join us never realising that she was arguing with Viktor and we would find her dead in her apartment later that afternoon.

'This is Mikky,' she says to her husband. 'Carmen's friend.'

He barely gazes at me but he looks around at our small group and his eyes rest on someone more important.

'Josephine, how thoughtful of you to come.' His mouth is filled with a row of white veneers as fake as his smile. Steven Drummond kisses my birth mother on both cheeks. 'It's wonderful to see you again. It's been a long time and this is so, terribly sad. It's a tragic day...'

'Stephen. I'm so sorry. Have you met Mikky?'

Josephine introduces me again and this time he looks vaguely interested and I'm rewarded with a wide smile and he shakes my hand. When she presents Eduardo as my 'novio' I feel my face redden.

'I met Carmen last year,' Josephine explains. 'I had lunch with her and your lovely daughter Yolanda. It was a flying visit to Malaga but very memorable one. Carmen was beautiful and you also have a delightful daughter.'

Josephine doesn't look at me. She doesn't tell him that she came to pick up a stolen painting on my behalf because I was lying half dead in hospital.

'Do you know Carmen's family, Josephine?' Stephen brushes past Yolanda to stand closer to Josephine, forcing her to step back out of his way and I imagine him at social conventions, meetings and charity dinners where he networks and name drops ignoring those who are of no use or value to him. I'm dismissed having fallen into this last category.

'They would love to meet you. They won't believe you're here. I think they are fans of yours. Come, let me introduce you. I remember once-' Stephen links his arm though Josephine's and she protests.

'No, Steven, this isn't the time to talk about me. Please don't-'

'Nonsense, it will cheer them up to know you thought so

142

much about Carmen and that you actually met her...' He steers her away and I hear him say. 'They're devastated, you can imagine. None of us can believe it, such a beautiful girl. So talented. Her father worked with me for years. We're like family. I've known Carmen all her life. It's a terrible, terrible, tragedy. It will do them good to know...'

Sofia drifts off behind them and I grip Eduardo's hand, heartened he's beside me and I rest my head against his shoulder and watch them disappear into the crowd.

A girl with long blond hair, a thick fringe and dark glasses appears beside Yolanda.

'I still can't believe it,' she gasps in heavily accented French. 'I only spoke to her that morning...'

'Don't torture yourself, Madeline,' Yolanda replies. 'Let the police deal with it. Do you know Mikky?' Yolanda says by way of introduction.

Carmen's secretary stares at me.

'I saw you when I came to Carmen's office,' I say.

She shrugs as if she has forgotten me and squints as if she has lost her contact lenses.

'That Inspector Barcos has been horrible,' she whispers. 'I'm sure Viktor wouldn't - it's not possible. The police are trying to say he - but you know it's not possible - I know him. He's the kindest man I've ever met.'

'Why has he disappeared then?' Yolanda replies.

'He hasn't disappeared. He's visiting his sick mother.' She pulls her designer handbag across her chest and directs the next question at me.

'You're delusional, Madeline.' Yolanda shakes her head and wanders off to join Enrique.

'You were with Yolanda when she... found her?' she asks me.

143

'Yes.'

'They seem to think it's my fiancé but it isn't – it wasn't him. He wouldn't do a thing like that. We're getting married.'

'Where is he?'

'He's gone to Russia. She isn't well.'

'Have you known him long?'

'It seems like a lifetime.'

'How did you meet him?'

'At the Easter procession – last year...It was love at first sight. We both knew immediately. I knew as soon as I saw him, he was the one.'

'And you introduced him to Carmen?'

'Carmen liked him. They got on well together and they had a lot in common.'

'Did he know her well?'

'They met a couple of times. A friend of his gave him something to sell but Viktor didn't realise it was stolen...and now...' She looks over her shoulder and whispers, 'They think he might have murdered her... but he wouldn't.'

'Why would he kill her?' I probe.

'That's what I say – why? It doesn't make sense.'

'Didn't Carmen meet him on Saturday afternoon?'

'No, I don't think so.' Madeline catches sight of Carmen's mother and says, 'The poor woman, I'm so sorry for her. I must go and pay my respects.'

After she leaves I lean against Eduardo for support. We move further under the shade of the tamarind tree and we're suddenly alone.

'Thank you,' I say.

'For what?' His forehead crumples in a puzzled frown.

'For being here.'

He shakes his head. 'I knew when I met you, that you were trouble and needed looking after but I never imagined this...'

'I know.'

'Is there anything else I should know, Mikky?'

I look into his trusting dark eyes. 'No.'

'Sure?'

'Yes.' I answer positively and slip my hand into his.

'I'm sorry I can't stay longer. Will you come back to Palma?'

I collected him from the airport last night. We had dinner together and stayed in a hotel overnight. I needed space and privacy and I needed love. Eduardo had been amazing.

'I'll stay here for a few days and I'll drive back next week,' I say.

I don't mention my plan to go to Bruges.

'Don't leave it too long, cariño. I'm sorry I couldn't get more time off but I've only just gone back to work after Tarifa.'

Jorge escorts Isabelle toward us. He holds her arm protectively at the elbow as they make their way through the crowd. He's dressed in full Guardia Civil uniform and it's only after he removes his cap and wipes his brow that I see the anxiety in his eyes.

'I have to go to work,' he says.

'And I have to get back to the twins. My mother never copes with them for long,' Isabelle explains. 'Come back to our villa, the gang are going to meet up later...'

They engage Eduardo in conversation and I use the time to study the people around us. I have the eye of a photographer and in a crowd I spot a tilt of a head, a secret smile, a knowing wink or an illicit, brief touch of a hand. I scan the scene filing it away in my head, identifying as many people as possible and linking their relationship to Carmen.

145

It's then that I see Father Ignacio. He's standing with another man - not a priest but a man in a dark suit and standing a few metres away from him, Inspector Barcos glares at me over his bushy moustache.

Chapter 9

"A great book should leave you with many experiences, and slightly exhausted at the end. You live several lives while reading." - William Styron

'I carried Carmen out of a nightclub once,' says Sebastian, a tall lanky, German. 'The taxi arrived and we all wanted to go home but she insisted on one more dance...'

'She knew how to move,' Yolanda agrees. 'She was a cool dancer...She loved that song: Dancing Queen.'

'Do you remember her at your birthday party last year?' says Enrique. 'She was–'

'We went to Paris together a few years ago,' says Lucia.

'She painted a beautiful portrait of–'

'Do you remember when she...'

Jorge and Isabelle have opened their home to friends to talk about and grieve over Carmen and their stories wind around me reverberating images and I imagine Carmen is still alive, still laughing and smiling. They're friends that I knew; the old gang but I can no longer relate to them and I move away toward the open terrace door.

I can't join in with their happy stories by comparison my memories are far sadder; hospital, healing the heart that Javier had broken, beating a guy at University who had pushed her and cut her head after we left a rock concert. Carmen had always made me feel protective of her but this time I hadn't been there to help her.

Had she always been a victim?

Could I have stopped it from happening or was her destiny sealed once she found me in Tarifa?

'Weren't you at University together?' Isabelle asks me, filling my glass.

I'm about to reply when a bald-headed guy called Jaime says, 'What about that time we went diving near Gibraltar? It was only afterwards when Jorge told them he was in the Guardia Civil that they let us off with a caution...'

'They thought we had been hiding drugs in tuna nets,' laughs Mariano who owns a bar in the back street of the city where we once used to drink.

Lucia wipes away a tear.

I don't want to hear their memories.

I don't want to swap my stories with them.

I slip through the open door wander outside onto the patio, into the cooler air and the quietness of the half moon. I zip up my leather jacket and stare across the city and the glistening sea. Although it was less than two weeks that I was kitesurfing in Tarifa with Eduardo, it seems an age ago that I had been care free and relaxed.

I turn at a sound and Yolanda appears beside me and by unspoken agreement we walk away from the door and across the grass to stand at the edge of the garden. The memories and laughter and the sadness of Carmen's funeral hangs over us and Yolanda is the first to speak.

'If there was one person who broke her heart it was, Javier. He didn't even send flowers,' she says. 'I'll never forgive him.

He damaged her for life.'

'He's still in South America,' I reply. 'Besides, she was always happier with you. You're kind and considerate.'

'We never had that excited euphoria that you have when you first meet 'the one', like when you think you might die if you can't be with them and every second drags until you're together again. It wasn't magical like that but I did love her and she loved me.'

'I know.'

'How did you meet, Eduardo?' she asks. 'You seem very happy.'

'I'm lucky. He's my guardian angel - my private nurse.'

'I can't believe Josephine Lavelle came to the funeral and that she knows my parents. They never said they knew her but I guess I'm not surprised. Papa seems to know everyone. She must think a lot of you to come here last year for you and to come here today-'

'Did you ever hear her sing?' I interrupt.

'Yes, I heard her a few times. Papa invited us once to La Escala.'

'I was never lucky enough to hear her sing. We only got to know each other last year and that was after her accident.'

'I didn't know you like opera, Mikky. You were always the rock and heavy metal type.'

I smile. 'I would like to have heard her but you're right, I can't bear crappy opera music. She's tried converting me but it's no good...'

'She didn't want to leave your side when Papa dragged her off to meet Carmen's parents.'

I never had the chance to tell Carmen the truth. I wish that I had confided in her so I take a deep breath and make a decision to tell Yolanda.

'We don't broadcast it but... Josephine, is my birth mother.'

Yolanda's mouth drops open and her grey eyes narrow. She stares at me. Her profile is illuminated in the moonlight then very slowly she asks.

'Is Eduardo a psychiatric nurse?'

'What?'

'You're sick, Mikky. You're nuts.'

'I don't have any mental health issues and I'm not on drugs any more.' My heart sinks. I know what she's thinking. 'You don't believe me, look!'

I pull out my phone and show her photographs. There's a particular one of us both taken after my operation to remove the letters: T-H-I-E-F that had been carved into my forehead. We are cheek to cheek smiling into the camera. The similarity is remarkable. We both have the same wide smiles, big eyes and the same nose.

'I have my father's colour eyes,' I say.

She stares at me.

'Cojones. You haven't got a great track record in telling the truth.' She turns away as if she's not interested and stares up at the moon.

'I'm going to find out who killed Carmen,' she whispers.

'That's a job for the police.'

'Don't you want to know who did it?'

'Of course but-'

'Viktor's got engaged to Madeline but I found out he's loads of girlfriends...'

'She's in love with him. I spoke to her this morning outside at the crematorium and she talked about getting married-'

'He's already married to a girl from the Ukraine. Don't you

150

know anything?'

'Obviously not.'

'Did you see the priest at the funeral? Was that your friend?'

'I didn't notice him,' I lie.

'Carmen was going to sell the book to Viktor once she had confirmation that it was worth millions. That's what they were arguing about on Saturday afternoon.'

'Why do you assume that?'

'Get your head out of your arse, Mikky! You know she wasn't happy. She was sick of looking after other peoples' artwork and artefacts and having nothing for herself. You know it killed her living in my apartment – literally,' she adds with a choke of emotion.

We both turn at the sound of footsteps and Isabelle appears on the terrace holding a cigarette.

'I thought you'd quit?' Yolanda calls and we walk over to join her.

Isabelle takes a sliver of tobacco from her lips and folds her arm across her chest. 'I started again after the twins were born.'

Her mobile shrills and she reaches into her pocket and fishes it out.

'Sí?'

She listens. She doesn't speak. Her eyes show concern and I watch her expression changing from raw emotion; shock - fear, knowing it's one that I would like to photograph.

'Okay. Drive carefully.' She pockets the phone and stares at me. 'That was Jorge. They've found a body near the crematorium and they think it was someone who was at the funeral today.'

The smell of geraniums fill my nose and throat. I'm suffo-

151

cating, I cough and choke. My head is hot and I'm dizzy.

'Are you okay?' Isabelle disappears and returns a few minutes later with a cool glass of water which I take with gratitude.

'Who is it?' Yolanda asks. 'Did Jorge say?'

The water is cold on my throat.

Isabelle shakes her head. 'He's on his way home now. I have to go and check on the twins. Don't mention it to anyone. Jorge said they don't know his name but he's a priest and he was blind. It seems like he tripped and fell but...'

I watch her back as she retreats inside and I inhale and exhale controlling each breath, stretching my chest cavity, hoping it will calm my shaking fingers but my knees buckle and I settle on the steps leading to the manicured lawn and I whisper.

'Oh, my God, Yolanda. We must tell Jorge about the Book of Hours. You must give it to him!'

She shakes her head. 'Don't be pathetic! Don't bottle out now, Mikky. Phone that expert of yours. Phone him now - the one in Bruges - let's go and show it to him.'

'And what do you propose to do with it afterwards, once you find out it's real or even a fake?'

'Carmen stole it for me. She did it to protect us so I wouldn't be beholden to my father. She didn't want us to reply on him. He thinks he can buy everyone. He's a control freak, Mikky. Money is power for him. Don't tell me you don't know what it's like not to have anything? This is my security, Mikky. It's mine and if you loved Carmen or if you're my friend, you will help me.'

'You can't walk around with it strapped to your body forever.' I glance down at her long black jacket where the book lays hidden.

'I will - just until we get it valued. Let's leave here as soon

152

as we can.'

Yolanda's slurring her words. She's slumped across the table talking to a few others in a similar state but I'm sober. My body is tense and I'm waiting and watching to see if she will let anything slip or will reveal the book strapped to her body. It's been a long day and a longer evening knowing that Father Ignacio is now dead.

I cannot believe it and I'm tense, waiting for the opportunity to speak to Jorge alone.

'Do you know what she said to me?' Yolanda bangs her fist on the table and the rooms goes quiet as everyone waits for another revelation, another story, about Carmen to fuel their morbid alcoholic-induced decline.

'What did Carmen say?' asks Enrique flinging an arm over her shoulder.

'Not Carmen - my bloody mother - Sofia, the Queen of Ballet. She said, she had an important dinner party to host for Papa with some new investors tomorrow night so they had to get back to Madrid...but then she said: This could be the opportunity for you to help Papa. Yolanda continues to imitate her mothers's South American accent: Well, you won't want to live in that apartment now that Carmen is dead. You'll have to sell it. Put it on the market and perhaps some ghoulish millionaire will want to buy it.'

Isabelle gasps and covers her mouth with her hand then she produces a lentil and beef stew and it distracts us as we gather around the pine table. Jorge, who's just changed into jeans and a shirt, slaps his beer bottle angrily on the table.

'What did you say to her?' Isabelle asks.

'I told her I haven't decided anything and that it's my apartment and I'll do what I like.' She sips more wine.

I haven't got anything to add to their conversations so I sit and dunk a chunk of bread into the gravy and red wine sauce. Isabelle's parents have been looking after the twins but now they've gone and she goes upstairs to check on them. I push my plate aside unable to eat more than a few mouthfuls. My heart is heavy and I shake my head when the guy sitting beside me, whose name I can't remember, asks what my plans are.

Nothing makes sense, and I'm tired and I find it hard to concentrate.

Jorge stands behind me and I feel his hands on my shoulders moving in a slow massage. It eases the pain shooting up my neck and I turn to look up at him.

'Will they assign you to the case?' I ask.

'Not at the moment.'

'I hope they catch him.'

He leans and whispers in my ear. 'Come with me.'

I rise and follow him from the room and outside into the garden where we stand looking over the neat lawn.

'Who does the gardening?'

'An old neighbour. It keeps him busy.' Jorge holds a cigarette in one hand and a beer bottle in the other.

'I thought you'd given up smoking?'

'I had.'

'Until the twins arrived?'

'Until you came back.'

I walk to the edge of the verandah to put distance between him and that comment and I wonder what it would have been like to be living in this villa with Jorge. He follows me and as we stand side by side gazing down at the twinkling city lights

154

I'm conscious of his spicy aftershave.

'It appears that Carmen was given a book. It's a rare book, an illuminated manuscript that they call a Book of Hours and could be worth millions if it's authentic. Did you know about it?'

I shake my head.

'We found a diary on the dead priest. I think you might know him. Father Ignacio. Wasn't he a friend of yours?'

I turn away, hardly daring to believe that he is gone.

'I met him when I was working on a project after University, on a restoration at a small chapel near Ubeda,' I reply vaguely.

'That was before you came to live in Malaga – before you met me?'

'Yes.'

'Have you seen or heard from him since then?'

'No.' I'm an accomplished liar. I just hope my name is not mentioned in his private papers.

'He was at Carmen's funeral.' He exhales smoke and stares at me. 'Did you see him?'

'No.'

I waft the smoke with my hand, batting it, like an annoying fly.

'It also appears that he met Carmen before she died. He gave her a rare manuscript.'

I would like to see Father Ignacio's diary. I sit on the step and after a few moments Jorge settles beside me.

'How did he die?' I whisper.

'It seems it was an accident. He was found face down. He drowned.'

'An accident?'

Having seen Father Ignacio navigate his way around I doubt

he tripped and I wonder if it was a way for him to end his life or for the church to cover up. Death by misadventure. Mishap or Guilt. I imagine Father Ignacio floating face down in the water and his arms spread wide, prostrate, as if embracing his punishment. Disillusioned and in despair.

'Do you think...?'

Jorge shrugs. 'The church wouldn't have it any other way.'

'It's too much of a coincidence – isn't it?'

Jorge puts his arm around my shoulder.

'So much death,' I say. 'What's it all for?'

'I don't know but I do think we've found a motive for Carmen's murder,' he replies.

'So you think someone was after this manuscript?' I ask.

Jorge nods. 'It appears so.'

'Viktor?' I ask. 'Or someone in the church?'

He shrugs. 'We're trying to find out who knew about it and where the book has gone.'

'It's not in the museum?'

'There's no record of the book being taken there,' Jorge says. 'And there's no record of Carmen going to anyone for authentication. Normally she would go to Bonhams in Madrid for this sort of thing. I thought you might know something. She didn't mentioned it to you? Would you know anyone–'

'What are you trying to say?' I move away and his arm falls to his side.

'You didn't talk to her about it?' Jorge persists.

'No.'

'And you don't know where the book is?'

'How would I?'

Jorge sips cold beer from the bottle. 'Father Ignacio went to her apartment almost two weeks ago.'

156

I cannot move. I cannot breathe.

'How well did you know him - really know him?'

'I worked in the monastery with him but that was ten years ago - before...before you and I met.' I want to add before we fell in love but I don't. Instead I swallow the knot in my throat aware that my core muscles are taught and Jorge is staring at me.

Does he want me to talk about the love we once had?

I stay silent.

'I think he gave her the manuscript that day he visited her.' His words are hushed and the truth rushes at me, bowling me over like a lone skittle.

'Why didn't she take it to the museum?' I ask.

This is the moment for me to be honest. This is the moment for me to tell the truth.

'We don't know.' Jorge flicks the burning stub into the bushes. 'The safe was open when we got there and you and Yolanda both say it was open when you arrived,' he adds. 'Neither of you took anything?'

'The murderer may have taken it?'

'Maybe...'

'Carmen never told me about a book or anything to do with her work,' I say.

'Why did you come back to Malaga, Mikky?'

'I - I needed to put some ghosts to rest.'

'Carmen didn't ask you for help? She didn't mention the Book of Hours?'

'She wouldn't have trusted me and you know why.'

I can't look at him for fear that my last night in Malaga will return to haunt me over again but I feel the heat of his intense stare, then Jorge sighs and stands up.

157

'Then she lied to you, Mikky. She lied to us all. I have to go and help Isabelle with the twins but be warned. Inspector Barcos will want to ask you and Yolanda a lot more questions now. This puts a whole different slant on her death - we have a probable motive and a valuable one. He wants to speak to you tomorrow so you'd better make sure you have a good lawyer. You were the last ones in the apartment and we only have your word that the safe was open when you got there and that you didn't take anything out of it. They want to point the finger at someone and so far they haven't got much to go on...'

I stand up and face him.

'But I haven't done anything wrong, Jorge. I haven't taken anything. I didn't know anything. Can't you do something? Can you look after Yolanda?'

He waves the empty beer bottle. 'I'll do what I can but I'm not on the case. Take care, Mikky. You're dealing with some very astute policemen who want to find answers.'

My world is collapsing under my feet. I'm floating floundering and wondering what to do when suddenly, he steps forward and pulls me into a hug. It would seem to be the most normal thing in the world for me to lay my head against his forehead but I pull away and he kisses me clumsily at the corner of my mouth. His lips are soft and his beard tickles my skin and for some reason I think of Judas's kiss on the night of the betrayal.

'Goodnight, Mikky,' he whispers.

After he goes inside I stand gazing up into the night sky, wondering if Carmen is now a twinkling star gazing down at me, laughing at my stupidity.

Carmen and Father Ignacio are both dead. I'm the only one who can link them with the illuminated manuscript that could be worth a fortune.

I shiver. It's as if I have been kissed by death. It's cold breath is on my skin, suffocating my face, tugging my hair and clawing my throat and from inside the villa comes a wave of laughter that fill me with nausea. I turn away and throw up over the roses growing at my feet.

Inspector Miguel Barcos-Lozano who I thought was fat and lazy isn't as 'simpatico' as I thought. His thick moustache covers his big teeth and with his hair slicked back and with tired red eyes he reminds me of a rat looking over a toothbrush.

'It's routine that we interview you again,' he says. 'Just to go over your statement in light of the recent changes and events. Memory is very often a strange thing. What we focus on and what we remember during a crisis or in case of violence or even when we are under threat, distracts us from the sequence of events or the details.'

'It's the third time.' I fold my arms.

'Did you know Father Ignacio?'

'Yes.' I tell him then how we met ten years ago, my restoration work and our friendship. I didn't tell him I fell in love or how my body became a gallery for dramatic biblical scenes.

'You weren't in touch with him recently?'

'No.'

I hold my breath and wait for him to call me a liar or to show me proof that I'd been with him in Carmen's apartment but he doesn't. He simply asks me another question and I believe that they have no evidence to say I'm lying. After every sentence he pauses for a few seconds, thinking of the implications of the information in my statement and although I consider myself to be an expert liar - all part of my dubious childhood - it's

159

now part of my character and testament to my adulthood.

Once again we go over the details of my arrival in Malaga and why I came here.

'So you just decided to come back?'

'I'd been kitesurfing in Tarifa,' I say and for some reason, call it instinct, I know he's verified these details with Jorge already.

'And you returned, why?'

'It's been four years. I wanted to lay some ghosts to rest.'

He skims over my statement and his lips move as he reads and I wonder what Jorge has told him.

'And when you came to see Carmen, she was alone?'

'Yes.'

'Was there any sign that anyone else had been to visit her?'

'I don't think so.'

'What did you drink?'

'Drink?'

'Did she offer you water or coffee?'

'We didn't drink anything – perhaps a glass of water – I don't remember.'

'And what did you talk about?'

'About my work in London and her work at the museum...'

'She didn't mention any particular piece of work?'

'No – well, not until...' I pause deliberately.

He leans forward and there is a flicker of interest in his dull rats eyes, so I say slowly.

'She said she was waiting for some Picasso's to be delivered from the Kunstmuseum in Basel. She was very excited about a new exhibition.'

I know it's information he already knew and it's not what he wanted to hear and I take pleasure how his shoulders drop and he sighs, and after a few minutes he continues with his questions.

It's the same format as the last time.

Did Yolanda and Carmen have any problems?

I don't know.

Did Carmen seem stressed?

Perhaps overworked.

'Did she mention Viktor or Madeline?

Not that I remember.

What did you talk about?

Family. Friends. The past. University.

We talk through Saturday morning – I said goodbye before I went jogging – the last time I saw Carmen.

What did she say?

I told her I was going to film the sunrise and she said: something like, Eduardo will love to see it and how lucky I am to have found someone so special. I think her exact words were: 'Let's have a coffee later?'

'So she expected to see you?'

'Yes.'

Her last words to me had been different but I don't share this with him. Her voice echoes in my mind when she'd whispered:

'I'm sorry, I ever dragged you into this mess, Mikky.'

'Did she?'

'Pardon?'

'She expected to see you?'

'Obviously.'

Then we get to how Yolanda and I found Carmen in the apartment.

'You didn't see or hear anything?'

'Yolanda and I took the lift. I think I remember hearing a

161

door closing upstairs but I'm not sure.'

He frowns. 'This isn't in your statement.'

'No?'

'No. You didn't mention it.' He checks the paperwork in front of him.

'I've been relaying it in my mind – I think I did hear a door from upstairs but it could have been one of the neighbours, I suppose...'

He scribbles a note then looks up over his bushy toothbrush.

'Did Carmen mention a book to you?'

'What sort of book?'

'A rare manuscript?'

'No.'

I can't tell him that Jorge told me about it. I don't want to jeopardise his career.

'Did she open the safe when you were there?'

'I don't think so...'

'You don't remember?'

'No. No, I'm sure, she didn't.'

'And Yolanda? Did you see her go into the safe at any time?'

'No.' We had agreed on this lie and I hope Yolanda sticks to it.

'You knew they had a safe?'

'Only when it was open and empty...when we found...' I feel uncomfortable.

'And Father Ignacio? How do you feel about his death?'

'Very sad.'

I'm in the middle of a thick web of deceit; complicit in Carmen's theft, Yolanda's lie and also in Jorge confiding details to me about Father Ignacio's presumable suicide that will be recorded as misadventure. It's all getting unnecessarily complicated.

'That's it then,' he says. 'You can go.'

'Go? Okay, thank you.' The relief must be palpable in my voice and I stand up. 'Will you keep Yolanda informed?' I ask.

'About what?'

'Carmen - and the person or people who...murdered her...'

'We're keeping her parents informed. They have advised us, they informed us they don't want us to - how would you say - mention it to anyone else...'

'But Yolanda is - was - her partner.'

'I know.'

'But she has a right-'

'Did she have a Civil Partnership?'

'No, I don't think so.'

'Then I'm afraid, the next of kin are... her parents.' There is a flicker of sympathy in his eyes. 'I'm sorry.'

I gather my rucksack from the floor and throw it over my shoulder. 'I'm thinking of going away for a few days. I need - space - some air and a change of scene. Is that alright?'

'It shouldn't be a problem if it's only for a few days. Your alibi checks out and we have to shift through all the information. We have your contacts details.' He checks the folder. 'Where are you going, anywhere nice?'

'To the north.'

'What for?'

'Kitesurfing.'

'Ah, yes, Jorge, tells me you are a kitesurfer...'

I smile and wonder what else Jorge has said about me. I imagine them chatting over a few cold beers finding out about me and I'm walking down the corridor conscious of his hot stare when he calls out.

'Just a moment. Would you mind if I check your phone?'

'My phone?'

'Yes, it's just a formality, really.'

I dig it out of my bag and hand it to him.

'Are you looking for anything in particular?'

'It's only routine.'

He scan reads my recent calls and my contact list and hands it back to me. He seems satisfied.

Fortunately I didn't call Carmen or Father Ignacio from my mobile.

'Just one other thing Señorita dos Santos, do you know if Yolanda is planning to sell the apartment?'

'I don't know.'

'Yolanda will have to pack Carmen's things? It might be quite emotional going back there. You might want to take someone else with you.'

'Thank you.' I smile. 'Just one thing, Inspector. How did Carmen die?'

'Die?'

'Yes.'

'A gunshot to the back of her head.'

'Like in an execution?'

'I suppose so, yes.'

'It was instant?'

'Yes. Why?'

'I would have hated her to suffer.'

Chapter 10

"A book is the only place in which you can examine a fragile thought without breaking it." - Edward P. Morgan

J orge comes with us to the apartment that I can't help but think of in my mind as the crime scene. The apartment is airless and oppressive but it's the smell that causes my stomach heave, industrial cleaner? Death?

The air is soulless and I feel the weight of death hanging over me like when Mama died. I was fourteen when she wrapped Papa's motorcycle round a tree and I had stood at the foot of her bed when we turned off the life support. Papa's sadness had overwhelmed me and like Yolanda today, I was unable to console him either. I pause in the hallway watching her gazing at the spot where we found Carmen's body. The sofa has been removed and although the blood stains on the floor have been wiped away nothing can erase them from my memory. She pauses holding onto the door frame but then she sways and I step forward and place my arm around her shoulder.

Her cheeks are wet and she brushes her tears away. 'I still can't believe it...It doesn't seem possible.'

'I know...'

Beside me Jorge's face is a mask. He loved Carmen. They had

been good friends and he remains stoic and silent as I steer Yolanda toward their bedroom and wardrobes, cupboards and drawers hang open.

'Come on,' I whisper. 'Let's get this done.'

'Chrissake, what a bloody mess!' she says. 'I gave her family permission to take what they wanted and it looks like they ransacked the place. Have they no respect?'

'Tell me what you need and I'll carry it down for you,' Jorge says.

She ignores him and pushes me away, throwing a suitcase on the bed, she works quickly, tossing clothes randomly pulling shoes and boots from the wardrobe.

'What about the paintings and all the other artefacts?' I ask.

'I'll put them in storage until I...decide. I'll get someone-' She moves quickly and deftly, anything she doesn't want to take, she leaves in a pile on the bed. 'I suppose I should stay and tidy up, but I can't face it - not today.'

'Leave it, I'll help you when I come back,' I whisper.

'It's ridiculous that I'm not allowed to go anywhere,' she complains to Jorge. 'Inspector Barcos won't let me leave Malaga. I need a break too. I need to get away for a few days. Why is he being like that with me?'

'It's because you were Carmen's partner. You might be able to help with her last movements and perhaps you may remember some conversations or meetings-'

'I've told him everything I know.' She grabs a handful of toiletries and returns to the bathroom en suite. 'I'm going to stay with Enrique. At least I won't be under such a police spotlight,' she shouts.

'Yolanda..' I say in reprimand when she walks back. 'Jorge and Isabelle have been kind to us both...' Jorge squeezes my shoulder and shakes his head suggesting I leave her alone.

'Is that all you want to take?' He picks up her suitcase.

'For now,' she replies.

I know she has no intention of coming back. She hasn't told Jorge but she's giving the key to a real estate agent so they can dispose of everything. In the days that we have stayed at the villa she has not confided in him and in the last few hours, I feel the atmosphere changing between them. She is turning more hostile and more resentful and I think it's because she can't come with me to Bruges.

We leave the apartment armed with bags and as Yolanda locks the front door Jorge leans over the stairwell and gazes at the drop below.

'It would be a horrible way to die but it wouldn't have been as bad as what happened to Carmen,' I whisper.

He's lost in thought then he rallies and presses the lift button.

'You're lucky you didn't arrive home earlier – both of you – it might have been a different story.'

'I wish I'd seen someone or something that would help,' I reply.

'You don't remember a single thing?'

'Perhaps a noise...'

'Noise?' He looks at me sharply.

'Up here – maybe a neighbour ...closing a door....'

'Did you tell the Inspector?'

'Yes.'

'Then it will be checked out.'

The lift arrives and we place the bags inside and descend in silence.

In the basement Yolanda opens the storage box and we load

my 4X4. It has the space and roof rack to carry Yolanda's skis, wetsuits and diving gear.

'You can use my place until you get settled,' Jorge says. 'There's plenty of room out back.'

'Enrique says I can store them in his basement.' She sounds angry and ungrateful.

'Have you decided what you are going to do... in the long term?' he asks.

'Not yet,' she replies.

'You need to be careful, Yolanda. We don't know who killed Carmen and I don't want them coming after you.' He puts his arm protectively around my shoulder. 'Or you.'

'You should give us police protection then.' She tosses a snorkel and flippers in the boot.

'There aren't enough resources—'

'That's a joke—'

He shakes his head unwilling to argue with her and so she slaps his shoulder.

'Don't worry. You know me, Jorge. I'm a tough old bitch—'

'And, I can look after myself,' I add, moving from his touch and climbing into my car.

Yolanda jumps in beside me and when Jorge raises his hand she faces the other way and stays silent until we are out of the garage and we join the traffic on the boulevard and then her mobile rings.

She checks the caller's ID and tosses it back in her bag.

'It's Papa – he's phoned everyday since Carmen died. He's spreading the word that my business is in trouble.'

We drive to Enrique's apartment in a tourist complex, on

the sea front, just outside Torremolinos. We unload the car in his basement and by the time we sit on the terrace drinking cava my shoulders are aching. I slump on the cane furniture, propping a pristine white cushion against my back and gaze over the park below and the sea in the distance.

Ricky, Enrique's partner, looks like a young Robert Redford. He produces cold meats and queso manchego and chunks of stone baked bread.

'You must eat,' Enrique says looking at me. 'You're losing weight and your face is gaunt.'

I pick up a slice of manchego and chew it slowly.

'Haven't they got any suspects? They must know something?' he says. 'Didn't Jorge say anything else?'

'You know me and Jorge,' Yolanda replies and a knowing look passes between them.

'Well, if you got on with him a bit better, he might tell you what's going on,' he says. 'And you'd know more.'

'I'd rather trust a snake-'

'Is it the Russians?' Ricky interrupts. 'Perhaps Viktor took the manuscript from the safe and that's the end of it. It'll just reappear and be sold to some drugs cartel like those two Van Gogh paintings that were found near Naples last year-'

'They'd been stolen from the Netherlands,' I reply. I'd followed the discovery of the paintings by the Italian police that had been found hanging on the wall of the notorious Camorra family who were closely affiliated with an international drug smuggling group.

'You wouldn't know who to trust,' says Enrique.

I think of the manuscript wrapped around Yolanda's waist. It's been over a week since she stole it and although I know Jorge must have searched our room in his villa, he never got close enough to Yolanda to feel it strapped to her body.

'What about your interview with Inspector Barcos?' asks Ricky. 'Didn't he say anything?'

'He seems to think the dead priest and Carmen's murder are related.'

'Are they?' Ricky reaches over and pours more cava into my glass.

'He wasn't murdered,' Yolanda explains. 'He was blind and he tripped. It was an accident.'

'It seems a big coincidence.' Enrique sighs.

'Maybe he stole the book that night. Didn't you say the safe was open? Maybe the priest came back to your apartment. Maybe he asked Carmen for the book back.'

'And the priest shot her?' Enrique laughs.

'Then it's the Russian Mafia...' Ricky says with finality.

They both fall silent and we all look at Yolanda who pauses with an olive in her fingers and says.

'When we arrived home the safe was open. It was empty. Anyone could have taken it...' She looks at me to validate her account and so I nod my head.

'Anything is possible,' I say. 'But would a priest kill Carmen - especially if he gave it to her in the first place? Father Ignacio wouldn't do that.'

I have no intention of telling them that I met Father Ignacio. The less they know the better.

'It could have been someone else from the church - someone who found out about the book...' she says. Her grey eyes are unfathomable and I would like to photograph her expression.

'What if the Russian murdered the priest as well?' says Enrique.

'It's possible,' she says.

'So, where's the book?' asks Enrique. 'Someone must have it.'

'The murderer must have it, whoever that is,' says Ricky.

I hold my breath and wait for Yolanda to confide in her best friends.

Ricky tucks his hair behind his ears and says quietly.

'Maybe there's someone else.' He looks at Yolanda and says in a conspiratorial tone. 'I know who it is. It must have been someone she knew because Carmen opened the door and let the person inside. There was no evidence of a struggle. She must have trusted whoever it was to walk around behind her...someone who would know the value of a book like that. Someone who might steal it...'

'Madeline,' Enrique whispers.

'Exactly! I bet it was her. I never trusted that French cow,' adds Ricky.

The following morning Yolanda unwraps the velcro from her body and lifts my T-shirt.

'I'm trusting you, Mikky. Just remember this is what Carmen wanted. We're doing it for her so her life isn't wasted. She helps me wrap the velcro straps around Salome's seven veils that she painted around my body then lowers my Foals T-shirt with a list of their tour dates and embraces me.

Her fingers pat my torso. 'Don't lose it.'

We walk downstairs and out to my car. It's barely 6am and Ricky and Enrique are still sleeping.

'Call me whenever you stop.'

'Okay.'

'Be careful, there's still someone after this book - a murderer...'

'Of course I will, and if you have any problems, go to, Jorge.' I climb into my BMW. My kites, boards and equipment are already packed in the boot.

'Jorge?'

'Yes.'

'No way.'

'Please Yolanda. He's Guardia Civil. He loved Carmen and he'll look after you.'

'Maybe.'

I leave Andalucia behind and cross the windmills of La Mancha – Don Quixote country – to Madrid, constantly checking my rearview mirror. I change radio channels and drive through the rain in the north and stop for a night in a small hostel made of dark stone and pine wood just outside San Sebastian. The following morning I'm on the road by 5am and the sun is rising sleepily in the sky when I call Eduardo before his early shift begins.

I pretend I'm in Malaga staying with Enrique and Ricky and looking after Yolanda.

He tells me he loves me and I say I will see him soon in Palma.

Then he says. 'I love the way you're caring and kind, Mikky. You're really thoughtful. You led me to believe that you weren't a good person and that you have no friends but it's not true. You know some amazing people and they all care about you. They love you.'

'It's not entirely true but I'm pleased you think that,' I reply.

'But I worry about you,' he says. 'Someone needs to look after you. All of this has been such a shock...'

His kindness increases my growing guilt so I say.

'I may take a break'

'I'll fly over next week,' he suggests.

'A few days on my own. I want to lose myself for a while. Take some photos and chill.'

'Where will you go.' The disappointment in his voice shows me that he understands.

'I may go to Bruges,' I say as if I am just considering the idea.

'Bruges?'

'Or Biarritz,' I say reading the road signs. 'I haven't decided.'

That evening as I cross the border into Belgium, my mobile rings and Yolanda's voice cuts through the car via the speakers.

'Nearly there,' I call cheerfully.

'Inspector Barcos came to see me in the studio this afternoon. He suggested I knew about the manuscript and he asked me if I took it from the safe. He suggested I've got a motive.'

'Maybe to steal the book but not to murder Carmen.'

'He says I could have paid someone else to...'

'No!' I slap the palm of my hand against the wheel. 'What does Jorge say?'

'He's not on the case.'

'Okay, well, it's only speculation. They have to explore everyone and all angles. Try not to worry,' I say, hanging up.

If Inspector Barcos suspects Yolanda then he may now also suspect me of having a motive too. Now I've left the country. The sooner I get this book authenticated, the sooner I can get back to Malaga. I have a sudden yearning to be back with Eduardo in Palma leading an uncomplicated and happy life.

It's late when I navigate the BMW through the narrow cobbled streets of Bruges, passing canals and medieval buildings with familiarity. This fairy-tale town with its picturesque market squares, almshouses, spires and churches is a world UNESCO heritage site. It was also once, my home. Ironically I took refuge here after my life exploded in Malaga. I drove and drove. I wanted to run away but I realised I could never run from myself and who I was or what had happened. Here in Bruges, I learned to block it all out. I focused on my work. I spoke to very few people and made no friends. I had to heal myself.

I stayed for almost a year picking up work; photography and sometimes I participated in more illicit dealings. I absorbed myself in art, focusing on restoration and the occasional piece of forgery.

It seems an age ago now but the streets are still familiar.

I find parking in Hoogstraat near the wealthy merchant's family home that's now been converted into a four star hotel. It has large ceilings, a spacious marble reception and a discreet comfortable lounge bar where I sit in a maroon, velvet Chesterfield and order a gin and tonic.

I text Yolanda and spend time browsing the internet while keeping my eye on the entrance.

Observation and looking over my shoulder are second nature to me. As a photographer and art thief, (retired) I'm used to surveying people around me, studying their faces and nuances. Even as a child I learned to look and listen, left abandoned for hours in the dark recesses of churches all over the country. I trained myself to be patient at an early age while my father gambled and drank his meagre earning and my mother seduced his friends and filled our lives with her jealous rages.

I became self sufficient and I learned the art of stillness. I glance up as a young, well-dressed couple enter the bar.

Honeymoon? Obviously lovers - not yet married.

I study their profiles and imagine how I would snap their photograph, and when the waiter passes me I order another drink and he nods discreetly.

The last person I expect to phone is Josephine and after a few seconds of hesitation I answer it.

'Hello darling,' she says. 'Where are you?'

'Hi, Josephine.' I smile as the waiter places a fresh drink in front of me. I suspect that Eduardo has already phoned her and it doesn't take long, until she says.

'Eduardo told me you're going away for a few days and I thought I might join you.'

'I didn't want to worry him.' I smile at her concern.

'I can understand, darling. Where are you? Have you left already?'

How well she knows me.

'I'm in Bruges. I had to get away for a few days, a change of scene.'

'Are you alright? I barely saw you after the funeral. I know you were busy and tied up with your friends and I didn't want to be a nuisance.'

'I didn't know you were friends with Yolanda's parents?'

'Not friends, darling. One of those acquaintances that you have in this life when you live in the public eye. Everyone is your friend when you are rich and famous and then they suddenly disappear when you need help or you're of no use to them.'

Her tone isn't bitter just matter of fact and I realise her life, although far more glamorous, hasn't been that different to mine: isolated and fearful – we have more in common than I thought.

We talk for a while and I reassure her that I'm fine and I'm happy that she cares about me.

Just before I hang up she says.

'I can join you for dinner tomorrow night. It would be lovely to catch up, Mikky. I could pop over on the Eurostar – just one evening – on our own – the two of us.'

In spite of myself I laugh. 'You've probably looked up the train times already – have you?'

She chuckles. 'How well you know me, darling. Book somewhere nice for dinner and I'll take you out.'

'This isn't so that you can persuade me to do that painting exhibition in New York, is it?'

'You're my daughter and I just want to spend time with you,' she laughs. 'But I might mention it and try and persuade you to use your talents.'

I'm flattered by her concern and persistence and by the time I hang up the phone I'm happy to be fussed over. I hadn't grown up with the luxury of caring parents and although this is somewhat new to me I'm secretly enjoying the attention of being pampered by my birth mother – at last.

In my room I unwrap the Book of Hours from my waist. I shower and with wet hair I lay on the bed with my back propped up against soft, white pillows and settle down with the masterpiece in my hand.

It's a medieval tome, an illustrated piece of delicate hand drawn art work that would have taken hours to create. I turn the pages of medieval history, studying the illustrated gold drawings and revelling in its magnificence. If it's not an original then it's an amazing replica and still worthy of admiration.

I close the cover with satisfaction and hold it against my breasts feeling my heart beating against it.

The vellum smells musty and I imagine the hours of meticulous detail that went into producing such a perfect piece of art work. I had forgotten how good it was to hold something so valuable and I'd also forgotten how good it was to be a thief – or as I called myself last year – an opportunist.

I dial Simon Fuller's number again but there is no answer. He hasn't returned my calls. He must still be in Asia and so, because of the urgency, I'm left with no alternative other than plan B and my old friend Theo Brinkmann, antiquities expert, fraud and conman.

If you don't know him he's as untrustworthy as your worst enemy. But he knows me, I helped him out a few times and he will remember that. More importantly, he has contacts that could – if necessary – help me sell it and that's what matters.

He will also tell me if the tome is authentic or not – or if it even matters – he could sell it anyway. I've known him to pass many fakes off as originals to unsuspecting investors from China and Japan. In the past I've helped him to forge documents and provide a false provenance trail. We were quite a team.

I dial his number and when he doesn't answer I leave a message then I close my eyes and my conversation with Yolanda earlier this evening reverberates in my mind.

'So what happens after we have it valued?' I asked.

'It depends,' she'd replied. 'If it's a fake – we can give it back

177

to the church.'

'But what if it's authentic? What do you want to do then?' I insisted.

'You'll have to find someone to buy it. Someone who will keep quiet and not implicate us in any way. Can you do that?'

This was my task - my responsibility.

Easy.

My friend Theo.

As I turn off the light, I'm already thinking ahead. To-morrow, Wednesday, meeting Theo and then dinner with Josephine. Thursday drive to Barcelona, catch the ferry and be home in Palma by the weekend.

It's a crisp spring morning. I leave the hotel and wander through the familiar cobbled streets marvelling at the window displays of hand made chocolates, fudge and toffee wrapped in an assortment of colourful ribbons and traditional decorated boxes with scenes of Bruges' canals on the cover. The Belgians take chocolate seriously and it's an important part of their economy. There's even an informal 'chocolate mafia' that keeps the price mid range in the shops for the tourists.

Although Easter is over there's still chocolates in trays, baskets, tins, and cellophane wrappers in the shape of chocolate chicks, as well as colourful dotted stiletto shoes, all shapes and sizes of animals, and sometimes more personal in the shape of breasts with a deep cleavage of white, milk or dark chocolate.

I browse the windows ducking and dodging back on myself, glancing through the reflected glass and sometimes pretending to be lost and when I'm sure that no one is following me, I slip through a narrow alleyway, cut across a small patio, and dart into a back street on the canal before coming out in a busy street off the main market square.

I enter the antique shop through the front door and the bell tinkles, fresh paint assails my nostrils and I sneeze. I don't recognise her at first. She's changed and although still elegant, her designer beige suit is now tight across her waist and her small eyes are framed by large tortoiseshell glasses. Her lips curl in the hint of a smile and she greets me like a well-established customer not knowing my needs but affording me the privacy of the backroom.

'Come through,' she says.

I follow Theo Brinkmann's daughter, Marina Thoss, along an airless modern corridor to the back of the building and a room filled with pine furniture. Large windows overlook a private court yard where an ugly grey fountain sculpture of woodland birds drink from a bowl of running water.

She pulls the shutters closed, flicks on a lamp and stares at me.

'I was expecting to see your father. I left a few messages for him.'

'He's not well and he's asked me to see you. Manuscripts and books are my area of expertise.'

'I would like to see him.'

'He's convalescing.'

'Where?'

'It doesn't matter. He won't see you. So? Where is it?'

Marina and I have never been friends and Theo's illness doesn't surprise me. He's been a heavy smoker all his life and he coughed his way through most days and nights when we worked together.

I hesitate then open my jacket and lift my Iron Maiden T-

179

shirt. I unwind the tape, removing the velcro and releasing the book, strapped in a waterproof bag.

I wasn't letting it out of my sight.

Marina Thoss doesn't blink but her owl eyes watch me with interest.

She takes it in her bony fingers and lays it on the table, and begins to slowly unwrap the hessian like it's expensive Christmas paper and she doesn't want to reveal the surprise too quickly. When she sees the calf leather cover a small exclamation of surprise falls from her tight, thin lips. She redirects the lamp and pulls on latex gloves. Very carefully she turns it in her hands and gazes at it's spine.

'A Book of Hours,' she whispers, 'a popular, devotional christian book from the middle ages.'

Marina meets my gaze with a rare smile. Her voice is melodious as she turns the page. 'Each manuscript is very often a collection of prayers or texts, sometimes even psalms, look at this picture of the Ascension - how marvellous. This is an amazing piece of work.'

I lean forward and gaze again at the fine pen work.

'This would typically suggest that it was made for a wealthy patron - it is particularly lavish in colour and it appears that the majority is written in Latin and not in vernacular; Dutch or English. See this? The inscription lining and panel stamps suggest that the binding was by Ludovicus Blok - do you see?'

She studies the book with interest pointing to small orna-ments of gold and coloured enamel etched into the frame of the drawing and she says. 'Characteristically towns appear in the borders. Here, see these branches and flowers? They add shade on the vellum making them deceptively lifelike rather like an illusion, and these tiny birds, insects and butterflies and strawberries evoke anecdotal scenes typical of the manuscripts from this region.'

She turns each page absorbing the details with a quick practised eye.

'There is beautiful symmetry on the pages, look how these martens and peacocks are displayed - this technique all adds a unique charm. As I would expect, there is a calendar of church feasts, an excerpt from each of the four gospels, the fifteen Psalm of Degrees, seven Penitential Psalms, a Litany of Saints, an Office for the Dead and The Hours of the Cross.' She speaks slowly turning each page lovingly and occasionally she holds it closer under the bright light, lost in thought.

I wait and watch.

She is absorbed with her assessment. Occasionally she picks up an eye glass and studies a particular drawing more intently then she looks up and asks.

'Where did you... come across this?'

'Your father and I have... an - arrangement,' I say. 'We worked together in the past and I trust him.'

She nods, closes the book and replaces it in the hessian.

'Well?' I ask. 'What do you think?'

'I think you should go elsewhere.'

'What?'

'I can't help you.'

'Why?'

'I'm not interested-'

I slam my fist on the table. 'I've driven all this way to see your father and now you tell me to go somewhere else-'

'Yes - and you can take your stolen property with you.'

'Your father-'

'My father is ill because of this type of business and I want nothing to do with it.'

'He's always said, he would help me–'

'He's sick and he won't help you.'

'So, why did you agree to meet me?'

She regards me closely. 'Because I was curious.'

'And now I've satisfied your curiosity? Now what?'

'Now, I want you to leave.'

'This is ridiculous.'

'Please go.'

I raise my voice. 'How do I know you will stay quiet, Marina? You're not like your father. How do I know I can trust you?'

'Because discretion is our business – that's how we've survived all these years.'

I take the manuscript and place it in the hessian cloth, then the protective waterproof bag and strap it to my waist.

'Name your price,' I say.

She hesitates for only a fraction of a second. 'I haven't got one.'

'You're making a big mistake. Your father would be very disappointed with you.'

'I'm not my father. I cannot be bought.'

'Shame on you,' I say. 'He was an honourable gentleman.'

'Probably, but only among thieves – not in the real world.'

'It was the real world for him.'

'That's why he's so ill. The stress has been too much for him and he can't do it any more.'

I'm furious. She's led me on and it's been a wasted journey. I can't even speak to Theo.

I'm at the door when she calls me and I pause with my hand on the handle.

'Mikky,' she warns. 'Be very careful, I don't know who else

knows about that manuscript but I do know that there are some people who will do anything to get their hands on something as valuable as that.'

Chapter 11

"A book is a version of the world. If you do not like it, ignore it or offer your own version in return." - Salman Rushdie

Bruges is busy. Tourists stand in my way snapping photos of the squares, churches and canals and it does nothing to ease the knotted anxiety in my stomach. I've come all this way to only to be let down. My heart is raging and I pace up and down the platform with frustrated, excited, nervous energy.

The manuscript is authentic.

I need Simon Fuller. He will advise me what to do next. I dial his mobile not knowing or caring what time it is in Asia but there's still no reply. I leave another message and ponder my options: return to Malaga with the book and give it to the church, give it back to Yolanda or hand it to the police and tell Jorge the truth.

I could also keep it.

I am after all – an opportunist. I could just disappear.

The passengers disembark from the train and when Josephine sees me she waves and hugs me tightly. Her hair is tied in a loose chignon and she wears a beige leather jacket and black jeans. I take her overnight bag and she links her arm companionably through mine and we walk toward our hotel.

'Are you sure it's not too far?' I ask.

She was shot barely two years ago and as a result she has little stamina and is often breathless. Her lungs are permanently damaged and it ended her career. She will never sing again but she told me last year that it was a small price to pay for having me in her life and I realise how much I must mean to her.

Catching sight of our reflection in shop windows, we're the same height and I wonder if strangers notice a similarity in our strong, over large features.

Now, I can't believe I didn't notice the similarity when we met and before she told me she was my birth mother. What's more surprising is that Javier, my flatmate who had been commissioned to paint her portrait, hadn't noticed the similarity either. I guess we had been too wrapped up in our own worlds: mine to steal a stolen Vermeer and his to become a well known portrait artist.

We walk slowly from the train station through the shopping streets and the busy squares pausing occasionally to admire a window display or a beautiful building.

'That's the Basilica with the Holy Blood,' Josephine says, pointing at a spire in the corner of the square.

I don't tell her that I lived and worked here with a conman, renovating stolen artwork and creating forgeries and we pause to watch the camera-snapping tourists.

'Do you believe that?' I ask.

'It probably gives people faith - if that's what they want to believe,' she replies.

'And you, Josephine - what do you think?'

'It's good to believe in something - don't you think?' She

smiles. 'I like Bruges. It's like Amsterdam but smaller and prettier.'

I look over my shoulder and take out my camera, snapping photographs, turning periodically, searching strangers' faces and taking ad hoc shots to study later in the quietness of my room.

'Are you looking for someone?' she asks.

'No, I'm just fascinated at how picturesque it all is.'

'Let's not be in a hurry, Mikky.' She pulls on my arm and I follow her to look in the window of another chocolatier where we giggle like schoolgirls over large breasts and penis shaped chocolate.

In the Market Square, Josephine stops to look up at the 12th Century belfry and my feelings are suddenly in turmoil. Everything seems so transient. These buildings may stand as testimony to the history of time but we ordinary mortals leave little presence on this earth.

Carmen is dead.

My hands begin shaking, a trickle of perspiration trickles down my back and my head rattles with unanswered questions.

Was stealing the book worth her life?

Why had Carmen wanted it so badly?

What did she want with me?

I brush away my tears and busy myself with my camera lens. It's all so final.

Poor Father Ignacio had been so tormented. He was filled with remorse and responsibility. Had he defied his belief and the church? Was he so disenchanted with his life and everything he'd done? Did he take his own life?

Could I have changed their destinies?

I turn away, leaving Josephine gazing in a boutique window

186

at manikins draped in fashionable spring wear. I'm not interested in the book or the money. I would willingly give it all up to have Carmen beside me and to walk through these streets with her. I would love the opportunity to sit and laugh like we used to - something that we didn't get the chance to do before she died - we had argued.

She been a different person to the Carmen I remembered.

She deliberately lied. I said I didn't want to meet Father Ignacio and she told Jorge I was in the port.

She hadn't trusted me.

She didn't tell me about Viktor.

Would I ever find out the truth?

'Are you alright?' Josephine links her arm though mine. 'You seem miles away.'

'I'm thinking about Carmen. If only we'd come back to the apartment earlier...'

'You can't blame yourself, Mikky.'

'I know - but I do. I feel as though I should have done more.' I step out of the way of a Segway. A tour guide followed by tourists in high-vis jackets glide past in snake formation on a modern excursion tour.

'Would you like to go on one of those?' Josephine asks.

'It's a bit tame for me.' I smile.

We walk arm in arm, both of us lost in our thoughts and I'm reassured by the warmth of her grip on my arm and the way her shoulder touches mine.

I should have told Inspector Barcos the truth. Perhaps I should give the book to Jorge and that would be the end to it. Instead I have immersed myself into this impossible situation, this ridiculous promise to help Yolanda because it's what Carmen would have wanted.

Why?

Because Carmen would have wanted this – I repeat to myself. I'm doing it for Carmen.

Am I?

I'm lying.

The truth is, I'm doing it because I want to see if Carmen would have got away with it. I want to know if her plan to steal the Book of Hours was better than my plan last year to steal a Vermeer. I'm an opportunist and having this valuable book strapped to me, taunts and teases me.

I could keep it.

We could have stolen it together. Maybe that's what Carmen wanted and that's why she involved me.

She knew that I would help her and she had no intention of returning it to Father Ignacio.

She needed me to get it from him, then she was going to use me to get it authenticated and to sell it illegally so that she would not get caught. I was the scapegoat in her plan. I would be blamed and I'm fooling myself thinking she came to Tarifa wanting to revive our friendship. She didn't care about my ghosts from the past.

She was using me.

At university we'd often debated stealing precious artefacts and who did art belong to? Good versus evil and the merits of honesty in the art world. We talked about the looting of archeological sites in the Middle East or South America and why a pittance was paid to the locals who often stole to feed their families. We talked about the middle men – the Janus figures – who on the one hand, plan and loot and on the other hand are often a respected face behind a western art gallery or even a well-known collector. We deliberated and discussed museums buying artwork; fake provenances and illegal shipments and I compounded my knowledge by working with Theo Brinkmann and Carmen knew that. She wanted my experience but Theo was now out of the picture and it is up to me to work out what to do now.

Did my relationship with Carmen hold any value or was it meaningless–

'Mikky,' Josephine calls. 'This way...' Somehow Josephine has unhooked her arm from mine and is standing in the glass doorway of our hotel, beckoning me to join her.

I smile sheepishly and walk back, happy to see her smile and feeling slightly ridiculous having been so lost in my head.

'Are you still thinking of Carmen?'

'Yes.'

'It must be so hard. Would it help to call Javier in South America?' She puts her arm around me and holds me close and I inhale the warm expensive scent that lingers on her skin and relish the love of her embrace. Tears well in my eyes and a knot forms in my throat.

'Thanks for being here,' I choke attempting to control my tears.

My goal was to find out if the book is authentic.

I know it is genuine. Marina has confirmed that.

Now I just had to find a buyer – and one that deals on the black market – and without Theo to help me – I must plan my next step carefully.

In the restaurant Josephine looks demure and glamorous in a violet print dress and a black shawl. It's hard to believe she was once a famous opera star until she is recognised and surrounded by a group of Italians asking for selfies and an autograph. Her Italian is fluent and they laugh. She's still retains the charm of the diva she once was and I'm proud that his woman who gave birth to me now calls me her daughter.

'I'm sorry,' she whispers as we settle at our table fifteen minutes later. 'I thought I'd be forgotten by now.'

'I'm pleased they hold you in such high regard,' I reply.

We order gin and tonics and read through the menu.

My mood is sombre and although Josephine understands my sadness, she is compassionate and endearing. She chats about her life in London and our friend, Gloriette Bareldo the famous soprano and her husband Bruno who I stayed with when I was recovering from my incident last year. Our conversation returns to Javier who is currently touring South America and of course her protege Andreas, a tenor she trained and who was in and out of my life, last year, as I recovered from my injures.

'He's doing a season in Berlin. He's doing exceptionally well. He's worked hard.'

The local dish of mussels in a garlic and white wine sauce are soft and juicy and I douse the chips in salt, savouring the versatile flavours on my tongue.

'Delicious,' I purr.

We talk about Eduardo. She has watched my relationship with him blossom and I know that they've developed an important friendship and are often in touch.

'How was your holiday? Did you love Kitesurfing in Tarifa?' she asks.

'Kiting gives me freedom and exhilaration. Out there I can live in the moment. There's nothing else to think about. I can go where I like. There are no rules or laws,' I say. 'Eduardo has great skills and he's trained me well, back to how I used to kite. It took a lot of training; running every morning and working out.' I pat my stomach and feel the book around my waist. 'It's been amazing and I feel healthy again.'

'Are you still running?'

'I try to make time every day - I'm pleased you suggested that we went there together. It was a good idea.'

'You said you used to go there all the time and you loved it and I can tell by the smile on your face that you haven't lost your passion.'

'It's also quite humbling, Josephine. The peace and calmness sometimes gives me time to think - alone in a vast ocean near a different continent is a great experience...'

After our empty plates are removed, I pull out my camera and show Josephine the video of Eduardo self starting, running into the waves and then a shot from above as he launches the board and jumps on.

'These images are taken from the drone. Aren't they brilliant? This is a front loop to topside and this one look - and this is board off.'

She lets out a small cry.

'Wow, can you do this?'

I scroll to a video of me that Eduardo took using the drone.

'This is me. These are Raileys; unhooked rolls,' I explain, watching my body twist and turn in the air.

'It looks dangerous-'

'There's nowhere like Tarifa,' I say. 'You'll have to come and watch us. It's the surfing capital of Europe - where the Atlantic meets the Mediterranean. The wind - the Pointe - if you get a downwinder and a wind speed of twenty-eight knots, it's amazing, like flying through the air.'

Josephine smiles and we're suddenly interrupted by a German couple. They apologise but as she has finished eating - would she mind - just a quick photograph - they saw her sing many years ago, one summer in the amphitheatre in Verona. They were on their honeymoon.

I offer to take a photograph of them all and I wonder if they notice the resemblance between Josephine and me. We have similar features but more than that, it's her expression that enthrals me, her eyes hold an inner beauty that is reflected by her gracious charm. She winks surreptitiously at me and I smile back.

They strike up a pose and I glance around the restaurant, scanning, picking up details; lovers giggling - sharing a quick kiss, a family group - celebration, two men - not gay probably business colleagues, an older couple and a table of four women.

Wait!

I look at the two men sitting behind Josephine.

Business colleagues?

One has a salt and pepper beard and dark hair. When she sees me staring at him he stands up and walks past the bar toward the toilet at the back of the restaurant.

'Mikky, take another one darling,' Josephine says. 'This lovely couple want one with their daughter - ah, here she is, come on, stand here beside me.' Josephine beams at a thirteen year old with braces on her teeth.

'Hold on,' I say, after I've taken it. 'That's lovely. Let me use my camera now.'

I return their phone and snap away with my Nikon for sharper images then I give them my business card. 'If you email me next week I'll send you some Jpgs.'

'Micky is a photographer,' Josephine explains. 'But she's

also an artist. She's having an exhibition in the autumn in New York.'

I fiddle with my camera, change the focus and snap photographs of Josephine until she holds her hand up to her face and laughs.

'Stop! Stop! Enough!' she protests.

I check the images to make sure I have one of the the stranger with the salt and pepper beard as he returns from the toilet. His angular face tilts in our direction and he nods to his dinner companion, another man in a matching, expensive grey suit. They leave the restaurant quickly without catching my eye and they're gone.

Over brandy and coffee Josephine raises the topic I expected.

'Will you please consider the exhibition, Mikky? I think it will do you good to get back to your painting again.'

'I have to go back to work,' I say, returning the camera to my case. 'I might go back to London but I should go and see Dolores first. I still feel bad that her art studio got wrecked last year.'

'I could set you up in a studio near me in London. You could paint...'

'Are you happy back there?'

'I think it's the right choice for me now. I'm catching up with lots of friends that I lost touch with-'

'Who abandoned you, when you needed them...'

'Who have embraced me into their lives again,' she smiles.

I sigh and wonder if her insecurity is a family trait that I've also inherited.

'I'll give you a lift to the train station tomorrow,' I say as Josephine pays the bill.

'That's kind, Mikky - thank you - and what are your plans?'

193

'I'll head back to Mallorca,' I lie.

The restaurant is only a ten minute stroll from our hotel and half an hour later, we're strolling down the Hoogstrat. The wind is cold and I pull my collar around my neck and when Josephine slips her arm through mine I realise I'm not shivering with cold - but with fear.

'You must come with me to the opera. I had no idea how much you enjoyed it the last time we saw Glorietta. We could go to the Teatro Real when you're next in Madrid. I'll see what's on. Maybe next month? Perhaps we'll go and see Andreas performing this summer-'

'I'm pleased he's doing so well-'

'I'll get tickets.'

'Don't bother - unless he's singing with the Foo Fighters.'

Josephine laughs and tugs on my arm. She knows I tolerate opera for her and it's not my thing.

'I know you don't mean it, Mikky. You really like opera, you're too afraid to admit it! Glorietta Bareldo would love to have you stay this summer. We though you might come to Italy in-'

The blow stuns me.

My head ricochets. I fall forward and strong arms push me roughly onto the bonnet of a parked car. My face is squashed against the hot engine and the metal burns my cheek. A heavy hand with a vice like grip is around my neck holding me in an iron lock while a another hand slips under my jacket and around my waist. His thick fingers are cold against my skin. He rips the tapes pulling the book free and I kick out. I struggle and lose my balance and he punches me hard in the kidney. I scream but my mouth is muffled against the metallic paint. He slams my head against the car and dazed, I slump to the ground.

Through the gap in the parked cars I see running black trainers. There's a squeal of brakes and my assailant leaps into the passenger side of a black Land Cruiser. He's still closing the door as it screeches around the corner, disappearing into a maze of narrow streets.

I struggle to my feet but my knees are shaking. I hold onto the car. My breathing is ragged and my body aches. My head is thumping.

'Josephine?' I shout.

She's lying motionless on the pavement. I slide over and crouch beside her. She moves slowly as if unfurling from a winter hibernation and I'm reminded of the violent end to her professional career. She clutches her chest, breathing slowly, appearing vulnerable.

'Are you okay?' I ask.

'I'm fine.'

I hold her elbow and help her to her feet.

'I'm fine, Mikky, just a little shaken. Are you alright?'

'Yes.'

'What happened?'

'We were attacked.'

'Let's get to the hotel,' she replies. 'We'll call the police.'

'No.'

'No? Oh my goodness look at your face...'

We stagger a few hundred metres along the road and into the reception. In the bright light Josephine looks closely at my cheek. 'It's bruised and burnt. I'll call the police,' she insists.

'Let's go to the bar and get some ice. I need a drink.' I pull on her arm.

The receptionist looks up and smiles.

'Is everything alright?'

'Fine,' I return his smile and pull on Josephine's arm. 'Let's not make a fuss.'

He seems bemused and confused by our behaviour but then he returns his attention to the computer screen on his desk.

'I want to know what's going on.' Josephine shrugs off my hand but she's the first to walk in the direction of the bar.

We sit at a corner table and I lean my head back against the velvet upholstered chair and close my eyes. My mind whirls.

I've lost it.

I've lost the manuscript.

I'm still shaking with anger and shock when the waiter returns with two large Courvoisier's and an ice bucket. I gulp the warm liquid and Josephine leans forward to dab my cheek with a cold napkin.

'What did they take? They were after something - what was it?'

'Money - he took my money belt,' I lie.

'You must go to the police.' Josephine looks composed but unhurt.

'No damage has been done.'

'What about your face?'

'It will be better by the morning.'

'They seemed to know where your money was? Was it a lot?'

I can barely speak. I can't believe I've been so stupid. How could I have let them take the book?

I should have fought harder - screamed - anything. I should have done something to stop them.

I sip the brandy and relish the heat on the back of my throat.

'He was a professional, you know that, don't you?' She is sitting so close to me that I smell brandy on her breath. The ice is cool on my skin.

'Really?' My shoulders stiffen.

'They were after something more than money,' her voice is low.

'It was only cash. I'll go to the police in the morning.'

'How much?'

'I was going to buy a new kite board.' I blush at my obvious lie.

'I hope they got what they wanted, Mikky or they may be back.' She tosses the napkin onto the table, her expression is unfathomable and I'd like to photograph it.

We finish our brandy quickly and in silence. I'm in a hurry to get to my room. I wasn't looking forward to telling Yolanda that I've lost the manuscript.

Yolanda picks up after the first ring.

'Where have you been? I've been calling you,' she says.

'Out for dinner with Josephine,' I reply, swinging my legs up onto the bed.

'Josephine?'

'She came on the train this afternoon to have dinner with me.'

'You're not on bloody holiday, Mikky.'

'I thought it might make my visit look more authentic - just in case someone was following me...'

'Who would follow you?'

'Well, the thing is-'

'What did Theo say? Is it authentic?'

197

'It's worse than that - Yolanda,' I pause. 'I've been robbed.'

'What?'

I tell her what happened. When she says nothing, I tell her how Marina - Theo's daughter - wouldn't let me speak to him this morning and how she said it was authentic but she didn't want to get involved. Then I tell her about the attack on the way home from the restaurant.

'One was driving and the other pushed Josephine out of the way and smacked my head against the car.'

'So who the fuck were they?' she shouts.

'I have no idea.'

'How could they know?'

'I've been so careful, Yolanda. I've been covering my tracks, taking so much care not to be followed - I can't believe it.'

'And they knew it was strapped to your waist?'

'Yes.'

'You're lying to me, Mikky. I know you are.'

'Ask, Josephine-'

'You're a bloody traitor. You've always been out for yourself and now you want keep this book. You're making it up. I should never have trusted you-'

'Yolanda, I promise you-'

'I'm sick of your lies, Mikky. You've spent your whole life lying and I don't believe your bullshit. Carmen might have fallen for it - but not me - you're sick in the head. You've no sense of loyalty - you're no friend to anyone - you're a fake - a sham- a worthless, selfish bitch.'

'Listen to me-'

'I'm not listening to any more of your shit! I'm going to call Jorge and tell him that you stole the book. That you took it from the safe and you've kept it all along. I'm going to tell him that you threatened me. I'm going to phone Inspector Barcos and tell him...'

'Please Yolanda, don't do that.'

'I'm going to tell him that's why you went to Bruges – you stole it and were going to sell it–'

'Please, Yolanda. Listen to me–'

But there's no answer.

She's hung up on me.

I call her back and when she doesn't reply I toss the phone on the bed and close my eyes. My head is thumping, my shoulders ache and I feel sick.

How much worse can this get? I say aloud but the bedroom remains silent with only the sound of a car engine in the street to keep me company.

I take a steaming hot shower to get rid of the touch and the memory of the man who groped my body and I stand with the water cascading over my head cursing my stupidity.

Who was he?

Who sent them?

Josephine was right. They were professional.

They had been watching us – watching me – since when?

I dry my aching limbs and rub moisturiser into the artwork that covers my body; my sleeve of Munch's colour, my shoulders, hips and waist and the beautiful and intricate patterns that are filled with hidden meanings and sentiments known only to me, then I lay on the bed with pillows propped up behind me.

Carmen would have loved Bruges.

She loved to travel and explore new places and cities. She was mesmerised with history, art and architecture and she loved museums and galleries.

Now it's all over.

Carmen is dead.

Father Ignacio is dead.

The manuscript is gone.

A wave of bile rises in my throat. I swallow hard and brush away a tear falling onto my cheek. I pick up my camera and study the images looking for the two men who sat behind Josephine in the restaurant. I take my time scrolling through the images when I pretended to snap Josephine's picture.

I zoom in on the two men. I focus on the one with the salt and pepper beard and I bring the zoom closer studying his features.

Do I recognise him?

I think of the faces when I've scanned the streets behind me, the funeral and when I went jogging in Muelle Uno. My cheek throbs and the combination of strong paracetamol and brandy makes my eyes droop. I imagine I'm running then I have a canopy in my hand and the kite is caught by a sudden gust and I'm swept high into the infinite blueness of the sky that gets darker and darker, navy then black...

When I wake up two hours later I'm still sitting up against the pillows. My head has fallen forward and my neck and shoulders aches. My temples are thumping but my head is clear.

I know where I saw the man with the salt and pepper beard. He was in the restaurant in Malaga the Saturday we had lunch with Sofia.

The day Carmen was murdered.

I'd left Yolanda and Sofia talking and I sat on the wall outside the restaurant. I bumped into him on my way back to the table. I was playing air guitar and I'd apologised.

Had he been following us - Yolanda or me?

Now he's shown up here.

He must have known about the manuscript.

I dress quickly throwing on torn jeans and my old Foo Fighters T-shirt. I had to find the manuscript before Jorge or Inspector Barcos find me. There was somewhere I had to go and one person who might still help me.

This time I don't bother retracing my steps and taking precautions, I go straight there, cutting up alleyways past the canals and over bridges and I am waiting outside the shop when she arrives. Once she turns the key in the door and has one foot in the door, I push her in the back. She stumbles and I follow inside slamming the door behind us.

'Oh my-' she gasps.

'We need to talk, Marina so sort out the alarm. Hurry up!'

She keys a code into the wall and I push her down the corridor toward the back of the building to her office and switch on the light.

'What happened to your face?' She looks frightened.

'Who did you tell about the book, Marina?'

She seems to take stock of what I'm asking and I give her time to piece the jigsaw together. I will know if she lies to me.

'It isn't that complicated to work out, Marina. Who did you tell about the manuscript?'

I take a step closer.

'I'm seriously pissed off. My friend Carmen was murdered two weeks ago. She was the Curator of Provenance at the Picasso Museum in Malaga and I found her - dead - in her apartment and now the police think I stole the Book of Hours. I have nothing more to lose, Marina, so...who did you tell after

I left here yesterday?'

'No one.'

'You're lying and I'm angry.' I bang the table with my fist.

She stutters. 'It's professional etiquette. You know I wouldn't tell a soul.'

'You're father would never have betrayed a confidence but you're scum–'

'My father is ill.'

'Where is he?' I lean over her and she takes a step back and holds up her hand.

'I can't tell you, Mikky.'

'Look at my face! I was robbed as I walked back to my hotel after dinner last night. I was in a restaurant and two guys were watching. They followed me. They knew I had it around my waist.'

'I didn't tell anyone. I promise you, Mikky. I want to get away from all of this - all this violence and crime. I grew up with it. My father - I can't begin to tell you what he's done and the mess and all the trouble he's caused our family but I want to lead a better life. I have a child and family that I love. I don't want to be involved in his seedy, sordid, underworld of crooks, fencing stolen property where life has no meaning and no value. It's not that I don't want to help you, Mikky - I can't. I love my family too much to throw it away. They're all I have.'

I turn away.

'Look at you, Mikky. They hurt you - they would do that to me - or worse to - my daughter. She's seven years old. I have to protect her.' Her pleading words hang in the air like invisible notes to a bird song. I'm angry but worst of all I believe her.

I think of my adopted mother and how she neglected me and

beat me. I still have the ugly eight inch scar on the back of my hand where she attacked me in a jealous rage. A mother must protect her daughter. It's her duty.

I collapse onto a stool and lean on the table my face in my hands.

'You're right, Marina. Nothing is worth this.'

She places her hand on my shoulder. 'I'm sorry,' she whispers.

I hitch my bag onto my lap and pull out my camera.

'Answer me this. Do you know either of these two men?'

I flick through the images I took last night widening the pictures on the screen with two fingers for a close up view.

'I might have seen one of them before.'

She takes it from me and concentrates on their face

'The one with the big hands looks tough. He looks like a thug. I don't know him but the other one looks familiar,' she frowns. 'The one with the beard. I'm sure I've seen him. Hold on.' She turns away and opens her MacBook on the table. She clicks on her browser and types in a familiar name.

Simon Fuller.

She's mistaken. I know Simon. It's not him and I sigh and turn away. She's wasting my time but she continues tapping the keyboard, clicking on various images and a row of faces appear on screen.

'It looks like him – no?'

I glance at the image on her screen with the image on my camera.

It's a match.

'Who is he?' I ask.

'I met him once, two or three years ago. He's a rare book dealer – from England. He does a few lecturers. I went to one a few years ago in Canterbury or somewhere. He's very knowledgeable about manuscripts and things like that...

I stare at his face fixing it firmly in my mind and his salt and pepper beard. It was the same man I saw in the restaurant in Malaga the day Carmen was murdered.

'His name is Nigel Howard,' she says.

'How did he know I had the manuscript around my waist?'

'He attacked you? He can't be involved,' Marina protests. 'He couldn't possibly be - he wouldn't hurt you. He worked with Simon Fuller for years.'

'Well, his friend with the banana fingers could have done. Thank you,' I say, packing my camera away. 'Now I know where to look.'

'What do you mean?'

'You hardly think I'm going to let him steal it - I'm going to get it back.'

Chapter 12

"There comes a time when you have to choose between turning the page and closing the book." - Josh Jameson

After I drop Josephine at the train station I sit in the car and check the Internet. After an hour, I decide I have two choices:

One, I can go to Malaga and try and talk my way out of this whole mess with Inspector Barcos and Jorge or Two I can try and find the manuscript.

Having little or no faith in the first option, I turn my BMW 4 x 4 in the direction of the Euro Tunnel, toward England and an address I found after Googling Nigel Howard.

While I wait in Calais for the train, I call Eduardo. He's working on an early shift so I leave a message. I haven't told him about the attack and I'm hoping Josephine will say nothing. The good thing about a mobile is that no one knows where you are, so I leave a message telling him that I'm driving slowly back through France and Spain to Malaga.

'I need time to think and to be alone,' I say. 'I love you.'

It's just until I have worked things out, I tell myself then I will be honest with him.

I call Yolanda's mobile. She doesn't answer so I call the

studio and speak to Enrique who says.

'Yolanda's selling the apartment. She's selling the whole lot - furniture and everything. She's keeping nothing. Jorge's helped her carry stuff and package the rest of the things to send to Carmen's family - but she's not good,' he says.

'How do you mean?'

'She's drinking a lot and working hard but I don't know how she concentrates. She's talking about the manuscript being stolen and she's making up stories-'

'Like what?'

He pauses. 'Well, this morning, she started ranting on about - well, she said, that you took it.'

'Me?'

'I think she's stressed. She stormed out of here about midday. She isn't happy.'

'She's under a lot of pressure. Look after her,' I say and hang up.

My mobile rings and it's Jorge and I decide to answer it.

'Hi?' I say.

'Hi Mikky, how are things?'

'Okay,' I reply cautiously.

'It's Father Ignacio's funeral today.'

'Oh.' I had forgotten.

'Inspector Barcos wants to speak to you.'

'Me?'

'When are you coming back?'

'I'm spending a few days with Josephine in Bruges,' I lie.

He met Josephine at Carmen's funeral. Isabelle is a big fan of opera and she was pleased to meet Josephine.

'He wants to see you,' he insists.

'Why?'

'Something about the time you got to Carmen's apartment when you came back to the coast. Yolanda says she got home around seven. She had driven back from Madrid…'

'What does that have to do with me?'

'You said you got to Carmen's around five.'

'Did I?'

'Yes but we found the taxi driver who drove Father Ignacio back to the monastery and he said it was just after six.'

'Really?'

'But you said you didn't see Father Ignacio – or did you?'

I remember looking down on the street watching Carmen wave him off even though he couldn't see her.

'I must have been mistaken with the time…'

'What did you do before that?'

'Before that? I was walking around getting to know the city…'

'He wants to speak you.'

'Does he want to phone me?'

'No, he wants you to come back to Malaga.'

'Okay.'

My board announces my train departure and I start the engine.

'Will you come back?'

'Sure,' I lie. 'I'll be back in a few days. It's a long drive.'

I ease the car forward and join the queue to board the train going in the opposite direction.

'How are you coping?' I ask, changing the subject. 'Everyone assumes that because you're a policeman you take it all in your stride but you and Carmen were good friends.'

'I think about her all the time,' he says softly.

'She loved you like a brother.'

'You always understood me,' he says. 'I'd like to see you. It would be good to talk – to talk properly. We never had a chance to say–'

'I've got to go, Jorge. I'm sorry–'

The traffic is easing forward and I know I will lose the signal inside the train. I'm relieved that Yolanda hasn't told them yet that I've taken the book and my heart feels lighter and my confidence grows.

'How is Yolanda?' I take a risk.

'Not good.'

'No?'

'She's – I don't know. Confused, angry, sad – a mixture of things. She really misses Carmen. We all do.'

'This can't be easy for you – being a policeman and not being involved in the case. Not being able to do anything–'

'What do you mean?'

'I understand how frustrated you must feel.'

'Didn't you know? I'm on the case now. I've been reas-signed.'

'No, I didn't. That's great! I'm really pleased, Jorge.'

'I'll sort it, Mikky, and I'll find the manuscript. That's a promise.'

'That's reassuring to know. I'll call you.'

The phone goes static and I hang up.

I drive on to the train and wait in the car. I drink my takeaway coffee and study the pictures of the two men in the restaurant.

Nigel Howard.

But who's the other man with the thick fingers? The man who ripped the book from my waist?

My iPad doesn't tell me who the second man might be but I know that once I get my hands on Nigel Howard there will be no more secrets.

I will get to the truth before Jorge.

Although I lived in London for a few years I didn't own a car so anywhere outside of London is foreign to me. I follow the directions on the SatNav that takes me to a small hotel outside Canterbury near Whitstable on the coast. It's somewhere for me to store my kites, boards and equipment and I take a hot shower and have a quick nap.

When I wake, I read Nigel Howard's profile again on LinkedIn that gives me a brief resume of his life and career. It appears he is well respected; an educationalist and an expert on rare illustrated manuscripts. Like Simon Fuller he also has links to the Canterbury Rare Bookshop so I decide that's where I will start my search.

I dress quickly, drive to the city centre and park below the old Roman wall that once guarded the city. I make my way along the cobbled streets, past timber framed houses to the Cathedral, a major pilgrimage site since the middle ages. It's a magnificent building and I'm distracted by it's beauty so I take my time walking slowly through the grounds and once inside I spend an hour studying the stained glass windows and intricate carvings noting the Gothic and Romanesque influence.

It's the headquarters of the Church of England and I sit for a while lost in my thoughts ignoring the tourists and guides around me and by the time I return to the main street, it's past eight o'clock and the city is buzzing with young people. Restaurants, pubs and bars are thriving with students and foreigners and I'm working out my best approach to Nigel

Howard when Eduardo phones breaking my concentration and I resent his interruption.

'Are you okay?' he asks.

'Just tired.'

I lean against the a wall and watch a family pass me. The toddler drags his heels and is pulled along by his irate mother.

'I miss you,' he says. 'Are you ever coming back to Mallorca?'

'Of course.'

'When?'

I don't say anything.

'Is it something I've done?' he asks. 'Is there something you want to tell me?'

'No, Eduard. I just have to - sort myself out. That's all. Carmen's death has really affected me and I need some time on my own.'

'You sure that's all it is?'

'Yes.'

'Would you tell me if it was something else - something about us?'

'Of course.'

I change the subject and ask him about his day and eventually I sit on the step of a closed shop. I'm happy to hear his voice and I think how my life has changed since we met.

Twice Eduardo had walked out and said he wasn't coming back unless I made an attempt to meet him half way or to improve my bad attitude. He said he wasn't pandering to me but that I could be me. I could be whoever I wanted to be and that I could start afresh. He made me realise I had a second chance in life.

Only this time with him and my birth mother at my side.

All I had to do was to trust them.

You can't be a victim all your life, Mikky,' he'd said, last year. 'This is your chance. You can decide what sort of life you want - one where you are bitter and where you dwell on the hurt and the injustices that have been done to you - or you can move on. Forgive but don't forget. Learn from it and become who you want to be. But if we are together you have to trust me - you have to trust us.'

He has given me strength and hope. He's encouraged me to speak my mind with reason and confidence and inadvertently I have begun to trust him but now I feel guilty for betraying his trust.

Why didn't I tell him the truth?

'Let's arrange some more time together,' I say. 'Let's go kitesurfing - can you arrange some time off? Just a few days?'

We talk for over thirty minutes, remembering our time in Tarifa and Kitesurfing on the Atlantic. When we'd concentrated on our skills and practised self launching, over and over, to be an independent kiter. We had competed together, Eduardo and I. I remember how I'd raced toward my board, grabbed it by its footsteps and chased into the sea, often after Eduardo, jumping onto the board and kited off, feeling my heart wild with exhilaration and excitement and the sun and wind on my cheeks, releasing the demons that collided in my head. But now, after Carmen's death, my life is tumbling backwards and I'm being sucked down, spiralling into a murky world, I don't want to be in. I know I'm responsible for her death. Carmen had needed me and I had let her down.

'I'll see if I can change a shift. I'll see what I can do,' Eduardo says, interrupting my memory, and just as he hangs up, he whispers, 'I love you, Mikky.'

I sigh, pocket my phone and follow the path along the river

Stour cutting through alleyways and pretty cobbled medieval streets.

Yolanda and Carmen dragged me into this mess and now I've lost the manuscript. Yolanda's words rotate around in my mind, echoing with nasty reverberation like a fervent angry anthem.

'You're sick in the head. You've no sense of loyalty - you're no friend to anyone - you're a fake - a sham - selfish…selfish…selfish…'

That's when I look up and see the crooked Tudor facade of the Canterbury Rare Bookshop.

The following morning I wake restless after only a few hours sleep. After a hot shower, I gaze at my reflection; my inked body and the empty space where the manuscript should have been strapped to my waist. I cover my burnt cheek and dark circles with tanned moisturiser and apply pink lipstick, thick eyeliner and hooped feather earrings and pull a black Arctic Monkey's T-shirt over my head.

By the time I get to the Canterbury Rare Bookshop in the eighteenth century building inside the Canterbury old wall, it's barely seven o'clock. A plaque on the door tells me the book shop was established in 1951 and although it's closed, I place my hand against the glass to look though the window at the wide selection of books; paperbacks to fine bindings and a good selection of original maps, prints and greeting cards.

I wander through the cobbled streets with names like Butchery Lane, Mercery Lane and Guildhall Street that are all relics of ancient trades during the medieval period. Old signs promote the reenactment of Chaucer's Canterbury Tales and pictures of robed Monks remind me of Father Ignacio and I wonder if he ever came here.

I walk through Hawkes Lane and Beer Cart Lane familiaris-ing myself with the alleyways and shortcuts and when I find an open coffee shop I sit in the window drinking coffee waiting until the streets are busy then I pay the bill, zip up my jacket and head outside where the air is fresh and cool.

The book shop appears empty so I spend a few minutes acclimatising to the dark and dusty interior, browsing though worn books and old manuscripts doubting there is much of any real value in the front and knowing anything worth a fortune would be locked away and kept safe somewhere in the back, out of reach from the ordinary shoppers and available only to those experts 'in the know' or 'with the money.'

Books cases are crammed and a narrow aisle leads me to a small table and rickety chair at the back of the building. I was hoping the shop assistant would be the man from the restaurant in Bruges but he isn't. He's willowy and thin with a raspy breath and his eyes are as black as coal.

'I was wondering if Nigel Howard was here?' I say.

He looks up from the book strewn desk and gazes thought-fully at me.

'Are you a student?'

I smile. 'I try to be.'

'Then you should know where he is.'

'And Simon Fuller?'

'He's away.'

'I wasn't sure if … I thought he was back…from China.'

'It's a long journey.'

I stare at him forcing a pleasant smile on my lips.

'I thought Simon was back yesterday,' I gamble.

'He's extended his trip.'

'When is he back?'

He turns away checking the spines of the books piled on the desk, reluctant to answer my question.

'And Nigel Howard?' I persist. 'How can I find him?'

He looks up from the book in his hand.

'If he wanted you to know he would have told you.'

'He's asked me to meet him. We were in Bruges...having dinner two nights ago but I lost his business card.'

He closes the book and places it back on the table, seemingly slightly modified, so I continue.

'And I can't remember the name of the man he introduced me to – so this is my first point of call to contact him. As he requested,' I emphasise.

'He was having diner with Mr Laroche.'

'That's right. I remember now. I don't have his number and I've driven all this way...'

He stares at me not knowing if I am telling the truth and then he sighs.

'Nigel Howard is not back until next Monday.'

I don't show my disappointment.

'Thank you.' I walk toward the door then as an after thought I return and say.

'He did say, I could speak to Mr Laroche in his absence. How can I contact him?'

Ian Laroche lives in the valley of the Great Stour River in the small village of Chilham about six miles southwest of Canterbury. Following the directions on the scrap of paper given to me by the humourless man in the bookshop, I pass the market square, Chilham Castle, a parish church from the fifteenth century and two public houses before arriving at a solitary and pretty cottage with wisteria covered walls.

It's almost midday and I sit in the car for a few minutes in the narrow lane feeling out of place. It's a Spanish registration BMW with two kite boards tied to the roof, hardly unassuming and inconspicuous but also quite unthreatening.

I take a deep breath and I walk up the front path and ring the bell.

At first I think there's no-one home and I'm preparing to walk back and wait in the car when I hear scraping from inside and bolts are pulled back. The door squeaks open. It's dark inside but I recognise the man instantly from the restaurant as the companion dining with Nigel Howard. I'm taken aback because he looks far younger than I remember. His shoulders are broad and his hands are like bunched bananas and I know immediately they're the fingers that unhooked the book from my waist as he slammed me onto the bonnet of the car.

'Good morning, Mr Laroche? Silas from the Canterbury Rare Bookshop suggested I contact you because Simon Fuller is in China...'

It's a swing in the dark and he looks as confused as I want him to be. He must recognise me but he doesn't show it, so I continue speaking.

'The thing is, I have a rare manuscript that I need authenticating,' I continue. 'I wanted Mr Fuller to look at it but as he's in China, I wonder if you would do me the favour?'

He holds onto the door unblinking and he replies in a deep voice.

'Who are you?'

'Mikky Dos Santos.' I hold out my hand but he doesn't take

it. 'The thing is,' I lower my voice and look over my shoulder as if this is confidential and I don't want the non-existent neighbours overhearing. 'It's rather a delicate matter...'

He doesn't blink.

'I was robbed last Tuesday in Bruges. I was carrying an authentic manuscript - a very old Book of Hours and it was stolen from me. I was punched and thrown onto the bonnet of a car. Do you know anything about this?'

He attempts to close the door but I block it with my black bikers boot.

'I think you do,' I shout.

He opens the door and steps outside to face me so I step back. We're well matched in height and shape but I have no self defence skills and I would be terrible in a fight; I lost the last round and the manuscript.

He takes in my short black hair, broad shoulders and fierce expression, then he says. 'I don't know who you are or what you want but go away! Get off my property before I call the police.'

'It will be me who calls the police, Mr Laroche. You're deal-ing with stolen property and I will make sure Nigel Howard's career - and your miserable life - is ruined.'

He clutches his fist but I back away.

I've riled him.

I walk quickly and with as much dignity as I can muster, and once I am out of his sight I run and jump into the car and with a squeal of brakes I'm off, accelerating quickly, my heat pumping as violently as a torrential tsunami.

I park on the verge outside the village and open the boot,

taking a gamble that if he leaves his house, he won't come this way but will head toward Canterbury. Within a few minutes I have the drone airborne and circling several hundred feet above his house. My arial view allows me to see his back garden, his garage and I'm hoping to see into his house.

The drone has sensors and will detect if it gets to close to an object so I concentrate on the screen, attempting to level it with a window but it's too dark inside to see. I raise it higher over the roof to the front of the house where I leave it hovering fifty feet in the air and it gives me an arial view of the surrounding area. I wait patiently and after twenty minutes when the drone's battery life is spent I leave it charging and walk the mile or so back to his house.

By turning up on his doorstep I wanted to spook him and get him to react but I spend the afternoon thinking I've wasted my time. I recharge the drone and send it back up but nothing. I wander up and down the lane and finally find a dip in the grassy bank and snuggle against the prickly hedge but Ian Laroche doesn't move.

It's beginning to get dark when he eventually comes out of the front door and opens the garage. He climbs into a black Land Cruiser and I know it's the same car from Bruges. I run back to my BMW just as he swings out onto the main road. I send up the drone and photograph his license plate then using Active Tracker, I lock onto his moving car. The Phantom 4 has a range of 5 miles the battery is recharged but I can't lose him. Rain splashes on my window screen and my heart sinks. Drones don't work well in the rain. I place the controller on the seat beside me and start the engine. The maximum range I can put between us is twenty-eight miles so I'm not too concerned - unless he drives to London. Using my SatNav I navigate the traffic and follow him.

I'm nervous but filled with adrenalin and I tap the steering wheel as I drive humming to Wolf Alice's, You're a Germ. Perhaps I'm on a wild goose chase but at least I'm doing something.

As we get closer to Canterbury, I lower the altitude to under 50 metres but lose the connection. I tap the console worried it might land on houses or a road and create an accident but then it flicks on again. I take a chance that Mr Laroche won't be looking in the sky to see if he is followed and I lower the drone so by the time we reach the city centre, I've narrowed the distance between us to six cars of separation. Taking a risk that he won't know my BMW, I follow him past the old city wall, several roundabouts but I'm worried about the drone's battery so I stop in a side street so I can track his progress and measure him against the map on the SatNav. He parks at the back of the Marlowe Theatre and he walks past the stage door.

The battery on the drone drops to under thirty-five percent. I navigate the menu to disable the drones return to home and auto landing features. I need every bit of flight time.

He stops near a pub near the river and looks over his shoulder.

The drone battery hits a critical level and before I get the chance to land the drone it runs out of power and it crashes to the ground several feet away from me. Two of its propellers are broken.

I find his black Land Cruiser, pull up the collar of my jacket, I follow in the footsteps of my suspect along the narrow path beside the Marlowe Theatre where posters advertise the National Ballet of Cuba. Scores of people are hurrying inside for the Friday evening performance.

I walk over a small bridge and fast running river and into a cobbled street that affords a beautiful view of the illuminated Cathedral. My SatNav takes me to a Tudor-style hotel with sash windows and a tavern advertising locally brewed ales. A crowd comes out of a restaurant and I step out of their way to lean closer to the hotel window. I peer into the bar and it takes me a few minutes for my eyes to adjust to the bright light.

Rain drops splash against my forehead and I'm tempted to go inside but I do a double take looking though the window.

He's here.

He's inside.

Ian Laroche is siting at a table on the far side of the room and his vice-like banana fingers are clutching a pint of ale. He's not alone.

I hold my breath.

I'm staring at the red hair and portly figure of Steven Drummond.

Yolanda's father.

Chapter 13

"It is what you read when you don't have to that determines what you will be when you can't help it." - Oscar Wilde

I turn away quickly exhaling with force as if I've been punched in the cavity of my chest. I lean against the wall too shocked to move. I lick my lips, my hands tremble and my heart is banging at my chest like it wants to escape.

Steven Drummond.

Nigel Howard and Ian Laroche stole the book of hours.

I wait until my heart settles and my breathing is under control then I risk looking inside again. They're leaning across the table in deep discussion. Steven Drummond looks annoyed. There's no sign of his fake veneer smile and he's firing questions at the other man whose ale remains untouched.

Steven Drummond integrated himself at Carmen's funeral. He slipped his arm through Josephine's and, against her will, led her away to meet Carmen's family as if it were a social networking event. Sofia had trailed after them her face a mask of expensive makeup and her lipstick set in a frozen half smile.

I'm overwhelmed by a growing feel of nausea and despair that rises from the pit of my stomach as I try and piece the puzzle together. Ian Laroche had ripped the manuscript from my body in Bruges.

Why was Nigel Howard in the restaurant in Malaga the day of Carmen's murder?

I stretch my aching neck muscles and walk away from the old hotel and stand on the bridge looking down at the stream watching the current ebb and flow listening conscious of stragglers heading to the Marlowe; footsteps, couples, cars - all the sounds fade in and out of my head and muddle my thoughts.

Nothing makes sense.

I pull my collar around my throat wondering if I should walk in to the hotel and brazen it out. I could accuse them of murdering Carmen. I could demand the manuscript in return for my silence but: Why kill Carmen?

Did Yolanda tell him I had the manuscript with me in Bruges?

I watch a piece of deadwood attach itself to the river bank and it lays tugging at the shore until dislodged by another twig and they float downstream illuminated by the overhead streetlamp.

Yolanda has never disguised her dislike of me. Did she know I'd be stupid enough to take the book to Bruges to it valued then she could frame me?

Trust - it's that word again.

I stare up at the Marlowe and imagine the audience watching the scene playing out on stage, and I hear their laughter as they applaud my stupidity. They're impressed with my pathetic performance and I take a small bow acknowledging my foolishness.

I've been framed.

I stand with my back in a doorway sheltering from the wind and rain watching the hotel entrance. I'm angry and I need a plan and I'm not relying on anyone else.

I'll sort this out on my own.

It's almost thirty minutes later when Mr Laroche turns and heads in the direction of the car park where I assume he will return to his car but when Steven Drummond walks past me toward the town centre my breath catches in my throat and like I've seen in the movies, I walk on the opposite side of the street, hiding; nipping in and out of shop doorways. I feel foolish but he doesn't turn around. Instead he turns into a luxury hotel with a Tudor facade on the main street opposite the Beaney Museum. I wait a few minutes then follow him inside. On my right is a modern and comfortable bar so I duck inside and watch him step into the lift. If he turned around would he know me? The doors close and he doesn't look up.

I settle in the corner of the bar with a newspaper and tonic water. Time passes slowly and although I study the faces of everyone going in and out, there's no-one that I could imagine he is meeting; no hookers and no businessmen, only couples hand in hand, head to the lift.

It's gone ten thirty and I stretch and yawn, wondering how long he might stay. The waiter looks at me so I order a coffee and I'm staring morosely out onto the street when she walks past. Only the pane of glass separates us and I gasp.

She enters the hotel and while she waits for the lift I study her neat chignon and her straight back. I'm unable to move.

I want to call out. I want to call her name but I can't.

My mouth won't work.

My birth mother is famous for her illicit affairs and I'd assumed her reputation had been greatly exaggerated. But I have eyes of my own. This is not a coincidence.

I know for a fact that Josephine Lavelle is going upstairs to

Steven Drummond's bedroom.

It's like death.

Something inside me has died. Feeling sick to my stomach I wait for Josephine to appear. I want to confront her, shame her, shout at her and although I wait until past midnight she doesn't come down, neither does Steven Drummond.

Feeling betrayed, angry and stupid, I drive back to my hotel and lay awake most of the night.

When did their affair start?

Is she working with him?

Does he have some sort of hold over her?

Did she manipulate me in Bruges?

Just after seven thirty I shower, towel myself dry and dress quickly.

I continue to try Josephine's mobile. It's been switched off all night and I'm sick of the automated message, 'the person is busy cannot take your call.'

Half an hour later I'm drinking coffee in the hotel dining room and I call again. This time I hear her voice.

'Hello darling, what a lovely surprise.'

The warmth of her tone takes me by surprise.

'Hi.'

'Where are you?' she asks.

'I have to go back to Malaga. Inspector Barcos wants to speak to me. And you?'

A modern day benefit of a mobile phone, no-one needs to know which country you're in.

'In London,' she replies.

We're both liars.

'How was dinner in Paris?' I ask wondering if she's still with Steven and his fake veneers.

'Lovely darling, Glorietta and Bruno flew in as a surprise. They were asking for you and I said we would meet them as Glorietta is singing in New York in October and I thought we could...'

Did she know I had the manuscript?

Is that why she wanted to meet me in Bruges?

Did she double cross me?

'You sound tired,' I say.

'I was at the theatre last night–'

More of her lies and anger wells up inside me.

'I need your help. I want to meet Steven Drummond, can you arrange that?'

There's a significant pause before she answers.

'Steven? Why?'

'I can't tell you.'

'Is anything wrong?'

'Isn't he your friend? Don't you mix with him – socially?'

'Not exactly.'

'Does he go to England?' I insist.

She hesitates and eventually she says in a resigned tone as if I should know and she shouldn't have to explain. 'Of course, he does, darling. His office is there.'

'I thought his business was in Madrid?'

'He also has an office in England.'

'He's an importer and exporter, no?'

'I think so...' Her voice trails off as if she's distracted. There's someone with her and I hear a voice in the background.

Is she being deliberately vague.

I want to shout down the phone and tell her that I saw her

going up to his hotel room last night in Canterbury but I don't, instead I say.

'I'm going to England. Can you arrange for me to meet him, asap?'

She replies with the same cold and angry tone.

'What exactly do you want, Mikky?'

'I want to talk to him.'

'Leave it with me. I'll see what I can do. I must go. I can't talk now. I'll call you later.' She hangs up without saying goodbye.

I think of Yolanda's beautiful mother, Sofia sitting in the restaurant in Malaga and her sad and resigned face at Carmen's funeral. What's the point of money and an extravagant lifestyle if you're with someone you can't even trust?

An hour later as I am strapping the surfboards to the roof, Josephine phones me back.

'He'll be at his office depot in Canterbury tomorrow at midday,' she says by way of greeting.

'Sunday?'

'Yes.'

'Thank you,' I reply, subdued by her coldness.

'I'm not happy,' she says.

I bet you're not, I think. She's been found out. I know about her affair.

'How are you going to get there by tomorrow, Mikky?'

'I'll get a flight,' I lie.

'I'll text you his address. I can meet you at Heathrow or Gatwick, if you like?'

'It's okay. I'll make my own way.'

'Then I'll book us a room in a hotel in Canterbury, leave it to me.'

'You're coming too?'

'You hardly think I'll let you go alone?'

'There's no need,' I say. 'I don't need you with me.'

'I insist.'

I spend the next few hours in a coffee shop on Whitstable sea front with Wifi access, drinking coffee and finding out as much as I can about Steven Drummond. I'd never thought to look him up before and to my surprise, although he imports and exports furniture for ex-pats around Europe, his sister business is far more interesting. It specialises in selling antiquities across the Indian Subcontinent and South East Asia to major museums and galleries around the world.

Upon further investigation it appears that a few years ago his associate smuggled antiquities from Kapoor. Steven Drummond was implicated in the theft but no charges were pressed.

He's a slippery snake.

I know that in 1972 the Indian Government took legal steps to protect antiquities trafficking but it hasn't stopped corruption. Having worked with Theo Brinkmann I'm familiar with how stolen treasure is smuggled. It's often labeled as a handicraft with similar looking items, sometimes box loads of them, and exported abroad. Custom and border police sometimes turn a blind eye or are not as vigilant as they could be but it's a difficult job to identify an authentic item against fifty handmade replicas for export. I Google him some more and it also turns out Steven Drummond sits on the board of a London Gallery near New Bond Street. He's in an ideal situation to distribute antiquities and artwork.

I stare vacantly out of the window of the coffee shop at the incoming tide where a kiter loops his kite 360 degrees. The bigger the loop the more power it generates and he makes a starboard tack for 600 metres before making a turn.

Steven Drummond hardly seems like a man who needs money - or does he?

I've met people like Steven Drummond who collect antiquities. They think it makes them look more interesting, more cultural and appreciative of fine art. They believe it gives them social standing and prestige but they'd sell a piece on whim with no regard to cultural value. In their world cash is king.

As I'm puzzling Steven Drummond and trying to make sense of his life-style, Josephine texts me his address so I pull up Google Earth and study the map. His office is in a retail park outside of the the city. Although he has offices in Madrid and Canterbury he also has outlets in Croatia, Istanbul and Varna where he deals primarily with the shipment of wood; oak, pine and mahogany and furniture.

It appears more recently he has diversified into wholesale transportation, large containers of trucks with bicycles, boats, motorcycles and even car tyres.

Later in the afternoon I drive back to Mr Laroche's house in Chilham. I wait in a side road and attach new propellors to the drone. Then I send the Phantom 4 into the sky, to check the house, garage and garden but there's nothing to see.

No-one is home.

I text Josephine and asks if Steven Drummond owns a house in the area and within minutes she texts me an address in Chestfield. When I tap it into my SatNav it leads me to a large mock-tudor home with a long gravel driveway near the golf course worth over one and a half million pounds.

Yolanda has never mentioned he had offices or a home in

England. She told me they went to Madrid or to his family in Scotland or Sofia's family in Argentina but never here. This property could hardly be a secret.

Why did he want Yolanda to sell their apartment in Malaga when he owns so much?

I check the console and although the video relayed from the drone shows me pictures of an amazing garden with beautiful shrubs and a neat lawn, the windows to the home are leaded light so it is difficult to see inside and I bring the drone back to recharge. I sit in the car and consider buying a smaller one, one that I could use for surveillance. Although it would be illegal it would offer me a far better insight into this man's life. I had to be one step ahead of him.

He is my enemy.

Father Ignacio had entrusted me with the manuscript.

I want it back.

My eyes become weary and with the lack of sleep over the past few nights I feel myself drifting off to sleep. I lean my head back and close my eyes, a sliver of sunlight peers from behind a cloud and warms the car and I yawn. I'm dosing off and in that moment between sleep and reality I realise it's not about the manuscript any more, it's about Carmen. Her face floats before my eyes before she became troubled and suicidal by her split with Javier; smiling and laughing. She was confident, happy and fun, and a talented artist who saw life through art, history and culture. She was gentle and calm.

I see a gun fired into the back of her head – I open my eyes. Where am I?

I blink. I'm sitting in a car park, a stone's throw from Yolanda's father's house and I know I'll do whatever it takes – I'll get him.

On Sunday morning I wake early refreshed after a good night's sleep. I run for eight miles along the seafront, sharing the promenade with early morning dog walkers, cyclists and bin cleaners in fluorescent orange suits.

Josephine sends me a text message to say she's delayed in London and is unable to join me and I smile and wonder if her absence had been deliberately planned; between her and Steven.

I shower and I'm finishing a warm croissant and cappuccino when Jorge phones me.

'How are you, Mikky?' he asks.

'I'm okay. Some days I struggle and I can't believe she's gone. What about you and Isabelle?'

'Isabelle is very sad - it will take time. Where are you? When will you get here?'

'In a few days. I just need to be alone.'

'Do you want me to meet you?'

'No.'

'You know I'm here for you, all you have to do is call me.'

'Thank you,' I reply.

'Inspector Barcos is getting very agitated. He wants to speak to you.'

'I'll be back soon.'

'Don't leave it too long or he will get angry.'

'Any news of the investigation? Have they found Viktor?'

'He's not in Russia. No-one knows where he is.'

'Madeline seemed to think he was visiting his sick mother.'

'His mother died when he was seven.'

'Any other leads?'

'Did you hear there was a young boy killed at the Easter processions-'

'I read about it in the SUR.'

'It seems he was working for a rival, Middle Eastern gang. There's a turf war going on at the moment and this young boy was caught dealing drugs big time through the Syrian gang in Marbella. Viktor wasn't happy with him–'

'Did Viktor kill him?'

'Probably.'

'Oh my God...' I hold my head in my hands. 'Carmen didn't stand a chance against thugs like these. Does she not realise how dangerous these guys are?'

'Viktor is an amateur compared to these other guys. Some of them have trained in the Soviet Union and their leader has commanded elite security forces. They pose on social media with their armoury and cars and they're notorious for cruelty and corruption.'

'And Viktor?'

'We'll catch him. Don't worry, Mikky. Let's talk when you get back. Let's have dinner together.'

'I'll call you,' I reply.

As I hang up, I hear the smile in his voice.

'I need to see you,' he says.

But it's Eduardo who's upset with me.

He's finished a night shift and he yawns loudly.

'Josephine said you're in England? You told me you were going back to Spain. What's going on, Mikky? Does this have anything to do with Carmen?'

'Yes.'

'Are you involved in anything...'

'No.'

'Would you tell me if you were?' he asks.

'Probably.'

'I can't help you if I don't know what you're doing. Josephine is worried about you,' he says. 'I'm worried about you.'

'I'm worried about Josephine.'

'What does that mean?'

'Nothing.' I sound like a sulky teenager.

I can't tell him about Josephine's affair with Yolanda's father. I can't tell him Steven Drummond has stolen the manuscript from me. I can't tell him I'm going to get it back and get even with Steven Drummond. It's awkward and tense.

'I'm sick of this. Call me when you're prepared to tell me what's going on.' Eduardo hangs up but there's no smile in his voice.

The depot office is on an industrial estate in Sturry where trucks and lorries park, unload and restock.

It's a few minutes before midday and a Spanish truck is in the loading bay. A group of men stand with clip boards checking crates and ticking items on a list and Steven Drummond separates himself from them and walks over to me.

He casts his eyes over my black dress, leggings and biker boots.

'Josephine is worried about you,' he says with a perfect white smile. He puts his hands in his pockets and rocks on his heels.

'You sent Nigel Howard to Malaga to steal the manuscript,' I reply.

'Did I?' His voice is deep and his Glaswegian accent strong.

'You also sent him and Ian Laroche to a restaurant in Bruges last Wednesday. They were following me. Ian shoved me against the car and stole the book.'

'You don't know what you're talking about-'

'I followed Ian Laroche from his home on Friday night. I saw him meet you in the hotel bar. He was the man who attacked me in Bruges and stole the manuscript from around my waist.'

I'm taller than Steven and I move closer to him.

'Why did you kill Carmen?'

He turns to check on the men loading the lorry and when he turns back, he asks.

'Is that why you're here?'

'I'm here because you stole my manuscript. I've come to get it back.'

His smile is charming but false. It doesn't reach his eyes.

'You've got cojones coming here and accusing me of-'

'It's not an accusation. I've got proof.'

He takes his hands from his pockets and steps closer to me.

'You're a bitch!'

'Does Yolanda know you killed her girlfriend?'

He regards me thoughtfully then his accent softens. 'Why do you think I would murder a young girl like that – a girl I loved and practically educated?'

'You need money and you want Yolanda to sell her apartment in Malaga.'

'Is that what she told you?'

'Carmen told me.'

'It's my apartment and it's about time they stood on their own two feet instead of galavanting around Europe and South America on a whim with no responsibility-'

'Yolanda works hard – she has her own business.'

He snorts a laugh. 'Tattooist to the Celebrities – how exotic. If it wasn't for me she wouldn't know anyone. I've introduced her to these people. I've made her famous. I've put work her way. She'd never have done it without me. She's a dreamer-'

232

His accent makes the vowels crisp and final.

'It's better than a murderer, thief and a liar.'

'What do you want?' he hisses coming closer to me.

'I want the manuscript.'

'I don't have your fucking book.' His round eyes glare at me.

'Nigel Howard was in Malaga the day Carmen died. He was in the restaurant when we had lunch with your wife, Sofia. He was also in the restaurant when I had dinner with Josephine in Bruges - the night I was robbed. That wasn't a coincidence. They stole the book to order - on your orders. It's what you do, isn't it? Looting antiquities and selling them around the world. Your import and export business is the perfect front and you distribute them through your art gallery in Bond Street-'

'Bullshit.'

'I can prove it.' I continue riling him, speaking calmly and slowly. 'You met Mr Laroche in a hotel in Canterbury on Friday night. Then you went to the hotel in the town centre....'

His cheeks turn red and he balls his hands into a fist. He steps closer, his eyes blazing.

He shouts, 'You little-'

'Do you want to hit me? Is that what you do? Do you beat women or just kill them like you did Carmen?' I nod at the men dressed in overalls with Drummond's Imports/ Exports hovering at the rear end of the truck watching us. 'Those men will see you, if you touch me.'

He blinks then steps away and takes a deep breath.

'You think, you can sell it on the black market and pay off all your debts. You have the motive for killing Carmen and I think the Guardia Civil will be very interested in your business dealings. You're lucky to get off the hook, the last time your friend in India almost got caught... I'll be back here tomorrow morning at eight o'clock. Have the book with you or I am going straight to the police with all the evidence. You won't survive the glare of publicity that I'll create. You'll wish you never met me.'

My hand is on my car door when he calls out.

'No one threatens me.'

I jump in and slam the door. My heart is thumping wildly. He'll probably have me killed within an hour but my tyres screech as I leave the parking bay. He'll have to find me first.

I imagine all the possibilities and every different scenario, and I tell myself he can't kill me. What would he tell Josephine?

My stomach churns when I think of my birth mother as one of his consorts. I never figured she would be at the whim of a wealthy man - controlled by money and manipulated for sex. Last year when I'd Googled her to find out about her past, I'd not believed what Karl Blakey had written and I try to imagine the lure and attraction for her with Steven Drummond. She had owned the world and she'd lost it all. I decide Steven is her passport back into the fast world of celebrities, drinking champagne and travelling the world.

I spend the rest of the day hiding, preparing and documenting the evidence I have. I make a video like a movie trailer; a last will and testament telling whoever sees it what has happened; how Carmen found me in Tarifa, Father Ignacio, and the Book of Hours. I record how Carmen wanted to keep it and how Yolanda stole it and I admit that I was curious to know if Carmen would get away with it, and I tell my future audience that I want to catch Steven Drummond and get the manuscript back.

It lasts under two minutes. I upload it to a programme on the Internet to be sent automatically to Eduardo, Jorge, Yolanda, Josephine and Inspector Barcos at a pre determined time: Monday at ten thirty.

The following morning, Steven Drummond's secretary, a woman in her mid forties with thick ankles and wide hips walks with me along the corridor of his offices. She opens the door and stands aside and I'm shown a modern boardroom with leather chairs. He's seated at the end of a long table and he quickly slides a photograph under the folder.

'So, you turned up?' He smiles and I want to thump him.

The secretary leaves and closes the door.

'What did you expect? That you would get away with murder and theft?'

He drums his nails on the table and continues to smile. His accent is strong and his red hair is slicked back in a Carry Grant style.

'You're out of your league, Mikky dos Santos. You shouldn't be here.'

'Where's the manuscript?'

I imagine him on a yacht in around the Greek islands, wining and dining with celebrities and businessmen doing shady deals for lots of money over expensive meals, and the tinny laughter of scantily clad companions.

When he doesn't reply, I say. 'I've made a video of the evidence against you.'

'What evidence?'

'You stole the manuscript from me.'

'You stole it from Yolanda,' he replies. 'Even the police know that.'

'Yolanda will tell the truth when she knows you're involved.

She hates you and when she knows you killed Carmen, she'll never forgive you.'

'Let's ask her.'

He nods to the far end of the room and I turn around. I'd thought we were alone but Yolanda is sitting quietly at the other end of the table regarding me silently with her cold grey eyes.

'Hello Mikky,' she says.

'Yolanda? What's going on?' I whisper. 'What are you doing here?'

Perhaps she's my ally and we can confront him together.

'Sit down, Mikky. Papa can you organise some coffee?'

Yolanda plays with the silver rings on her fingers and I see their similarity; narrow eyes and red hair and lack of integrity.

'You took the book,' she says.

'It was stolen from me. Your father took it. His friends were following me.'

She shakes her head and Steven pauses long enough to laugh and when he leaves the room I'm disturbed further by the sly smile on his lips.

'Why did you give me the book then get them to steal it? Did you want to frame me?'

'Jorge has been trying to contact you. He's worried about you. He thinks you might finally have lost the plot completely.'

'Why?'

'You stole the book from the safe.'

'You gave it to me.'

'No. You stole it from the safe-'

'I wouldn't know how to open the safe. I didn't even know the combination-'

'All beside the point, Mikky. Inspector Barcos believes me.

236

Sit down.'

I reach for a chair and allow the impact of her words to sink in.

'You've stitched me up. Why?'

Steven Drummond returns with two cups of coffee and places them on the table.

'Was this something you planned, with him?' I nod at his smiling veneers.

'We're all working toward the same common goal.'

'What goal is that?'

She raises her head and says to her father, 'Do you want to explain it to her?'

Steven sits at the table, smoothes his tie against his large stomach and sighs.

'Carmen stole it for me.'

'I don't believe you.' I shake my head and look at Yolanda. 'You don't believe this bullshit, do you?'

'I only found out last night when I flew here, let him explain.' She places her hand on mine.

'This had better be good.'

His voice is deep and his accent strong. 'She contacted me after the priest had been to see her. She knew that she had the opportunity to keep the book and she thought that as I wanted them to sell the apartment it would be a way of, how shall we say, appeasing me.'

'And you agreed?' I say to Yolanda.

'She knew nothing about it,' he interrupts. 'Carmen never told Yolanda that she had it or that the priest had been to her. But when she telephoned me with the idea of selling the book, I told her I wanted to see it. Get it authenticated and she was supposed to show it to Nigel - that day in Malaga - but she didn't show up. Nigel flew down to authenticate it but she wouldn't meet him.'

'So you killed her?'

'Viktor Gruzinsky killed her,' Steven adds. 'Viktor cultivated her secretary Madeline to get to Carmen. He intimidated her French boyfriend - a boy called Alain who he threatened and he went back to Paris. He sent Madeline a text to tell her it was all over. She was bereft and that's when Viktor stepped in and seduced her.'

'You wanted Carmen to sell the book of hours to Viktor?'

'She bottled out.'

'So, you stole the manuscript from me in Bruges.'

'I took it for safe keeping. I wasn't sure what you were going to do with it-'

'And, you know all about this?' I turn on Yolanda.

'I didn't know Papa was involved in any of this until last night.'

He smiles. 'It's a happy coincidence that Yolanda is angry with you. She didn't know if you had stolen the book or if you were telling the truth and understandably she went to Inspector Barcos, and to your friend Jorge who is now on the case.'

'You have no proof I stole it or even that it was stolen from me. I'll tell them the truth,' I say, thinking of the video I've programmed to be emailed in a few hours. 'It's my testimony against yours.'

'You ran. It's as simple as that - straight after the funeral. You disappeared with the manuscript that you stole from the safe. You went to Bruges. Nigel Howard has already spoken to Marina Thoss and she's desperate to keep her record clean. She'll tell them how you went there with it strapped to your waist demanding to see her corrupt father. You haven't got an alibi, Mikky.'

'Josephine was a witness to the attack.'

'They will see it as an elaborate ploy to fool Josephine and for you to keep the manuscript. Josephine will know you've been lying.'

I look at Yolanda. 'Why was he forcing you to sell your apartment in Malaga? Isn't that why Carmen wanted to steal the manuscript and sell it - so that you two could afford somewhere nice?'

'It wasn't as simple as that,' Steven answers for her. 'I didn't want them to just sell the apartment. I wanted her to move back to Madrid. Carmen's talents were wasted down there. She should have been working in Madrid at the Prado or the Thyssen or even the Sorolla Museum. She was worth more. She was better than she knew. She was talented and gifted. She was well respected - anywhere would have been better than Malaga and the Picasso-'

'That's ridiculous-'

'Even the Archaeological Museum would have been better, anything - anywhere in Madrid but she wouldn't listen to me. She wouldn't do as she was told. She-' he raises his voice.

'She loved her job,' I interrupt.

'She needed to be here.' He bangs the desk. 'I wanted her in Madrid where it all happens. Where she could have made something of herself. We could have worked together. We could have done so much more-'

'You wanted her to help fence your stolen antiquities and sell it through one of your organised crime channels? Like Viktor Gruzinsky? You're a Janus figure. You need help in disposing of stolen goods, someone to create false provenances to provide reassurance that the art you're selling hasn't been looted or are outright fakes-'

He smiles. 'You're clever. You're better than I thought-'

'You organise local criminals in South America to loot archaeological sites then you organise transport and false documentation and you smuggle them through multiple borders across the world, selling them to museums and collectors, making the object legitimate in the open market.'

'Bingo!' He claps his hands slowly.

'There must be multiple people across the world all linked together so you make a profit,' I continue. 'A web so carefully concealed, a network of corrupt thieves. How do you get away with it?'

He shrugs. 'They're a series of people who don't know what happens to the artefacts before or after so they can never know the complete picture. There're rarely paper trails, no-one says exactly where it originates or it's final destination, so it's almost impossible to sort out the black market from the white market. There's only this lovely middle grey area and it's so broad anyone runs the risk of buying looted or illegal artefacts.'

Yolanda's expression doesn't change and her eyes remain cold and hostile.

'Why take this risk when you have so much?' I ask.

'Everyone is doing it. You would too, if you could. It's not my fault - if it wasn't me, someone else would be doing it,' he laughs. 'There should be greater due diligence by the authorities. They make it so easy. It's far better than drugs and human trafficking. It's a white collar crime. It's not really serious just a few artefacts here and there that governments and institutions can't look after properly.

'It's lying, cheating and stealing,' I argue. It's invariably non-violent and respectable but it often befits members of the social elite who are financially motivated and believe they are above the law. These people are also notoriously difficult to catch and to prosecute. He's in denial of his responsibility to the art world and of the legacy and culture of counties and continents. 'A young woman is dead because of you–'

'You're not going to blame me for Carmen's death. I'm not responsible.'

'You are and you can't justify your illegal actions. Are you not ashamed?' I turn on Yolanda, 'Did you know about this?'

'No.' She won't look at me.

'And now? He's going to get away with it?'

She shrugs. 'Carmen's gone.'

'You've framed me.'

'You deserve it,' she whispers.

'What did I do to you?'

'You know what you did – four years ago – the last time you were on the coast...'

I shake my head to block out the painful memory.

'You trashed our flat. You were stoned. You were out of your head.'

'So, this is your way of repaying me?'

'Girls, let's not get carried away with the past – this is about the present and of course – our future.' Steven slaps the table to get our attention.

'Future?' I look at him.

'Yes –our future. You want to get the Guardia Civil off your back and I can help you.'

'Why would you help me?'

'Why not? You're the daughter of a close friend.'

'You know she's my...' I can't finish the sentence and I know by the look that passes between him and Yolanda that she told him. 'This has nothing do with Josephine...'

'If it came out that you are a thief and you stole the Book of Hours it wouldn't do her a lot of good. She's had enough bad press and once they know her daughter is a–'

'Josephine is well over her reputation and what the public think. You'll find there's more to her than that. She waited thirty-one years to meet me. She's not going to let me go that easily.'

I level my gaze at him. They maybe lovers but I haven't entirely given up on Josephine yet.

She's still mine.

He sits folds his arms. 'Well, let's say that you're going to help me because it will save your sorry arse from going to prison for a very long time. Pay attention. I'm going to tell you what you're going to do to sort out this very messy situation.'

Chapter 14

"Keep reading books, but remember that a book is only a book, and you should learn to think for yourself." - Maxim Gorky

He slides the manilla folder across the desk to me.

'Study it closely. It might save your life.'

I take the photograph from the folder that he'd hidden when I came into the boardroom. I gaze at the profile of a man, mid forties, shaved head, steely deep-set eyes, pale complexion with dark mole under his left eye.

'Have you seen him before?'

I shake my head.

'That's Viktor Gruzinsky,' he says. 'Madeline's boyfriend.'

He slides another picture across the table of the two of them, arm in arm, walking along the sea front of Malaga. 'Have you met her?'

I recognise her long hair and heavy fringe.

'Only at Carmen's funeral.'

He nods. 'Good. You're going back to Malaga and you're going to set up a meeting with Viktor. It will be a simple swap. Three million euros for the manuscript.'

'You want me to do what Carmen was going to do before she bottled out?'

'Well done.'

'Isn't he in Russia or Siberia or somewhere?'

'Madeline knows where he is. They're in love. He'll come out of hiding for this manuscript. He wants it so badly that he was prepared to kill Carmen for it. Don't you want to catch her murderer?' His words chill me.

'After they argued in the Parador he followed her back to our apartment–' Yolanda's voice breaks.

I take a deep breath, concentrate on Viktor's profile.

'Why three million?' I ask.

'There's a Russian oligarch who's willing to pay twice that and Viktor needs the money.'

'Why not sell it direct to the oligarch?'

'It's too complicated at the moment. Let Viktor sort that out. I'm not a greedy man.'

'You're setting up a network in Malaga to send artwork into Russia? Is this the sweetener? Where you work out if you can trust each other?'

'Something like that.' He leans on his elbows on the table and opens his palms. 'The choice is yours, Mikky. I have friends in the police. I've told them you've been threatening me. My workers who were loading the truck yesterday are witnesses. You even used your mother to set up a meeting with me–'

'She's not my mother – she's my birth mother.' It's suddenly important for me to distance her in my life, to make her feel somehow less important.

'Whatever.'

'I won't do it.'

'This is the only way you're going to get out of this mess. It's your choice, Mikky. It's my word against yours and quite frankly – everyone knows – you're not to be trusted. You're a liar.'

'You want me to go back to Spain where the Guardia Civil are looking for me. Find a Russian who has murdered my friend and is now in hiding in Siberia or somewhere and arrange with his girlfriend – who is probably being watched by the police – to swap a rare and stolen manuscript for three million euros?'

'Yes,' he smiles. 'You've got it. Clever girl.'

'Then what?'

'Then you're off the hook. I'll tell that nice policeman that you were once in love with – Jorge – that it was all a mistake but I'll only protect you, if you get the money and the Guardia Civil aren't involved. They mustn't know about the swap and afterwards, Yolanda will swear she never saw the book and that you're innocent, won't you Yolanda?'

She nods. 'Of course.'

I stare at Yolanda in disbelief. 'You want me to go back to Malaga, make the exchange and get you money? Is that what this is all about – money? Is this why Carmen lost her life and why Father Ignacio died?' I shout.

'Life is simple. And yes, it's all about money.'

'Don't you have a heart? Are you really this ruthless?'

His snowy white teeth form a snarling smile.

'Carmen didn't want to move to Madrid. You were forcing her. She'd have kept the book and bought an apartment before she did a deal with you.' I look at Yolanda and add softly. 'You could have afforded your own place.'

It didn't make sense.

Carmen must have phoned Steven Drummond when I was in Malaga.

'Why did she tell you Father Ignacio brought her the manuscript?'

'She owed me everything. She was in debt to me. She wanted for nothing as a child. I brought her up and paid for her education. If it wasn't for me she would have been a scullery maid in some back street in Madrid like her whore of a mother.'

Yolanda glares at him but he continues speaking.

'Since she was a child. She was more mine than anyone else's. You see, I paid for her private education and I looked after her. She was quick and intelligent and she had a passion for art, she recognised its value and she loved collecting. I bought her an old quill and ink set when she was eight and I could see how she loved it. I knew then she was destined-'

'You groomed her?'

'Her father knew that my help would come with a price and the debt would be repaid one day. They lived a luxury lifestyle, holidays abroad, expensive clothes while I funded her artistic talents - all those apartments in Florence, Rome and Milan while she studied, painted and travelled. I mapped out her career. She owed me big time and she never let me down until-'

'Me. Until she moved in with...me,' Yolanda interrupts him.

'She deserved better. She was worth more-'

'She was selling stuff for you?' I can't believe it.

'Only a few very minor pieces of artwork. Nothing too serious and nothing that would cancel out her family's debt. Nothing on the level that she was supposed to-'

'Stuff that you stole or had looted?'

'Me and other people, delicate jobs, you know the type...' he smiles. 'You know how this business works.'

'Did you send Carmen to get me?'

'Only to get the book out of Father Ignacio. Silly fool wouldn't give it up without you being there.'

'You killed him.'

'I'm not a murderer.'

'He felt responsible.'

'He was weak.'

I turn on Yolanda. 'And you knew about his? You knew Carmen fenced stolen goods?'

Her eyes are cloudy with tears and she shakes her head looking bewildered as if she is making sense of it all. 'Not until last night, when he told me.' She nods at her father.

Steven's deep, voice fills the room. His eyes are also filled with tears and he speaks haltingly and with hesitation.

'Carmen was strong, intelligent and educated. She was a woman who made the most of the opportunities that were given to her. She didn't squander her life on crap - becoming a third rate tattoo artist for Would-Be Celebrities and cruddy footballers and their cheap wives. She made something of herself. She was a successful career woman; clever, capable and she was astute. Quite simply, she was the child I never had. I loved her...'

Yolanda stands and pushes her chair roughly aside. 'Believe me, Papa. Sometimes, I wish it were me and not Carmen who'd died, too.'

The plan is that Steven Drummond will transport my 4x4 back to Malaga in one of his containers and when I complain about my kite-surfing gear he silences me with a raised hand and a meaningful stare.

I don't have a choice.

It's mid afternoon when Yolanda and I fly in his private jet to Madrid. Steven Drummond says that neither Inspector Barcos nor Jorge know that I have been in England but they might be keeping tabs on the airport in Malaga.

From Madrid Yolanda and I take the AVE to Malaga, and in the early evening light Yolanda sits morosely gazing out of the window, acting as my bodyguard constantly glancing around at the strangers on the carriage.

'You should wear a cap or something,' she says. 'The Guardia Civil are probably looking out for you.'

'I'll give it some thought,' I reply.

I watch the rolling countryside get drier the further south we travel and I remember the familiar scenes of my childhood, travelling like gypsies never settling, always moving on, finding new work or looking for a new school. I think of Papa, the man who raised me, now living in Estepona. On my last visit to Tarifa I'd passed the entrance to his property but I'd never even looked in the direction of his home. I felt no emotion, no connection, no warmth and certainly no love.

Where did it all go?

Hadn't I loved him once?

I recognise the familiar buildings on the outskirts of Malaga city and although I know it well, I realise I don't belong here any more. There is nothing here for me now. When I came back to the mainland in February to go to Tarifa, I drove down from Barcelona and avoided Malaga. Eduardo and I had been happy kitesurfing, drinking beer and eating tapas every evening until Carmen had come to find me.

Steven Drummond had sent her.

She'd asked me to return to Malaga. She said she needed my help. If only I'd have known how serious it all was and what she wanted me to do, I would never have agreed and she might still be alive and things might have been so very different.

Yolanda leans across the small table.

'Take this mobile to contact, Viktor, me or Papa. Our numbers are in there.' Yolanda slides a new phone across but I continue to stare out at the countryside.

Spain is the land of my youth. It's where I grew up. We'd travelled like nomads, constantly on the go, moving on, finding another job, new friends, somewhere else to rest. I hadn't known any stability and I'd never learned to make friends, even now I struggle and I decide I will speak to Eduardo as soon as I can.

I miss him.

'Tell me when and where the swap will take place and I'll give you the manuscript,' Yolanda whispers as the train begins to slow.

'What if I call, Jorge and tell him that you have it and that you lied all along and that your father is a crook?'

'You won't, because like me, you want Viktor to be caught. He murdered Carmen and you want to get him. That's the only thing we have in common.'

We regard each other across the table.

'Is that why you're going along with your father's plan? Did he set it up?' I ask.

She looks blankly at me.

'Your relationship, did he encourage you to be together? Did he think that she would bring out some good in you?'

'Papa hated that we were together. She was his protege and I was his embarrassment. He couldn't hide how much he loved her. When Carmen and I fell in love and we decided to live together it was Carmen who told him. He was furious but she stood up to him. He put the apartment in my name - but it was for her - he bought it so that she would be safe and happy.'

'Didn't it bother you that your father loved Carmen so

249

much?'

She looks away concentrating on the passing apartment blocks and glimpses of busy roads. 'I got used to it. I grew up with it - always being compared with this other girl I'd never met. The chauffeur's daughter was always so pretty and popular: Carmen's doing so well at school. Carmen's at University. Carmen's Graduation. Carmen's studying art. Carmen's in Malaga. Carmen's at the...'

'You weren't jealous?'

'I loved her.'

'Did she know what he was like?'

'She laughed it off - played it down. She never took him seriously, that's why our relationship worked. She never gave a damm about him. She used to laugh at him behind his back. She took what she wanted from him. She knew he was a control-freak and if you didn't do as he said, you were cast from his inner sanctum. He's got the false smile and he knows how to integrate himself with wealthy people or those who can give him something but I was never valuable to him - until my business took off and the celebrities came knocking on our door, then he relied on us to impress them. It was Carmen who encouraged them to buy expensive artwork to impress others. That's why he wanted us in Madrid. We were useful to him.'

'Neither of you wanted to go...'

'I had no idea he was pressurising Carmen but he was bullying her. He wanted me to sell our home but I never trusted him. I know what he's like. As soon as anyone displeases him they're cast aside and he wants nothing to do with them. They don't exist. He blanks them. He has no regrets. He never apologises. He's never wrong-'

'He's arrogant and bigoted,' I say. 'If you never apologise

it means you're never wrong and he's not God. He's just an arsehole.'

'He appears kind but he only gives something if he's getting something back. There has to be something in it for him. He offered to buy us an apartment in Madrid so it made him look good. That's why Mama thought he was being kind but it's all control-'

'Does she not see through him?'

'She's aware of his faults but she's loyal to him. At first he used to pretend he was kind just to impress her. She only ever saw the good things he did and not the manipulative and nasty way he tries to control everyone. Now I think she sees him for who he really is - that's why she isn't happy.'

'Can't they divorce?'

'It's not as easy at that. Mama is still useful. She's still highly regarded in Argentina and her family are very wealthy and influential.'

I'm thinking how Buenos Aires would be the perfect hub for exporting and importing artefacts all over South America but Yolanda continues speaking.

'I, on the other hand, am very different. He never wanted me in his life. I'm of no use to him. I'm discarded - an outcast - unwanted and completely useless. He said, I was a parasite and I lived off third rate celebrities and that I was lazy. He even told me once, that he didn't want me in his life.'

'He's not a kind man.'

'You'd better not cross him, Mikky. He's dangerous and vindictive. He used to be in business with his brother, my uncle, and they fell out over money and he sent some thugs to sort him out. It wasn't nice. It split up the family and my uncle still lives in fear, so there's no telling what he would do to you.'

The train pulls into the station and it glides to a stop.

I gather my black jacket and my leather holdall. 'Thanks for the warning,' I say.

'Don't forget the mobile.'

I pick it up and stuff it in my bag. 'I'm sorry, Yolanda.'

She looks at me quizzically. 'What for?'

'Four years ago. I trashed your place. I was out of order.'

I don't wait for an answer, instead I step out of the carriage and lose myself in the hoards of people - all strangers like in the London underground or the Metro in Paris or Madrid. I'm anonymous and unseen.

I walk with long determined strides. I'm back in Malaga with a job to do and my ghosts won't haunt me this time.

I have phone calls to make.

This time I won't fail.

It's late when I make my way to an area that I used to frequent, in the seedy back streets and to a hostel with no star ratings. It's the only place where I know they won't ask for my ID.

Memories tumble into my consciousness and I'm fearful and wary, uneasy at the emotions that rise in me but I'm resolute. My past and the demons from four years ago have gone. I'm stronger now. I won't be guilt-ridden and I look around with the eye of a sober person, untouched by drugs, and see it's shame and squalor and inhale the bitterness of urine and hash in the dark streets.

The prostitutes, mostly from eastern Europe, look hollow-eyed and sick, many of them hooked on drugs - probably coke or liquid skag. The pimps looks the same, only slightly older and more worn. They watch me like hyenas with sly empty eyes and my body tingles, but I walk tall with my arms at my side ready to defend or to run. Part of me would welcome violence. I could take out the anger and aggression that churns through my body that I can't get rid of even after a long run. I'm suffocating with frustration and rage, manipulated and played like I'm someone else's puppet but this time I will turn it all to my advantage – this time, I will win.

First, I must consider my options, plot and plan.

With my room key gripped in my hand I climb the narrow, dimly lit stairs and throw my bag on the blue and pink nylon cover. I open the window and look down into the street illuminated by dull lights and watch the occasional car or Vesper cruising below.

I open my bag and pull out hair dye and a bottle of whiskey and a packet of sponge cakes. I check the Internet connection and order a few things online that I will need, including new propellors for the drone. I might need some more spares.

Afterwards I shower in the bathroom that's barely big enough to rub myself dry with an ingrained stained towel. I pull back the bed cover and although the sheets appear clean I brush off two long, blond hairs that are clearly not mine.

I check my phone and see a missed call from Jorge. I sigh and lay with my hands under my head staring up at the ceiling considering my choices.

Do I have any?

We all have a choice.

There are always options, so why is Josephine having an affair with Steven Drummond?

At the funeral I thought she was Sofia's friend. How little I know of the social elite and the insincerity of their lives but none of it matters now. I must focus on my task. If I take the emotion out of the situation, as I learned to do as a child, and think only of what is important then I can structure my actions constructively. Stick to the facts.

I want the manuscript – but then what will I do?

Return it to its rightful owners – the church?

I want Viktor. Apart from wanting to kill him, I would be happy if he received a heavy prison sentence for Carmen's murder and I also hold him responsible for Father Ignacio's death.

But what else do I want?

Who else?

Steven Drummond?

I'll tell Josephine the truth and hopefully she might see she's been making a mistake in having a relationship with him. I hope she'll stay away from him but what if she continues to see him?

He's a psychopath; glib superficial charm, lack of remorse, emotional shallowness but what if she's in love with him?

I can't emotionally blackmail her and give her an ultimatum – Steven or me – that would make me as controlling as him; just as vindictive and just as nasty. Josephine has to live her life, the same as I must live mine and I hope we'll be able to mend our relationship and rebuild the trust between us.

Steven's a psychopath but he blends into normality and disguises his lack of moral scruples and indifference to other people's suffering. The white collar crime he commits is as subtle as his illness. He knows what other people feel but he doesn't feel it himself. He absolutely doesn't care. That gives him an advantage. He will understand what Josephine is thinking and he will use her against herself.

I pace the room, staring periodically out of the window.

And what about Eduardo?

Can a sincere and loving relationship be based on dishonesty?

He's everything I'm looking for - kind, patient, understanding and strong - mentally and emotionally. He's good for me but what can I give him in return.

Who am I?

I will tell him the truth. He deserves that much. I will even tell him about the painting that I stole last year. I'll tell him about The Concert and the truth behind the fire and the beating that almost killed me - and I'll tell him about the Book of Hours and how Carmen and Yolanda have drawn me into their web of deceit and then he can decide if he thinks I'm worth keeping.

But what if he wants nothing more to do with me?

I sigh.

There's a shout in the street, running feet, a dog barks then a Vesper squeals past. A rumble of thunder gets louder and I wonder if it's an earth tremor but a sudden flash, lights up the ceiling and illuminates the squalid, cruddy walls.

I'll be lucky to sleep at all here.

I check my watch, eat a small cake and toss the wrapper into the basket. Eduardo's shift will soon be over. He doesn't know that I'm a suspect. In fact, unless Josephine has said anything, he doesn't even know about the manuscript.

And Jorge?

He's giving me a chance to come forward. He may have been protecting me but now he's on the case it will be about his personal and professional ambitions. He'll want the truth. He's tough. He gets what he wants. He won't be stalled for long.

Outside thick smacking drops of rain begin to splatter against the window so I make sure it's closed. Across the road a streetwalker in a mini skirt hides in the shelter of the doorway. She must sense movement at my window because she looks up, but her gaze is quickly broken by a cruising car. It stops in the overflowing gutter. There's a short discussion and she opens the passenger door and climbs inside.

A shudder runs through me, a tremor, a suppressed memory and perspiration breaks out onto my forehead. I'll never be able to tell anyone. Perhaps if I'd told Jorge then things might have worked out differently and my life would be completely changed but I didn't.

I ran.

I ran from him and I ran from the truth.

Five minutes later I dial Eduardo's number and my hands are still shaking. When he answers I keep my tone deliberately light.

'What's a girl got to do, to get some attention from a gorgeous guy?'

'Jump on a plane to Palma,' he replies. When I hear the smile in his voice my heart grows lighter and I feel safe again. I swallow repeatedly so my voice will not shake and he won't hear the sadness in my heart.

I can't tell him how much I love him.

I just hope that after this is all over and he knows the truth, he will still want me.

On Tuesday morning with my hair dyed silver grey, I head to a cheap boutique and buy a black mini skirt, white vest and purple jacket and although I look similar to the girls smoking on the street corner, they eye me with distain.

I wait in the street near the Picasso Museum until Madeline appears. Her hair hangs like a curtain down her back, and a thick fringe and round glasses cover her face. She totters on high heels with a Louis Vuitton handbag over her shoulder and in a few strides, I'm walking alongside her.

'I want to speak to Viktor,' I whisper. I slip a note into her hand. 'It's urgent – don't mess up.'

I disappear between a queue of tourists and hide around the corner. It's a long day, hanging around, looking over my shoulder, watching and waiting but finally at six thirty Madeline leaves the building.

She heads in the direction of Muelle Uno and I follow her, stopping periodically to check to see if she is followed. I use my camera to hide my face and just like a tourist would do I snap pictures as I walk; the Cathedral and the missing tower that was never finished because the money that should have been used to build it was diverted and used to fund the Spanish conquest in South America, the narrow streets and Gothic building facades.

In Muelle Uno the terraces are busy. Madeline heads to the cafe where I had coffee with Jorge only two weeks ago and sits with her back to the wall looking out at the moored and expensive yachts glistening in the marina. I walk past her table and sit inside. If the Guardia Civil is on her tail or suspect me then I expect them to swoop down. There's a back door and I wait. I give the waiter a note and ten minutes later Madeline pays for her coffee and comes inside pretending to look for the toilet. She doesn't see me at first or doesn't recognise me so, I stand up and indicate a chair for her to sit down.

'Hello, Madeline.'

'Mikky?' Her small mouth opens in surprise. 'I - I didn't recognise you,' she stammers. Her French accent is heavy and although she speaks good Spanish we speak in English.

'I'm on the run. Sit down,' I whisper, glancing over her shoulder at the busy promenade.

She turns and follows my gaze. 'From who?'

'The Guardia Civil.'

I give her a few moments to absorb this information. 'I stole the manuscript.'

'What?'

I know she heard me but I say. 'I've got the Medieval manuscript - the Book of Hours. The one that Carmen had in her safe.'

'You took it?'

I laugh. 'Yes.'

'Where is it?'

'I have to know I can trust you. Carmen trusted you, Madeline-'

She nods earnestly. 'I loved her.'

'I know you did.'

A few tears spill down her cheek and I place my hand over hers. She delves into her handbag and wipes them away with a clean tissue.

'It's been such a strain,' she sniffs. 'They're chasing the wrong man. They're looking for Viktor-'

'They think that whoever killed Carmen must have stolen the book from the safe in her apartment but that's not true. I know he didn't do it.' She wiggles her bottom on the plastic seat to get closer to me. 'He promised me. It wasn't him.' Madeline screws up the tissue in her hand.

'Carmen told you about the manuscript and you told Viktor?'

'Yes.'

'And you arranged for Viktor to meet Carmen?'

'They met a couple of times. She liked him.'

'She told me she thought you were a lovely couple,' I lie.

'Really?' Her smile lights her glistening eyes.

'So why did they argue?'

'I don't know,' she says simply. 'Viktor wouldn't have killed her-'

'I know...'

'Oh Mikky, I'm so pleased you believe me. Viktor is a gentle giant. He wouldn't hurt anyone. I know they say awful things about the Russian mafia but he's not involved not like some of them - those Middle Eastern guys in Marbella are scary. He really isn't like that-'

'I understand and, I'm sure you love him more than anything.'

'I do...' Her eyes are shining brightly.

'That's why I've come to you. I need your help. You need to contact him for me-'

'I don't know where he is.'

'Don't lie to me, Madeline. This is urgent and he will want to know. You must tell him I have it.'

She looks doubtful before replying. 'The police don't know, I know, where he is...'

'Good, and we're not going to tell them, are we? What I want you to do is to tell him that I have the manuscript. He told Carmen that he already has a buyer. I can do the deal with him now. I can swap the book for the money.'

'But how? How can he...?'

'He - what? Trust me? Look.'

I hold out my mobile and show her a sixty second video of me taken yesterday by Yolanda in Steven's office with dated copies of El Pais and The Sunday Times, and I'm turning the pages of the manuscript.

'Ask Inspector Barcos about me - or Jorge. They'll tell you, I've gone missing. Why do you think I've dyed my hair and I dress like this? Madeline, you must tell Viktor and we need to do this urgently. The longer I'm in Malaga, the higher the risk, they will find me. Can you get hold of him today?'

She pauses, then nods.

'Good. Tell him we can do the swap on Thursday. That'll give him time to get the cash together. I'll let him know the details.'

I stand up but she places her fingers on my arm.

'He'll want proof the book is authentic - that it's the same one.'

I pause. 'Okay, I'll get it. Just make sure he's still interested because if he isn't then I have someone else who will bite my arm off for it,' I lie.

'Give him first option, Mikky,' she pleads.

I slide a piece of paper across the table with my new mobile number.

'If I don't hear from you by midnight, I'll assume it's all off.'

That evening I'm sitting in the corner of the small bar beside the hostel eating ham, egg and chips and drinking red wine when Josephine calls my mobile. I've ignored three calls and two voicemails in two day and I can't put her off any longer.

'Hi Mikky, where are you?' she asks.

'What do you want?' I reply.

'I'm sorry I couldn't come to meet you and Steven on Sunday. I've had to sort something out and it's been quite difficult.'

'Is your lover's wife causing you problems?'

'What?'

'You think I don't know about you?'

'Stop talking in riddles, Mikky. What do you mean?'

'I know Steven Drummond is your lover.'

She pauses and takes a deep angry breath. 'No, he's not and I'm sorry you see it that way. I expected more from you.'

'I tell it like I see it.'

'You're smart and intelligent - not everything is how it appears.' Her voice softens. 'What's going on, Mikky? Has this got something to do with Carmen's death?'

'Hasn't your boyfriend told you?'

She sighs. 'Steven Drummond is not my boyfriend and I want you to tell me what's happening. Where are you? What's this got to do with him? I want to see you. Are you still in England?'

'No, I have to do something-'

'Does this have anything to do with those men who attacked you in Bruges? I'm not stupid, Mikky. I thought you were going to ask Steven for help. Speak to me, maybe I can help.'

I drain my wine glass and mop up egg yolk with a piece of bread.

'I can't tell you, Josephine. I'm really sorry but it's something that I've got to sort out.'

'Does it involve Carmen and what happened to her?'

I pause. 'Yes.'

'Are you in danger?'

I sigh. 'Not really.'

'That means you are. Okay, what can I do to help.'

In spite of myself, I laugh. 'You're such a trooper Josephine, I really do admire you.'

'We're in this together, Mikky. Let me help.'

'You've done enough. Thank you for arranging that meeting - it was what I needed and what I suspected.'

'Steven is involved?'

'He's not a nice man,' I reply.

'No-one is all good or all bad. You should know that. Even the most vilest people in the world have a charming or good side...'

'He a psychopath. He's charmed you. That's why he gets away with doing bad things. You could have picked someone better looking to shag,' I say.

'Don't be crude. Besides, he is not my type and Sofia is my friend. She's been very kind to me.'

'Then isn't that rubbing her nose in it?'

'It's not as simple as that.'

'You'll be denying that you went up to his hotel room next.'

'His what?'

'His hotel room - I saw you in the hotel in Canterbury last Friday night. You followed him up to his room.'

'You were in Canterbury?'

'I saw you. You lied to me.'

Silence hangs in the air and I wonder if we've lost the connection. I'm about to cancel the call when she says quietly. 'It's not how it looks.'

'You stayed the night...'

'It wasn't like that-'

'Karl Blakey wrote about your affairs. You told me he made it up to slur your character. You told me he lied. I'd have believed you, if I hadn't seen it with my own eyes.'

'I will tell you what happened Mikky, but only if you promise you will say nothing to anyone. You can't even tell Eduardo and certainly not Yolanda. Then you can tell me what's going on with you. Deal?'

'Tell them what?'

'Sofia is very ill. She's had a breakdown and she's depressed. I was with her on Friday. We went to the Marlowe Theatre in Canterbury to see the Cuban National Ballet but at the interval she disappeared. I was worried and I didn't know where she had gone, so I called Steven. Presumably she'd checked into this hotel before and when he got there he found her in a terrible state. He called me and told me where they were and after the performance I went to the hotel to help her. Eventually we persuaded her to see a doctor and I took her up to London in the early hours of morning. Steven arranged a car for us. I was with her when you demanded I send you his contact details, so you can imagine my reluctance and worry...'

'Is she alright?'

'She's in a private clinic.'

'Will she be okay?'

'I hope so.'

'And Yolanda doesn't know?'

'Steven's told her that she's on holiday with a friend in the Caribbean or somewhere. After Carmen's death, Steven wasn't sure how she would take the news that her mother is ill. He said Yolanda is selfish and she doesn't care about anyone but herself and I can't interfere, Mikky. Steven promised me to secrecy.'

'So Sofia is your friend?' I mutter.

'Yes she is, and if it helps – you're right. He's not the most handsomest, kindest or most charming man I've met. In fact, he's quite repulsive and emotionally stunted. He has complete lack of empathy and he won't take responsibility for his actions and certainly not for the way he treats Sofia. I really don't know what she sees in him but it's not for me to interfere.'

'He's got money, Josephine. She's blind to his faults. He gives her the lifestyle she enjoys.'

'So he pretends but it's a heavy price to pay and as we both know there's much more to life than money and an extravagant lifestyle. So, now it's your turn, Mikky. Tell me what's going on. I need to know the truth.'

Chapter 15

"A book is a dream that you hold in your hand." - *Neil Gaiman*

It's a hassle having three mobiles; my own, the one given to me by Yolanda and now one I bought on the Internet. I sit on my bed and label them carefully, using sellotape and coloured paper so I don't get muddled waiting for Viktor to call me. He has another two hours until the deadline at midnight.

The phone Yolanda gave me rings and it's Steven. 'You have two days, to deliver or I phone the police.'

'I can't do it in that time.'

'You haven't got a choice.'

'I don't even know where he is.'

'Find out. I've got Jorge's number in my hand.'

'Madeline is going to contact Viktor. He might not even be in the country.'

'Not quick enough.'

'I'm waiting for Viktor to phone,' I raise my voice.

'Get hold of Madeline again.'

'Get off my back, Steven. I want the Manuscript. It will need verification. Can Nigel Howard do that? I have to get Madeline to trust me and I have to prove it's the authentic book of hours.'

'Nigel has disappeared.'

'Where to?'

'It doesn't matter but he's gone.'

'What if Viktor thinks he's being duped?'

'He won't if you do a proper job.'

'If Madeline or Viktor think for one minute that you or Yolanda are involved then we won't even have a deal. I've told her I am on the run and in hiding. If you want the money from Carmen's murderer then you will have to trust me-'

The line is dead – he's hung up.

I lay on the bed and put my arms behind my head and stare at a giant stain in the corner of the room where the ceiling meets the walls. When the person upstairs flushes the toilet I think it gets bigger like a dragon with a fiery tongue and thick long tail and it reaches to the curtain rail.

I jump when my mobile rings.

Viktor is on the phone for less than two minutes – the traceable time for mobiles. My palms are perspiring and my hand is shaking. My mouth is dry and I may be sick. He's the head of the Russian mafia. He murdered Carmen and he wants something I don't even have. I can't mess up.

'I want Madeline to see it,' he says.

'The price is four million euro.'

'It was three million.'

'It's gone up.'

He pauses. I watch the seconds tick past on my watch.

'How can I trust you?'

'Do you want it or not? We can do the swap the day after tomorrow.'

'Thursday.'

'Yes or no?'

I will get my life back and assuage the guilt that I'm carrying. I'm doing this for Carmen and if I fail, I too, will die.

'Madeline must see it tomorrow.'

The following morning Yolanda slips me the manuscript. She sits beside me on a bench and I take take the book then wander along the quay to my rendezvous point. I sit near the open window and gaze out past the gently flapping palm trees and settle my gaze on the blue horizon where a cruise ship navigates its way toward the Port.

Last year, when I was in hospital I laid in bed gazing out at palm trees and blue sky dreaming of paella and cold beer. Eduardo visited me before or after his shift to check my progress and we formed a fragile friendship, teasing each other, and he made me laugh. I'd felt safe flirting back knowing he had seen me in the worst possible condition with ragged letters scored into my forehead and the religious and iconic artwork tattooed across by body. I was confident he would be repulsed by the bloody head of St John the Baptist across my breasts and Salome's leering smile but he wasn't. His gentle humour and persistence made me feel secure and once I was discharged Josephine rented a villa where I could recuperate. Eduardo spent many evenings with us until one night, after dinner we made love. It had been a long time since I'd felt a warm and loving touch and it woke in me a passion that I thought was dead. Afterwards Eduardo held me gently until my tears subsided and I'd slept in his arms.

'Mikky?' Madeline slides into the seat in front of me. 'I didn't recognise you. You've dyed your hair again?'

'I'm experimenting...'

'Redhead?'

'Not my best look.'

'Have you got it?'

'Here.' I indicate the bag on my lap.

A waiter hovers beside us and Madeline orders orange juice. If only Eduardo were here.

'Let me look at it.' Her voice is curt. 'I don't have long.'

'Don't take it out of the hessian bag.' I caution her sliding it across the table.

She gives me a withering look but I return her cold stare. She opens the chequered bag from El Corte Ingles and opens the hessian.

'Viktor trusts you?' I say.

'Of course.' When she looks up, sunshine is reflected in her glasses and she blinks before replying. 'I checked your story out. Inspector Barcos does want to speak to you.'

'It's why I must be careful.'

She studies the book and eventually puts it back. She slides it back across the table and without taking her hand from it she says. 'He wants it authenticated on the day we do the swap.'

'Impossible.'

'He's insisting.'

'It won't happen.'

'He wants Simon Fuller – the man Carmen was going to use.'

'Simon's in China.'

'According to Viktor, he's back in England.'

I shake my head. 'I can't involve him.'

I don't add that it would be too dangerous.

'Then the deal is off.'

'What were Viktor and Carmen arguing about up in the

Parador the afternoon she died?'

She seems taken aback with my sudden question and blinks quickly.

'I need to find out, Madeline.'

'Why?'

'Because if Viktor didn't kill her, then it may lead us to who did.'

'You'd better get Simon over here.' She stands up.

'Tell Viktor that when I call you tomorrow - he'll have twenty minutes to meet me.'

'What about Simon Fuller?'

'He'll be here.'

'That won't be enough time-'

'Tell him to be waiting from midnight tonight.'

'What if he can't-'

'If he doesn't show there's no swap.'

'If you think-'

'Just tell him, Madeline. These manuscripts don't come along every day of the week.' I pat the El Corte Ingles bag and as she hoists her Prada handbag onto her shoulder, I say.

'Are you really that in love with Viktor?'

'He's my fiancé.'

'Do you think he loves you?'

'I knew as soon as I saw him that he was the one.'

'He got rid of Alain - your last boyfriend. He set you up to get to Carmen. Did you know he followed you at the Easter procession?'

'Bullshit.' She totters away on high heels.

I pay the bill.

Outside Ian Laroche is waiting for me. Last Friday in the hotel bar in Canterbury with Steven Drummond he was dressed in a smart suit. Today he's dressed in a pale blue T-shirt which reveals his bulging biceps and wide shoulders. He stands silently beside me as I wait at the kerb. A white Renault appears and Yolanda leans out of the window and takes the bag. Ian Laroche climbs into the passenger seat.

'What happens next?' Yolanda asks.

'I need my car urgently. Let me know when you've brought it back from England.' I turn on my heel and walk away feeling the warm sun on the back of my head, wondering how many eyes are watching me.

Back in the hostel I make some phone calls then lay on the bed and gaze up at the ceiling. The dragon stain has spread, turning into an elongated crocodile with muscular legs and it now reaches to the soiled curtain rail.

How did Carmen think she would get away with it?

My mobile rings.

'Viktor has agreed,' Madeline confirms.

'I'll phone you after midnight with instructions,' I say. 'And by the way - you're not invited.'

I make a couple more calls then I phone Eduardo. His name is last on my list but only because his shift is over. He has two days off before going back to a day shift.

'We lost a young girl tonight.' He sounds tired. 'She was knocked over by a truck. She was fourteen.'

The resignation in his tone make me realise that Eduardo's working day consists of life and death. This is the first time he's mentioned a patient and I imagine the frown across his eyes. 'Her family are devastated.'

Suddenly I have a vision of Mama lying in hospital when they

270

switched off her life support and I shiver. The proximity of death has always hovered over me and I stare at the anguished, silent scream on my arm. 'I'm sorry, Eduardo.'

'I wish you were here,' he whispers. 'Are you coming home, Mikky?'

'I have to do something then I'm all yours.'

'Do you mean it?'

'Yes.'

'Do you want to tell me about it?'

'You know I love you, don't you?'

I can hear a smile in his voice when he replies, 'So, you haven't met anyone else who'll have you, then?'

'You're my angel.'

'Yeah, yeah, yeah! I bet you say that to all the nurses. Hey, did I tell you Josephine called me yesterday? She said she saw you last week – in England.'

'Oh.'

'You never told me you were over there...'

'It was only a quick visit.'

'Mikky, I'm not going to play cat and mouse or twenty questions with you. I would like you to be able to trust me and tell me the truth. I have no hidden agenda. I don't want anything from you. I just want to be with you but only if that's what you want too. When you lie to me, I feel the trust–'

'I haven't always lied...'

'You have evaded facts, Mikky. You told me you were driving back to Malaga but you were in England. I can't live with someone or have a relationship that isn't honest. All relationships are based on trust. I don't know what you want and sometimes I don't even know who you are. I'm prepared to help you in any way possible but if you won't let me – if you

271

don't let me in and let me help you, then we won't get very far.'

'I will let you in,' I say.

'Where are you are now?'

'I'm in Malaga.'

'Truthfully?'

'Yes.'

'Where are you staying? With your friends?'

'No. In a hostel.'

'Have you met Jorge again?'

'No.'

'Mikky, I'm not doing this - I'm not playing your game-'

'I'm in Malaga and I'm not seeing Jorge or any other man. I promise, Eduardo.' I think he may hang up. 'I can send you a selfie with the cathedral in the background?' I swing my legs off the bed and search for my boots. 'I'll do it now if I have to. So you'll believe me.'

'I don't need a photograph for that.'

I take a deep breath and realise I am standing metaphorically at one of those crossroads in my life. For the first time I have someone special in my life who I don't want to lose and like Josephine, he's a large part of my life but I'm frightened. Trusting him or Josephine will make me vulnerable. I cannot be hurt any more.

'You may not recognise me, now. I look different to how you last saw me.'

'How do you look?'

'Today I'm a pelirojo - tomorrow I will be-' I turn the packet on the bedside table to read the instructions. 'Silver.'

There is silence until I ask, 'Eduardo? Are you still there?'

'I'm hanging on by a thread but this connection is about to

be severed unless you tell me everything–'

'Please don't be angry with me...'

After I hang up from Eduardo, my heart is lighter. I wait at the back entrance to El Corte Ingles and play air guitar to Wolf Alice's, Moaning Lisa Smile and perform like the inimitable Ellie Roswell, singing and rocking in my imaginary world until my white 4X4 BMW comes to a halt and Ian Laroche climbs out and slams the door.

'I hope you haven't stolen anything.'

'It's all still there. Can't you see?' He nods at the boards still attached to the roof rack but I open the boot, check my bags and hold out my hand.

'You could at least thank me.' He drops the keys into my palm and I climb into the car.

'Mr Drummond wants to know when the swap will happen,' he calls.

'I'll need the manuscript in the morning before Yolanda goes to work.'

'She'll be going with you.'

'I don't want her with me.'

'Mr Drummond insists.'

'What about you? I suppose you want to hide in the boot?'

'What are the arrangements?'

'I'll let you know.'

'He approves the plan first.'

'He either wants the money or he doesn't. So, tell him to get off my back. I'm not dressing like this for the fun of it.'

'He–'

I hold up the palm of my hand. 'Two people are dead. He

273

hasn't done a very good job of protecting anyone and I'm not trusting him to look after me.'

I drive off heading to the multi storey under Muelle Uno where I navigate the underground parking. I park between a navy Ford Focus and a Red Fiat. I lock the door then pretending I've dropped something I bend down and leave the keys on the front wheel.

I walk quickly checking that I'm not followed toward the train station. They are building a new Metro and the streets are a mess, so I make my way through the scaffolding and hoarding and I'm just in time to board the next train. After a few minutes I arrive at the airport and I continue to look over my shoulder.

In the queue I go over the details of my plan and contemplate all the things that could go wrong but I can't think of anything better.

I will have to make it work.

When it's my turn I pass over my Internet reservation to the man in the smart uniform and smile, hoping he can't see the anxiety in my eyes and the fear in my heart.

I park the hired grey Skoda in a small gap wedged up against the bins. I lock it and look over my shoulder. I've done a mega detour of the city from the airport and now I'm confident I haven't been followed, I relax my shoulders and stretch my neck. I'm tired and hungry.

Inside the seedy bar where I've eaten a few meals, the no smoking rule seems to have been conveniently forgotten, and a fog of fried chips and strong coffee hangs in the air. I pick up a stained SUR and sit at an empty table by the far wall. Beside me a one arm bandit jingles periodically, competing with a football game on TV. When a goal is scored a groan erupts and the barman shouts above the hissing coffee machine and raises a fist, and customers complain and shout at the screen. Malaga is playing a league game and they're losing.

One of the other girls eating alone calls out, teasing them for supporting the losing side but I ignore their banter and order small plates of pimientos padron, ensaladilla ruso and pulpo a la gallega.

I wash it down with red wine diluted with white lemonade happy to be anonymous. I've put my plan into place and eat slowly, thinking through the details and the timing, anything could go wrong.

The door opens and I glance up. He's not dressed in his Guardia Civil uniform but I'd recognise his powerful shoulders and confident gait anywhere, as he ambles inside and leans on the bar.

I hide my face behind the SUR hoping he won't recognise me as a redhead.

Jorge sips a beer, discusses football and joins the banter. I never imagined he would come back. This area is contained like a gehto for drug dealers and pimps, no-one bothered you, if you didn't bother them. Four years ago he'd been working under cover. He tipped me off that night but I'd been lured with the promise of cheap cocaine and I couldn't resist. The dealer's front teeth were black and his unfocused eyes bloodshot. His friends had been dirtier, unwashed and full of drugs. Only one guy – the first one – seemed hesitant. Memories tumble over each other, clawing and scratching wanting to be remembered and I begin to shake. My mouth dries and my heart beats in the base of my throat. Then my mobile vibrates on silent.

It's Josephine.

I must focus. I won't be distracted by my past.

I must do this one final task.

The phone stops and it pings with a message.

Tomorrow after it's all over, I will tell Josephine.

Jorge waves to the barman and leaves.

He didn't recognise me and a sense of elation and surge of optimism ripples through me.

I wait for my hands to stop shaking then I pay the bill and step into the dark street. I double back on myself checking the side streets, walking I circles and a few girls give me a curt nod or they sniff their sleeve. I know their pimp is watching. If there was any sign of police they would be gone.

The fat night porter doesn't look up from his computer and I imagine him watching porn. The stairs creak and as I unlock my bedroom door, my phone rings again.

'Aren't you going to answer that?'

His voice cuts through the darkness.

My fists clench.

The lamp momentarily blinds me.

Jorge eyes are dark and angry.

'How did you get in here?'

'It's hardly the Bank of Spain. What are you doing here, Mikky?'

I throw my bag on the bed and leave the door ajar while I brush my teeth and gargle loudly. When I come out of the bathroom he's standing by the window.

'I hardly recognise you,' he says.

'I thought I'd got away with it.'

'I'd know you anywhere.'

'How did you find me.'

'You rented a car at the airport.'

I flop onto the bed. 'So? Are you going to arrest me?'

'Why don't you tell me what you're planning, instead?' He wanders around the room opening the rickety wardrobe and looks under the bed before stepping into the bathroom.

'What makes you think I'm planning anything?'

'Erm, now let me think. Well, hiding in this seedy dump of a hotel, your hair colour is not one that you would have chosen and of course, the rented car tends to give it away...'

'Quite smart for a policeman. You've done well. Your career has really taken off.'

'I didn't think of looking for you here. I never thought you'd come back...'

I look up sharply. It's the first time he's made reference to that night and my heart begins an irregular solid beat. I dig my finger nails into the palms of my hand and when I realise I'm biting my lip I turn it into a smile in spite of the bile clawing up my throat.

'Tell me what's going on.' His voice is soft and melodious. 'I can help you.'

It would be easy to succumb to his charm. He was the nearest I had come to a proper relationship in my life. Before him, I'd had many lovers, men and women but they were borne out of a necessity to satisfy my sexual urges and not out of any form of commitment, love or devotion. Jorge had been different but I'd refused to live with him. I wasn't capable of giving myself totally and wholly to one person - not after Father Ignacio so I coated my emotions with an armour of indifference that I fed with cynicism to thicken it's growth and speed.

'I've missed you.' He stands only a few feet from me.

I could reach out and place my arms around his neck. I

277

imagine the tanned hardness of his body and the tenderness of his kiss.

'I couldn't help you the last time, Mikky and I'm sorry. I'll never forgive myself. But this time I can. Please, tell me what's going on. It's what Carmen would have wanted.'

He's right. It is what Carmen would have wanted. She had encouraged me to like Jorge. It was because they were friends that I had the confidence to stay with him for those two years. She loved him as a brother and she loved me. I remember her saying to me: He loves you, Mikky. You can trust Jorge. He won't hurt you.

But what if he didn't believe me?

The memory still fills me with fear and he seems to read my mind and squeezes my fingers.

'Yolanda stole the manuscript,' I whisper. 'She opened the safe to take out some money and she found it - that morning - on the Saturday before Carmen...'

'You knew about the book?'

'Carmen came and found me in Tarifa. Dolores, my friend in Mallorca, told her I was there kitesurfing so she went to the hippy camp and asked them where to find me. I was on the beach at La Bolonia and she said she needed my help.'

'So that's why you came to Malaga?' He stares at me and I wonder if he thought I'd returned for him.

'She knew I'd lived in Bruges and I knew people who would get it authenticated.' I tell him about meeting Father Ignacio and how Carmen wanted to steal it. 'She wanted to sell it on the blackmarket and buy an apartment for her and Yolanda.'

He nods but says nothing.

'After Carmen's funeral, I took it to Bruges to get it authenticated.' I tell him about Marina Thoss and the photographs I took in the restaurant and how how I was robbed.

'Marina, she told me she recognised Nigel, so I went to Canterbury.' I tell him how I followed Ian Laroche and I get to the part about looking through the window of the hotel and Jorge leans forward. He rests his elbows on his knees and watches me intently. Gone are the eyes of my the man I once loved and instead I'm looking at Jorge the detective. He's taking account of everything, listening to the details and the nuances in my body language and tone.

'He met Steven Drummond,' I say.

Jorge exhales heavily.

'His wife Sofia and Josephine are friends, so I got Josephine to arrange for me to see him and when I got there Yolanda was there too.'

He knows I'm telling the truth and I breathe a sigh and un-burden myself telling him everything including how Yolanda and I flew to Madrid on Steven Drummond's private plane, caught the train and how, this morning I showed Madeline the manuscript.

I pause to let him to absorb the information and he stands at the window.

My shoulders sag and the knot in my stomach begins to untwist. I stretch my shoulders and my neck, wondering if the prostitute downstairs on the street will see Jorge in my room.

He turns to face me. 'You were very brave going to Steven Drummond,' he says softly.

'I was convinced he was responsible for killing Carmen.'

'He didn't kill Carmen,' he says flatly. 'The Russian bandit killed her. He's used the gun before. She let him into her apartment.' Jorge scratches his beard, rubs his eyes and yawns loudly.

Outside a moped whines, travelling too fast and for a second I remember the sound of the motorbike as my adopted mother careered drunkenly down the dirt track from our caravan to the main road.

The room is silent and I hear my own heart thumping.

'She didn't stand a chance,' I say. 'She couldn't have given Viktor the manuscript. Yolanda had taken it.'

Chapter 16

"A book is a device to ignite the imagination." - Alan Bennett

I pull out the whiskey bottle from the bedside cabinet and wash two beakers under the tap in the bathroom. Jorge sits beside me on the edge of the bed. He's exhausted and deep in thought.

We clink glasses and I say.

'Steven Drummond wanted Carmen and Yolanda to live in Madrid. He wanted Carmen to work with him, selling his looted treasures.'

I explain about his illegal business and how he wants to set up a network smuggling artefacts in and out of the country.

'I think he wants to set a route up with the Russians – to ship stuff to Eastern Europe. I think the Book of Hours was the first deal, to cement the trust between them.'

Jorge sits silently beside me absorbing my words, thinking of the implications of a new network for antiquities trafficking and art crime, working out the logistics and the details. I know he will check the facts against my theory.

'Did Yolanda tell you that I stole the manuscript?'

'She told Inspector Barcos.'

I smell whiskey on his breath.

'You believed her?'

'She was always jealous of your friendship with Carmen. You had a bond that she couldn't understand.'

'She never forgave me for trashing their apartment.'

'You did make a mess of it. We looked for you everywhere – afterwards. Why didn't you come back?'

'I thought you all hated me.'

'It wasn't your fault.' He takes my hand and holds my fingers to his lips but I turn away as a tear escapes down my cheek. I wipe it quickly away: shame, relief, guilt.

'You're still a good listener,' I mutter.

'I'm not a detective for nothing,' he smiles back.

I move my hand away and he leans back on the bed and crosses his arms behind his head. He gazes up at the ceiling and I wonder if he can make a shape or animal from the stain in the ceiling.

'So, Steven Drummond wants you to swap the Book of Hours for the money?'

I sigh. 'Yes.'

'Well, that's not going to happen now, Mikky. We know you don't have the manuscript and there's nothing to prove. I'll call the team and tell Inspector Barcos. We can take the manuscript from Yolanda and we can get Viktor. That's what police do. That's what I do. I catch the bad people.'

'You can't or you would have done that by now. You need me,' I continue speaking quickly. 'You can't find him without me.'

'This is retribution for Carmen, isn't it?'

'No.'

He sits up. 'The past is past, Mikky. Let me handle this. We'll

282

pick him up.'

I check my watch. I'm beyond tiredness and the whiskey has made me light headed.

'It's almost one o'clock, Jorge. Hadn't you better get back to Isabelle and the twins?'

'I can arrest you. I can get this place pulled apart. I can have you followed. You can't get away, Mikky. So tell me what have you've arranged.'

I yawn. 'Midday tomorrow – today now –'

'Where?'

'Outside the cathedral – on the steps.'

'He's just going to turn up with the money?'

'Yes.'

Jorge laughs. 'He's going to turn up with three million euros and you are going to hand over the manuscript?'

'Yes.'

'Is this as far as your plan goes?'

'What's funny?'

'This is an international gangster – a Russian bandit with contacts all along the coast and you think you'll get away with this? You think he'll just show up with a bag of money?'

'Ian Laroche is ex SAS. He'll be there. He never lets me out of his sight when that book is around.'

Jorge stands up.

'Get some sleep, Mikky. You look terrible. Meet me for breakfast at seven o'clock in the bar beside the Picasso Museum.'

'Okay.'

On his way out he leans forward and brushes my lips with his and his beard tickles my cheek.

When I wake a few hours later, I check the Internet for the weather, wind direction and speed then I shower and dress with care. It takes me a while to get ready and to feel comfortable and when I pull on my Parker jacket it's barely five o'clock.

I've only had a couple of hours sleep and my eyes are raw and itchy.

Today's the day.

I leave the hotel in the dark and the night porter who is snoozing with his mouth open and his chin on his chest doesn't register me walking past.

Outside it's cold and quiet.

I drive the rented Skoda through the narrow streets, glancing at my mirrors taking the risk that I can trust Jorge. I park and take the drone from its bag. It's ten past five when I dial Madeline's number.

'Viktor has twenty minutes to get to the main entrance of Muelle Uno. Tell him to park and wait.'

'I don't know if-'

'Just tell him.' I regulate my breathing. Except for the occasional taxi and moped. It's quiet and I shelter in the doorway of a closed shop on the street corner.

When a white Mercedes pulls up I walk over and tap on the driver's window. Viktor lowers the glass. His cold grey eyes regard me silently. His head has been recently shaved and I see the mole under his left eye.

'Give me your mobile.' I hold out my hand.

He pauses.

'You want the manuscript don't you?'

'Yes.'

'This is just me and you Viktor. I'll give it back to you

afterwards. No-one else. Okay?'

He hands me his phone and I pass him a mobile I bought on the Internet.

'This is how I will contact you. If there's anyone following you or attempts to get near me, I'll call the Guardia Civil so follow my instructions carefully.'

He takes the mobile.

'Drive up to the Parador. I'm watching you. If you have any of your mafia bandit friends around then the deal is off. Go now! You have seven minutes. I'm timing you,'

I watch his car disappear then I use my mobile to call Yolanda.

'You know where to meet me. Thirty minutes.' I hang up.

I sit in the Skoda, pick up the control and raise the Phantom 4 into the air. It glides across rooftops and skims trees and the four cameras give me an arial view of Viktor's Mercedes winding its way up the narrow hill. I track its progress until his car pulls into the hotel car park and I call the mobile.

'There's a red Fiat 500 on your right. The key is on the front right wheel. Get in the car.'

He steps out, bends down and finds the key. He opens the door and sits behind the wheel.

'Take out one million euros and put it in the bag on the passenger seat.'

'Why?' His voice holds the trace of an accent.

'Just do it. I have to check the authenticity of your money just as you want to check the manuscript. You have three minutes.'

I lower the drone and look over his shoulder and watch him put the bundles of cash in the bag. He's so engrossed in his task he doesn't notice it.

'Tell me when it's done.'

'It's done.'

I raise the drone and track him from a height above his head.

'Put the bag in the boot of the red Fiat, lock the car door and put the keys back on the front tyre.'

He pauses.

'Hurry up, Viktor.'

'How do you...?' He squints and looks up at the brightening sky.

'There's a navy Ford Escort on your left. The key is on the right front wheel. Get in and drive it down here.

'I-'

'Just do it, Viktor or the deal is off.'

I tuck the phone under my chin and watch him on my screen.

The drone is hovering 500 metres above his car. The four cameras are focused on him. I have him on audio in the car and when he drives along the Boulevard in the navy Ford, I say.

'Head toward the motorway - toward Marbella.'

'You're joking?'

I hang up and after a few seconds the Escort moves into the road joining the early morning drivers and I pull out after him.

I dial Josephine's mobile. She answers on the second ring sounding sleepy as if I have woken her. It's not yet six thirty.

'Where have you been? I was calling you all last night,' she says.

'I had an early night,' I lie.

'Are you alright?' she asks.

'I'm good. It's going to be a beautiful day and I need you to do me another favour.'

I hang up knowing I can trust Josephine.

I navigate the quiet streets until I get to a suburb of Malaga where fisherman's houses have been turned into fish restaurants. As a child I remember fishermen sloshing up from the beach in wellingtons, slopping water from heavy buckets with their catch and fresh fish was weighed and gutted, baked, boiled or fried before being served at wonky, mismatched tables. The flavour of succulent crayfish, slippery wet octopus, wide mouthed grinning turbot and glistening sea bass still stays with me but Yolanda standing in the bus stop brings me back to present day.

She opens the passenger door and climbs in.

'You're five minutes late.'

'Have you got the manuscript?'

'Of course.' She lifts up her shirt to reveal the book strapped to her chest. 'I'll be glad to get rid of the bloody thing.'

I pull into the road, conscious there's a motorbike, white Renault, a blue van and two lorries following and it take a few minutes until I settle a few cars behind the navy Ford Escort.

'Where are we going?' She looks at my profile but I glance in the rear view mirror not sure if I'm consoled that Ian Laroche is driving the white Renault behind me.

'Have you contacted, Viktor?' she asks.

The motorbike turns off the motorway and a black Mercedes and a green Seat overtake.

'Is he meeting us?'

I don't reply.

'What time?' she insists.

I remain silent.

'What do you think I'll do? Tell Papa?'

'Have you got your mobile?'

'You told me not to bring it.'

I don't comment.

We pass the next twenty minutes without speaking. I keep my eyes on the rear view mirror as well as watching the drivers who overtake, trying to memorise faces and license plates. As we approach the outskirts of Marbella I dial Viktor's number. We listen to the ringing tone in his car and when he picks up, Yolanda sits up straighter.

'Stay on the motorway to Estepona.'

'Where are we going?'

'Surprise.'

I don't give him chance to reply before I hang up.

'Is that Viktor?' Yolanda scans the road ahead. 'He's in front of us?'

'In the navy Ford Escort.'

'How did you manage that?'

'I rented it.'

'Where's Madeline?'

I shrug. 'At home in bed? I don't know. I told her she wasn't invited.'

Yolanda swivels around to look out of the back window.

'How do you know we're not being followed by his - friends or the bloody Russian mafia?'

'I don't.'

'For christstake, Mikky,' she shouts.

'What did you expect? I don't want you with me-'

'I didn't expect this stupid plan. Where are we going?'

'Stop shouting.'

She squirms in her seat. 'This is bloody dangerous. They could be following us. Why are we going to Estepona?'

'So he can't have an army of people ready and waiting for

us.'

I feel the heat of her gaze on me. 'It doesn't mean he can't call anyone.'

'I have his mobile.'

She stares at me with an open mouth. 'How did you get that?'

'I asked him for it.'

'This is a stupid. You're fucking nuts!' She gazes out of the window and the sunlight catches her auburn hair and I'm momentarily distracted by the depth and intensity of its rich colour. I would also like to photograph the confused puzzle in her eyes.

'I should never have taken the manuscript,' she says.

'It's a bit late for that now. Don't think about it.'

'I think about nothing else,' she replies quietly. 'It is all my fault.'

'We could all have done things differently.'

'She was my partner.'

'She was my friend.'

Yolanda looks away. 'Papa bullied us. He wanted Carmen to do the deal with Viktor but she bottled out. It was her reputation that was at stake. She let him down. She owed him. But she wouldn't sell his stolen artefacts. He told me, I killed her. He told me it was all my fault-'

'No, you didn't-.'

'He made me feel worthless. I killed her. That's why I told him you had the manuscript and you'd gone to Bruges.'

'It doesn't matter now.'

'He didn't care about her. He pretended he loved her but he only wanted what was best for him. I should have known what was going on. If only she'd have told me. Why didn't she? I could have done something. I might have saved her...'

'There is never one reason why something happens, Yolanda. There's always a number of reasons that coincide together, sometimes it's circumstances or things we don't know about let alone expect and the situation changes. We have no control over it – even though we think we do – we don't know what's going on we make assumptions – sometimes wrongly – and we have to adjust.'

I think of how badly I judged Josephine and the wrong assumption I'd made with her and Steven Drummond.

I indicate and overtake a Mini to keep up with Viktor who suddenly accelerates and continue talking as a red convertible overtakes us.

'Don't blame yourself, Yolanda. You can't live the rest of your life with guilt'

'Are you being kind to me?'

'No.'

Viktor is speeding up. I'm doing 150km well over the 120km speed limit so I dial his number.

'Slow down, Viktor. This isn't Formula One.'

'Tell me where we're going,' he shouts.

'Then you can tell your friends and have a little army waiting for us? I don't think so. Slow down and don't break the speed limit or the police might catch you with all that money.'

'We're nearly at Estepona – then what?' he shouts.

'Be patient.' I hang up.

It's just past eight o'clock. I've missed my breakfast date with Jorge and I wonder how long he will wait before he realises he should not have trusted me.

Five minutes later I phone Viktor.

'Keep going on the motorway toward Algeciras.'

He groans as I hang up.

Yolanda's phone bleeps.

'That's an unusual sound for someone without a phone.'

She pulls it from her bag. 'Hello, Papa. No. I don't know where we're going. She won't tell me.' She holds the phone out to me and says. 'He wants to speak to you.'

'Sorry. It's illegal. I'm driving,' I smile at her.

'She won't speak to you,' she says into the phone. 'I don't bloody know. We're following him. Don't bloody shout at me. I could be surrounded by Russian mafia for all you care. What? I'll ask her.'

'He wants to know, does Viktor have the money?'

'Hope so.'

'She thinks so. I'll call you when I know something. Yes. I know Ian is following us and so does Mikky. It's not a big secret. I'll tell you when I know. Okay. I'll call you. I'll tell her - yes.'

She sighs and throws her phone into her bag.

'He says if you mess this up, you're dead.' She grins at me and adds. 'He's a bit dramatic but I think he really means it.'

'I think they'll be a queue of Russians that will get me first. He'll have to wait his turn.'

'You're a ballsy bitch,' she says. 'I admire you for that, even though I've always hated you.'

It's a throw away comment, a disposable sentence and a mindless confession - she hates me. She's always hated me.

It goes around in my head and it's like a discarded plastic wrapper bumbling along in the wind, rolling along dusty pathways of my mind, gathering speed and kicking up memories.

I'm hurt and instead of hiding, I'm goaded like a bull by the matador and I'm prodded into action and I lower my horns and say.

'Even when you inked me – you hated me?'

'You were just someone to practise on. I made you look good so that Carmen would be impressed with me.'

''You should have advised me against John the Baptist's severed head. It's not the most erotic attribute to my body.'

'You were resolute. You hated yourself.'

'You could have suggested a pretty butterfly...'

'I thought if I did what you wanted, cover you in religious paintings and old masters replicas, then no-one would want to sleep with you–'

'I didn't want to sleep with anyone...'

'You went from sleeping with everyone to becoming a nun. I know you met Jorge but people like you don't change. Was it because Carmen lost interest in you?'

'Carmen? Carmen was never interested in me.'

'That night you trashed the apartment...'

The memory makes my hands tremble and my palms are suddenly perspiring. I flick on the air conditioning and rub my hand across my forehead.

'You were stoned. You were off your head with drugs,' she continues.

'I–'

'I don't know what Carmen saw in you. Oh, I know you saved her after Javier dumped her at University, God, I was sick of her telling me that story but I hated you even more when I saw how pathetic you were that night. How you were trying to hang onto her...'

'Hate is a very strong word. Don't you mean jealous?'

'She loved me, not you.'

'We never had a relationship. We were friends, that's all–'

'But that night I saw you. You were in bed,' she raises her voice.

'That night was different.'

'You were looking for attention. You wanted her.'

'I was out of control and she helped me–'

'It wasn't as if you'd led a charmed life, was it? Wasn't your father living around here somewhere? Didn't he live down this way?'

She looks out of the window as if she might see him working in the fields.

'Back there, he has a garage in Estepona.'

'Don't you see him?'

'Not since last year.'

'And what about Jorge?'

'Jorge?'

'Why didn't he save you? Why did you try and ruin our relationship?'

I drive for a while in silence leaving the question hanging in the air. I turn up the AirCon unwilling to unzip my Parker feeling uncomfortable in my clothes.

'Jorge was working under cover. That night there was a drugs bust and Jorge was going to take Alexi down. The Russian mafia controlled the black market and the Guardia Civil–'

'I paid protection money to Alexei…he threatened to smash in my shop.'

'Alexi was the head of the Russian mafia back then. Jorge told me to stay away but a guy I'd met a couple of times, told me where I could score some high quality coke so I went to meet the dealer in this bar…' The quiet purr of the air conditioning fills the car. My throat is dry and my voice soft and hoarse. 'I was set up.'

'What happened?'

'Alexi was killed and Jorge's cover was blown. Somehow they found out I was Jorge's girlfriend and they reeled me in...but it was a trap.'

In the rear view mirror I watch a red convertible pull out but then it changes it's mind and turns off the motorway and I continue speaking.

'Alexi's bodyguard was there. He wanted revenge. The pimps on the street brought along some friends and they wanted...I...I...struggled. I tried to fight them but they were stronger and I couldn't...' My words hang in the air and I try to disassociate my words from the images carousing through my mind.

I don't tell her about the stench of vomit in the alleyway or the giant shadows on the wall as they leaned over me or the pain that ripped through me.

'Are you saying...' she whispers.

'They held me down.'

'My God.'

Her hot eyes bore into me and I'm filled with shame. I fight back my tears.

'So you came to our flat?'

'Carmen helped me...wash...I was...she held me.'

'You never told Jorge?'

I shake my head and take a deep breath. 'That night Carmen called Papa. She told him what had happened but he told her, I was a slut. He said I deserved everything they did.'

Yolanda says. 'Then I came home?'

'I was raw and in pain.'

I remember how Yolanda had started shouting. She pulled me violently from Carmen's arms and her roughness made me retaliate. I went berserk, releasing the violent and pent-up demons inside me and I trashed their place. Then I fled.

'Why didn't Carmen, tell me this?' She chews her thumb nail.

I don't know the answer and so I dial Viktor's number.

'You're doing very well, Viktor. Stay on the motorway and head toward Cadiz.'

'I need the toilet,' he says.

'You'll have to tie a knot in it.'

'You're fucking joking–'

I cut the connection.

Chapter 17

"The only important thing in a book is the meaning that it has for you." - W. Somerset Maugham

We drive in silence past Algeciras and we descend the wide, sweeping hills filled with wind turbines rotating solidly in the breeze. Below us the town of Tarifa lays tucked against the coastline and across the eleven kilometres of The Straits of Gibraltar, the rugged pink and purple Rif Mountains of Morocco catch the sunlight. It's the most southern point in Europe where the Med meets the Atlantic and it's a kitesurfer paradise where virgin sandy beaches are buffeted by the Mistral, the Sirocco or the Poniente.

We follow the navy Escort along the flat road that runs parallel to the Atlantic where rough scrubland provides food for roaming cattle, horses and a few sheep and a sense of excitement wells up in me.

The conditions are ideal: a full moon and strong Poniente were forecast and I'm suddenly confident.

'Take the next left,' I say to Viktor.

I brake as he slows down.

Yolanda sits up in her seat.

'The beach of La Bolonia? It's a dead end. There's only one road in and the same road out.'

'Exactly.'

'We've driven all the way here to come to the fucking beach?'

'It's the only place he couldn't stake out in advance.'

'But there's no escape.'

'Exactly.'

'You're bloody nuts.'

We turn off the main road and drive over the rocky hills of the Sierra de la Plata and Lomo de San Bartolomé for several kilometres then I stop the car at an acorn tree where black pigs sniff and grub around in the dirt and watch the navy Ford Escort disappear over the last hill to the Roman ruins of Baelo Claudia.

'Tell Ian Laroche to wait here. Viktor mustn't see him.'

Yolanda takes out her phone. 'Park on the left near the pigs,' she says.

'Stay here with him,' I say.

'No.'

'If Viktor catches sight of you then he'll bottle out of the whole thing. If you follow me or mess up, your father won't be happy and neither will I. It's between me and Viktor. I've given him my word and so far he's done as I asked.'

'What if he's armed?'

'Then Ian can get him on the way out. He has to come past here. There's only one way in and one way out, so give me the manuscript. I have a more important job for you.'

She looks at me quizzically and I reach into the back of the car and pull out the Phantom 4.

'You can watch and track everything with this. You can call me if there are any problems. I need you to film it all. We need the evidence against him.'

I lean my hip against the car door to stop it from slamming in the wind and place the Phantom 4 on the ground.

'Have you used one of these before?'

'I have,' says Ian Laroche who appears beside me.

It takes me a few minutes to launch it and I take it high into the sky.

'It's windy but you can see everything. Check the main road and the car park. I've locked it on to Active Tracker and to Viktor. Look!'

Ian Laroche takes the console from me and we stare at the screen watching the Ford Escort pull to a stop in the empty field beside the boarded up beach bar. It's still early in the season and won't open yet for at least a month.

I raise the drone higher.

'Now look! Here at the road. If any of his mafia people turn up, you'll see. Call me. Tell me what's happing. Now, give me the manuscript.'

'How the hell are you going to get it authenticated out here?' Yolanda unstraps it reluctantly. Her mouth is cast downwards in grim resolution and she won't meet my gaze as I take it from her and tuck it into the front of my Parker.

'Don't bloody lose it,' she says.

'I'm expecting a red Fiat 500. Let it come past.'

I check my watch and glance at the hill. 'That's the only car allowed down here. Anything else – stop them.'

'Who's in the Fiat 500?'

'Simon Fuller.'

'Are you serious?' Ian says.

'You planned all this?' Yolanda stares at me. 'Simon's agreed to come here?'

'He's my friend.'

'But Viktor is dangerous-'

'I didn't tell him that.'

'For chrissake, Mikky. Are you still taking coke?'

'Have you a gun, Ian?'

Yolanda laughs. 'He's ex SAS. You should see the kit he has in the back of his car.'

'Good. Then you'll be safe. Wait here with Ian and if there's any trouble. Just get out and drive like the wind.'

'Trouble? You're joking. How can there be any trouble when we're in the middle of bloody nowhere?'

I look at the console. Viktor's standing beside the boarded up beach bar waiting. He's surveying the scene before him; a windswept and deserted beach where there's nowhere to run and nowhere to hide, and when I climb back in the Skoda, Ian Laroche is already on his mobile phone.

My time is counting down.

The sand is trickling away.

Over the hill the beach stretches for miles in front of me to the east toward Tarifa and to the west to massive sand dunes. It's a windsurfers and kiters paradise. Out at sea a colourful shoal of kites swirl and circle, and a couple of tuna boats bob on the rough current, only a few deserted houses in a ribbon development along a dirt road stand as testimony to summer residence.

But now. In the middle of nowhere, there's only me and Viktor. He stands buffeted by the wind with a rucksack slung over his shoulder and an angry frown. His bomber jacket billows, filling with air like a puffer fish. The wind caresses my face, stroking my cheeks and teasing my skin, whipping my short grey hair across my cheeks. Behind my sunglasses, my eyes are sore with tiredness. I stand for a few minutes and calculate the distance to the sea, probably seventy five metres, perhaps one hundred metres. I look along the length of the beach to where a mini sandstorm is only knee-high.

'If you're messing with me - you're dead.' His words get blown away on the wind but it doesn't detract from his menacing tone.

I don't look up. I don't look for the drone. I walk slowly, glancing over my shoulder, hoping for the red Fiat to come over the brow of the hill. My heart is pumping like a raging steam train as I move closer toward the killer of my friend until we stand five metres apart.

'Where's the manuscript?' he shouts.

He's shorter than me but wide and strong. His bald head shines in the sunlight and his piercing deep grey eyes crease in a squint. His mouth is large and thick lips give him a feminine appearance, and when his jacket blows open, there's a hand gun tucked in the pit of his arm.

'I have it.'

'I'm not giving you the money until I know the manuscript is authentic,' he growls.

'I'll give you proof.'

'How?'

'Simon Fuller will authenticate it for you.'

He follows my gaze to the narrow road.

'Trust me,' I shout.

'I'm bored.' He places his hand on his hip, moving his jacket aside.

'Be patient. You're the one who wanted it authenticated.'

His voice holds the hint of an Eastern European accent. 'So, you're the gofer for Steven Drummond? I didn't think he'd let his own daughter come here.'

'You're right! Not after what happened with Carmen,' I shout back. 'Why did you have to kill her? Is the book that important to you?'

A red Fiat glistens in the sunshine and proceeds cautiously over the hill.

'You're not as clever as you think, Mikky dos Santos but if Simon Fuller checks out, then we've got a deal and I might give you something else.'

The Fiat comes to a stop and a man with a thin angular face, wearing jeans and boots climbs out of the car. I haven't seen Simon Fuller for a few years but I would know him anywhere.

The three of us stand as if we are at the points of an equilateral triangle, until I beckon Simon to follow me to the wooden shack.

'Who's she?' Viktor pulls out his gun.

I spin around.

The driver's door opens. Her hair blows in the wind.

'What the ... what the feck is she doing here?' I hiss and my heart fills with fear.

This wasn't part of my plan.

I can't protect her. I can't protect my birth mother.

They had flown over from England together last night and I'd instructed her to let Simon Fuller come alone. She was supposed to wait at the Parador in Malaga.

Now, as Josephine raises her hand and blows me a kiss, Viktor looks up at the drone hovering in the sky above our heads.

Simon Fuller is six foot three with not a pick of fat on him and a grey goatee. He zips his black NorthFace jacket to his chin and picks his way across the dust and sand.

'Put your gun away, Viktor,' I say.

The lock on the beach bar is already hanging loose and I push open the door. Inside it's dark and dusty. I thump open a window and brush my hand across the top of the bar removing a thick layer of sand, dust and a complicated spider's web.

Viktor's heavy footsteps follow us.

I hug Simon quickly.

'I need you to authenticate this manuscript.'

I unzip my Parker and pull it from my waist.

'Who's in the car? Who's she?' Viktor asks.

'She's my driver,' Simon answers. 'I don't drive.'

I can't believe I overlooked such a catastrophic mistake and I've put her life in danger.

Viktor pulls a phone out of his inside pocket.

Who's he talking to?

I took his mobile.

'Keep your eye on the driver. If she moves – shoot her,' he says.

I can't speak. My lips are stuck and I swallow non existent saliva in my dry throat that's clogged with sand.

'Hurry up,' Victor says, pocketing his phone.

Simon removes the manuscript from the hessian and spends a few minutes turning the pages of the book then he glances at me.

'The is amazing… it's similar to the Hours of Joanna of Castile that was the only devotional manuscript to survive from the collection. This codex – and this coat of arms belongs to Joanna and her husband Philip the Fair. There were rumours of a missing manuscript. I believe it could be a second one made for the Queen - Juanna la Loca, that went missing. It was thought to be in the possession of a wealthy family from Galicia before the Civil War. It was said, it was entrusted to Monks in a Monastery either in Granada or Cavadonga in the north. There were so many rumours-'

'Stop with the history lesson. I'm not interested,' Viktor interrupts. 'You wouldn't want to lie to me. I'll find you wherever you go.'

'This is an important part of Spain's cultural heritage,' Simon protests but I snatch the manuscript from his hand and nudge him to the door.

'Go back to the car, Simon. Get out of here and take Josephine with you.'

'Will you be alright?'

'Yes - go - now!'

'It belongs in Spain.'

'I know. Go!'

I follow him to the door and stand on the wooden veranda watching him climb in the car and when Josephine starts the engine she raises her hand. Viktor stands beside me like we're friends waving goodbye to our guests and we wait until the red Fiat disappear over the crest of the hill.

Then he turns to me.

'Do I make the swap or do I kill you?' He opens his jacket and I am staring down the barrel of his gun pointing at my chest.

'You were careless, Mikky. You've under estimated me-'

Above us the drone hovers.

He holds out a hand. 'Give me the manuscript.'

The drone sweeps low and Viktor looks up. He steadies the gun with both hands and shoots. The Phantom 4 slithers from

303

side to side, buffeted and winded by the volley of shots and it crashes to the floor sending a plume of sand gusting in our direction.

Viktor grunts with satisfaction and when I look at his wry smile my heart seems to sink into the sand beside the drone.

It's only now, I believe my plan is seriously flawed.

Chapter 18

"I divide all readers into two classes; those who read to remember and those who read to forget." - William Lyon Phelps

The drone lays dead at my feet shot in ragged pieces. Viktor raises his gun and shouts. 'You brought me all this way – to this isolated fucking beach – for what? Could you possibly be so stupid?'

I take a few paces and back away but we're both distracted by the roar of a powerful motorbike coming over the hill. The rider in a leather suit and black helmet is driving recklessly fast and it swoops down to us kicking up sand in its wake.

I use the diversion to slip the manuscript inside my Parker and I run. Gunshots follow me as I slide behind the grey Skoda and in front to the beach bar the motorbike sprays sand into the air and skids to a stop.

The rider lifts his visor.

Mikky, come on.' Jorge holds out his hand.

Viktor pokes his gun out from inside the wooden shack.

'Where's Yolanda?' I take a step out from behind the car.

'Back there,' he nods at the crest of the hill. 'Let's go.'

I pause wondering if Viktor will shoot Jorge or me first.

'What took you so long?' Viktor moves outside.

'Come on, Mikky. Let's go.'

I'm a few metres from Jorge when Viktor shouts.

'You're not going to trust him are you?' Then he adds. 'You're still after the manuscript, Jorge?   Killing Carmen wasn't enough for you?'

Jorge releases a gun from his holster but Viktor continues shouting against the wind. 'She didn't want you involved. She wanted to pull out of the deal-'

'He's lying,' Jorge shouts.

'So he went to her apartment to get the manuscript but when she opened the safe it was gone. You panicked and you killed her.' Viktor opens his duffle bag and holds up a plastic bag. 'Look!'

It looks like a revolver inside with a silencer attached.

'Give me the gun, Viktor,' Jorge climbs off his bike.

'I told Carmen you were greasing both sides but when you signed on to work for Steven Drummond that was the final straw for her. She didn't trust you but she didn't have to die.'

The white Renault comes roaring over the hill and Jorge lunges for me. I dodge and in a few quick strides I'm crouching behind the Skoda and a volley of gunshots echo as Viktor fires wildly from inside the bar. Jorge ducks behind his motorcycle as the Renault pulls into a skid, the wheels skidding dangerously fast.

Yolanda flings open the door. 'There's a sniper up there. Ex SAS and he'll shoot.'

She points up at the hill and I imagine Ian Laroche crouching in the shrubbery watching the scene through the sights of his powerful rifle.

Viktor calls out from the doorway. 'Here's a present for your father. It's the gun Jorge used to kill Carmen. His prints are

306

still on it. He wanted me to get rid of it.' Viktor dangles the plastic bag and it sways between his fingers, taunting and teasing.

Yolanda moves cautiously forward, one step at a time.

'Don't do this Yolanda. He's winding you up. He's lying.'

'That's why we argued. As soon as she knew you were involved she wanted nothing to do with the manuscript or any other stolen artwork. She was frightened - of you.' His voice is carried loudly on the wind and the truth of his words slice through my heart.

Yolanda pauses.

'He's lying,' Jorge growls.

Viktor tosses the plastic bag out of the door and it lays in the sand between them.

I stand up from behind the Skoda.

'Why did you have to kill her? I shout.

Jorge's shoulders slump and he rubs his forehead. 'Steven sent me to get it. I thought she was lying to me when she said the safe was empty-'

'You shot her and blamed me.' Viktor stands on the wooden verandah. 'You gave it to me hoping I'd be caught but it's still got your prints on it.'

Jorge holds out his hand to me. 'I've come to save you.'

In three strides Yolanda picks up the plastic bag. She lifts it to the sky as if trying to see the prints then she turns.

'Why?'

Jorge holds out his arm and aims his gun at Viktor.

'What about her?' Viktor nods at me. 'He sacrificed you - did you know that. Four years ago he sent Alexei's bodyguard after you so he could kill Alexei.'

Jorge takes off his helmet and drops it on the ground.

'He's crazy. It's not true. '

I frown and I'm drawn to a memory of another night when they said I was crazy. I swore and tore at them but I was no match for their strength and as I was held down someone was in the shadows was watching. I called out. I begged. He didn't look away but then he's gone.

My shameful memory is replaced by anger.

'You were there that night,' I shout.

'Don't listen to him, cariño, you know me better than that.' He looks defeated but then he leaps forward and grabbing Yolanda, he wrestles her to the ground, grabbing the plastic bag from her grasp.

Viktor fires. Yolanda screams.

Jorge raise his gun and shoots but Viktor dodges inside. The wood on the doorframe splinters.

Yolanda lays face down in the sand. Jorge kneels against her, using her body as a shield and aims the revolver at me. Suddenly a red dot wavers between his eyes and blood pours from a hole in his forehead. His body crumples and he falls backwards into the sand and his eyes stare up at the blue sky in bewilderment.

Yolanda groans. I run crouching low and drag her back behind the Skoda.

'Viktor?' I shout, pulling off my Parker, I wrap it around her bleeding shoulder. I unzip my rubber suit and tuck the manuscript against my chest.

A bullet hits the back window, glass shatters over us and I duck.

Another gunshot then it's silent.

I risk a quick look, Ian is running down from the hill, crouching and poised like an SAS trained operative.

A bullet pings on the bonnet and I duck.

'Come out, Viktor!' Ian shouts.

'It's you against me,' Viktor replies, 'and I'm prepared to take my chance...'

'Yolanda?' Ian shouts. 'Where's the manuscript?'

That's when I kick off my biker boots and bending low I run for my life. I tuck my head down and aim for the sea. Behind me an explosion rocks the ground. A massive bang is carried on the wind and I've gone fifty meters when I pause to look over my shoulder. The beach bar is engulfed in flames and black smoke billows into the sky.

I run, pumping my arms, pushing my body, straining the muscles in my calf and shins. Eduardo trained me well and I'm fit. I race, dodging and weaving putting distance between me and Viktor. I weave a haphazard path in the wet sand. I'm conscious of the rubber wetsuit rubbing against my skin and the manuscript tucked against my chest. It isn't a suit of armour. A bullet could puncture my body and leave me sprawling on the ground. I'm in the open, vulnerable, sucking the wind into my lungs, panting hard, and running for my life on a deserted beach with nowhere to hide.

A powerful engine bellows into life. Viktor sits astride Jorge's motorbike and he tosses a grenade into the hillside then he revs the engine and turns the motorbike in my direction.

Yolanda's blood is on my hands and the wet sand eats at my feet, pulling and clawing my toes. I stumble but the roar of the motorbike forces me to my feet and I'm filled with terror.

A bullet whizzes past my head.

I duck, weave and run, calculating the distance looking for my goal and I catch a glimpse of it. Although it's fifty metres away and weighed down with sand the pale blue and yellow kite flutters, caught up in the wind, like it's waving, beckoning and calling to me. My spirits soar and I'm energised. I spot my harness and I slide to my knees, scrabbling in the sand with my left hand. I'm twenty-three metres from my billowing kite and I secure the harness around my waist. Ten seconds. I grab the kite bar and, as I run to the side of my kite, I connect it to the harness. Twenty seconds. The wind is on my left and I pull on the line connected to the wing tip furthest away from me. The kite billows with life and the sand weighing it down blows off and the canopy rises. Thirty seconds. Wind is trapped inside and the tip of the kite canopy lifts from the floor, bellowing and shooting up toward the sky as it launches above my head. Forty seconds. My board is near the shore. I grab the foot strap with my left hand and head for the ocean. I steer my kite and it lifts me a little off the sand and simultaneously, as I release the foot strap, I quickly grab the front rail of my board. Fifty-five seconds. It's on the water in front of me and I lead with my right foot but my back foot doesn't quite make it and I grip the rail, wobbling precariously, finding my balance.

Shit!

I've practised a million times.

The icy shallow waves splash over my toes and suddenly the board slides suddenly under my feet. One minute.

I breathe out with relief as my body absorbs the moguls of the undulating sea swell. A soaring sound by my ear causes me to look up. A bullet hole has ripped my canopy. I need to accelerate quickly downwind. I tense my body pointing my front right foot downwind and throw the kite continuously in 360 degree rotations, looping as I chase behind it, like a waterskier chasing the boat.

I glance at the shore. Viktor sits astride Jorge's motorbike firing indiscriminately but I keep focused, looping continuously pulling away from La Bolonia and east, past Valdevaqueros beach toward Tarifa, hoping not to feel a bullet in my back.

I pull away, gaining speed, feeling safer. It's a rare spring tide and new moon. The extreme high and low tide will guide me safety into the still water of the lagoon that appears near the campsite. I'm buzzing with my great escape. The race of a lifetime. I revel in solitary and freedom; sunshine is on my face, the salty sea on my lips. My short grey hair whips around my cheeks and adrenaline surges in my body filling me with exhilaration. I'm feeling strangely euphoric, and as I join the throng of multi coloured kiters, whirling

roar overhead and a helicopter swoops and circles low, blocking out the sun and I'm caught in its cold, dark shadow. When it tilts back and swoops up toward La Bolonia, the Guardia Civil ensign shimmers in the sunlight underneath its belly, and I ride into the smooth waters of the lagoon and glide up onto the beach. Stepping out of my board, I self land; releasing my kite bar from my harness and I weigh my kite down with sand amongst the anonymous crowd of kiters, saluting its performance today. It was a ride I'll never forget.

When I look up a familiar face smiles; Eduardo, my Adonis walks toward me. His blond tousled hair and gleaming eyes are filled with love and devotion, and when he pulls me into his arms, I wrap my arms around his neck and kiss him firmly on the lips.

'You took your time,' he whispers.

'I was having fun.'

'You found it all where you asked me to leave it – all laid out for you?'

'It was perfect.'

'I wasn't happy about breaking the lock on the beach bar. We'll have to buy a new one–'

'We probably won't need to.'

He frowns and I ask.

'Is Josephine okay?'

'She and Simon are on their way back to the Parador.'

'Good.'

He strokes a silver strand of hair from my eyes. 'Not your best colour.'

'What colour would you like me to have tomorrow?'

'I've always liked pelirojos–'

'Dream on...'

Epilogue

It's August and almost thirty five degrees. I pull myself out of the swimming pool and drip my way to the sun chair under the fir trees on the patio of the villa that overlooks Palma's imposing cathedral that glistens in a shimmering heat haze. I towel myself under the wooden rafters of the pergola that's entwined with pink and purple sweet smelling bougainvillea and slip a Queens of the Stone Age, T-shirt over my dark hair.

Bruno hands me a glass of chilled proseco which I accept gratefully and I stand for a few minutes looking over Eduardo's shoulder watching him add saffron to the dish of simmering paella.

'You sure you know how to make this?' I tease.

'It's my grandmother's trusted recipe.'

'So you don't need my help?'

'Thankfully no. You can have the day off.'

He strokes a drop of water from my nose and kisses my cheek.

It's my birthday and I couldn't ask for a better present or better company; Glorietta Bareldo, the world famous soprano, and her young husband Bruno have arrived from Italy. Dolores my ex art teacher and her thirteen year old granddaughter, Maria have driven down from Arta and Simon Fuller and Josephine who have decided they've more in common than music and art have flown over from England.

Josephine picks up the discarded El Pais, her cheeks already have a hint of a tan and says.

'I thought Steven Drummond was one of those people who would always escape justice.'

'No-one should be beyond or above the law.' Dolores breathes out a plume of smoke from a long cigarette holder.

'Or get above themselves,' adds Maria. 'He sounds vile.'

Simon strokes his goatee. 'You hear about these Janus figures in the art world. They're normally well known and popular, and they're a disgrace to our industry. They're invariably responsible for the paintings of dubious provenance that hang in museums, banks and colleges around the world. It gives us all a bad name and it makes me feel more determined to stamp out this sort of thing.'

'I'm a firm believer that good will always triumph over evil.' Eduardo turns from the barbecue and waves a spatula in the air.

'You would,' I laugh. 'You only ever see the best in everything and everyone.'

'I never met Steven Drummond but I know he sold antiquities to our friend Dino Scrugli, now Dino is worried that some of the artefacts he bought might be fakes - or even stolen - and he paid a fortune for them,' adds Glorietta. She's dressed in a multicoloured sarong that emphasises her curvaceous figure.

Bruno raises his glass to his lips. 'It must be a worry for all collectors. Perhaps many of the pieces in Dino's collection will be identified as replicas or worse, as cheap imitations. How would anyone know?'

'It's become easier to spot a fake,' explains Simon, 'and art experts have much more technology at their disposal now; radiometric dating, infrared spectroscopy and gas chromatography...the balance of power is about to change with the breakthrough of more forgery detection in diverse fields. Authenticators will soon be using Artificial Intelligence, Bitcoin and protein analysis-'

'It all sounds very complicated,' interrupts Dolores.

'It's the development of technology that I, and many others, like to call progress,' Simon smiles. 'It will help stamp out this sort of thing.'

'I hope he gets what he deserves,' says Maria, sipping orange juice and leaning her arm on Josephine's shoulder to study the grainy black and white image.

'What happened to Viktor?' asks Bruno, pulling the bottle from the ice bucket.

'The Guardia Civil picked him up on the beach,' I reply. 'Presumably he's saying nothing and Madeline says she will wait forever - well, until he's released but he's wanted for a list of crimes in the Ukraine and he may even be deported.'

I hold out my glass for a top up.

'How's Sofia?' I ask Josephine.

'She's gone back to Argentina. She has a sister and other family members who will help her recover. Yolanda went with her and I'm pleased you saw her before she left.'

Carmen had been monosyllabic in the hospital. Viktor's bullet had grazed her arm and her life had collapsed around her: Carmen was dead. Her father was an international antiquities smuggler and her mother was clinically depressed.

'She still wanted to blame me for going back to Malaga,' I sigh.

'It will be easier for her, easier for them both, to start a new life in Argentina,' Josephine adds. 'It's Isabelle that I feel sorry for, she's a young widow and she'll have to raise their twins

315

under the shame of her husband's legacy.'

When I'd handed the manuscript to Inspector Barcos and gave him my full statement I asked him what will happen with Steven Drummond and he'd shrugged. He wasn't surprised Jorge had been added to Steven's Drummond's payroll to oversee the shipment of smuggled artwork and artefacts. He told me that he'd suspected Jorge for some time of being involved in illegal profiteering and working with the Russian bandits.

'There's nothing the Guardia Civil can do. Steven Drummond hasn't broken any laws in Spain. We have no evidence of what he might do and now that we've caught Viktor I would think that's messed up his plans to import and export stolen artefacts through Spain.' Inspector Barcos was resigned to everything, including his imminent retirement.

'Until he finds someone else to help him,' I replied.

'Maybe - but we can't do anything at the moment. Be thankful, Señorita dos Santos, you were very lucky to escape with your life and Spain is very fortunate to have the manuscript back. God must have been watching over you.'

'God expects everyone to help themselves,' I replied but he had simply shrugged and smiled then checked his watch. Our interview was over and he wanted to go home.

I move my chair further underneath the shade of the fir tree and watch Eduardo prepare salad; dicing onions, slicing peppers and peeing avocados.

'They need to set up an international task force to help monitor stolen art,' he suggests. 'There must be lots of people who would work voluntarily; scholars, professionals and even the public.'

'There is the Art Loss Register,' Simon replies.

'I mean a specialist team to crack these sort of cases,' Eduardo says.

'Mikky could run it,' Maria says with teenage enthusiasm. 'And I could help.'

'Not a chance,' says Eduardo frowning. 'She's promised she's not getting involved with any stolen art work - ever again.'

'Exactly - and besides, I'm going to keep her very busy.' Josephine says. 'Your art exhibition in New York will keep you out of mischief.'

'We'll have to fly over for it,' Dolores says.

'Can I come? I've never been to New York,' says Maria.

'I'll check my calendar for December,' agrees Glorietta. 'I'm dying to see your new work, Mikky.'

When the conversation turns to art and they're talking about Georgia O'Keeffe's new exhibition in Madrid I turn my attention to the picture on the front page of the national newspaper and raise my glass in satisfaction at Steven Drummond's pale and haggard face as he's led away in handcuffs.

'Happy Birthday to me,' I mumble.

As soon as I knew Steven was untouchable I couldn't let things rest. I couldn't let him walk away unscathed from the damage he'd done to so many lives so I did it for us all; Carmen, Yolanda, Sofia, Father Ignacio, Isabelle and her twins and even for Viktor and Ian.

The one million euros that Viktor left in the Red Fiat outside the Parador that Josephine kept safe for me has paid for Steven's demise and it was money well spent.

I set up a deal involving Madeline at the Picasso and Marina Thoss in Bruges. As an anonymous dealer, I bought an ancient Egyptian deity, forged the provenance and sold it to Steven's gallery in Bond Street for twice the price. When he tried to sell it for a five million euro profit to a Chinese investor, it was declared as an obvious fake and Steven was denounced as a fraud. It didn't take long for experts like Simon Fuller and Nigel Howard to expose Steven's reputation and his integrity was suddenly under the spotlight. On further investigation the Metropolitan police found evidence to suggest Steven had a history of illegally importing and exporting rare artefacts, and a complicated network of looters operating in South America channeling stolen goods through Argentina, through London to dealers in Asia.

According to El Pais, the Guardia Civil had suspected Steven Drummond was using Madrid as a new networking hub and they were tipped off... and Steven Drummond would go to prison for a very long time.

I lean back in my chair and raise my glass. The vivid white eight inch scar on the back of my left hand and Edvard Munch's deeply disturbing The Scream wrapped around my other arm suddenly feel less emotionally harrowing and, for the first time in my life, I'm not riddled with anguish, soul searching or psychological torture that has chaperoned me throughout my life.

Today I am thirty three.

It's my first birthday with my birth mother and without thinking I get up from my seat and wrap my arms around her neck in a loving and warm embrace.

Josephine hugs me and my silent tears fall onto her chest, all the years of abuse, despair and heartbreak surge from my body in a tsunami of emotion and I'm exhausted, cleansed and filled with a sense of renewed energy as if I've been reborn, stronger and wiser.

Her breath is warm on my skin and she speaks so softly it's only me who hears her precious words.

'I love you, Mikky.'

Through my teary eyes I return her smile and marvelling at the similarity of our features.

'I love you too,' I whisper, then I tilt my head at Simon and say in a louder voice.

'Is it too late for me to ask for a sister?'

THE END.

Afterword

Janet Pywell's books:

Culture Crime Series:
Golden Icon – *The Prequel*
Masterpiece – book 1
Book of Hours – book 2
Stolen Script – book 3

Other Books by Janet Pywell:
Red Shoes and Other Short Stories
Bedtime Reads
Ellie Bravo

For more information visit:
website: www.janetpywell.com
blog: janetpywellauthor.wordpress.com

STOLEN SCRIPT:

Book three in the Culture Crime Series features unconventional heroine Mikky dos Santos, a protagonist who is brilliant, idiosyncratic and who does not always do the right thing.

Artist and photographer, Mikky dos Santos is brilliant but rebellious. After a personal catastrophe in New York she insists on going to Greece to authenticate a valuable parchment where she makes a promise to return it to the Jewish museum in Rhodes. But time is running out and Nikos Pavlides isn't giving up the Torah easily. He's also hiding a deeper, darker secret and, as he plays a deadly game, the stakes are raised. Faced with drug dealers and human traffickers with no regard for life, Mikky's survival instincts kick in as she uncovers the sordid reality of the truth and its savage consequences.

Fighting for her life, how will Mikky fulfil her promise? This enthralling, fast-paced thriller is an emotional roller coaster of shocking twists and turns...

Set in America (New York), Turkey (Izmir) and Greece (Rhodes) this exciting novel will keep you turning the pages.

It's a deadly game...

Expertly researched, each book in the series gives a harrowing glimpse into the hidden world of violence, greed and jealousy within the arts.

About the Author

Hello,

I was Director of a marketing company and I worked in the travel and tourism industry for over thirty years before writing full-time.

I am currently writing my first Culture Crime Series.

Having published two books of short stories and a romance, I am now working on a variety of writing projects including a comedy script, drama for theatre and a film script.

If you'd like to join my mailing list for information on new releases and updates on my work then please subscribe to my newsletter.

You can connect with me on:

🌐 http://www.janetpywell.com

🐦 https://twitter.com/JanPywellAuthor

📘 https://www.facebook.com/JanetPywell7227/

🔗 https://janetpywellauthor.wordpress.com/

Subscribe to my newsletter:

✉ https://www.subscribepage.com/janetpywell

36373827R00182

Printed in Great Britain
by Amazon